THE CONTRACT

By the same author

City of the Sun
Where the Dead Lay

THE CONTRACT

DAVID LEVIEN

BANTAM PRESS

LONDON • TORONTO • SYDNEY • AUCKLAND • JOHANNESBURG

TRANSWORLD PUBLISHERS
61–63 Uxbridge Road, London W5 5SA
A Random House Group Company
www.transworldbooks.co.uk

First published in the US 2011 as *13 Million Dollar Pop*
by Doubleday, a division of Random House, Inc., New York

First published in Great Britain
in 2011 by Bantam Press
an imprint of Transworld Publishers

Illustration of garage © Paul Simcock / Getty Images
Illustration of man © Hughes Léglise-Bataille / Getty Images

A CIP catalogue record for this book
is available from the British Library.

ISBNs 9780593065808 (cased)
9780593065815 (tpb)

Addresses for Random House Group Ltd companies outside the UK
can be found at: www.randomhouse.co.uk
The Random House Group Ltd Reg. No. 954009

The Random House Group Ltd supports the Forest Stewardship Council®
(FSC®), the leading international forest-certification organization. All our
titles that are printed on Greenpeace-approved FSC®-certified paper carry
the FSC® logo. Our paper procurement policy can be found at
www.randomhouse.co.uk/environment

Printed and bound in Great Britain by
CPI Mackays, Chatham, ME5 8TD

2 4 6 8 10 9 7 5 3 1

To my sons: Joseph, James, and Robbie

1

Frank Behr walked two steps ahead of the principal toward the blacked-out Chevy Suburban. The winter had cracked a few weeks earlier, and the night air swirling around them had lost its bite. The report of their hard shoes on concrete reverberated off the walls of the underground parking garage of the Pierson Street office building. The principal was half a foot shorter than he was, so looking back, Behr had a clean view of the amber-lit geometric rows, now mostly devoid of cars due to the late hour, that spread out around them.

"Yeah . . . yes," the principal said into his cell phone, "it's going to happen. Tomorrow morning, tomorrow afternoon latest. Shugie's just getting the press conference together."

The principal was Bernard Kolodnik, a prominent businessman with a real estate and property development background who was so smooth and successful in his dealings that he was admiringly known around greater Indianapolis, and throughout the Midwest, as "Bernie Cool." Fit at fifty, Kolodnik had a strong jaw, blue-gray eyes, and hair the color of steel-cut wheat.

"What? What?" Kolodnik said, fighting reception that was growing choppy as they got farther underground. "You're crapping out on me, Ted . . . Ted?" He clicked off the call.

"Damn things," Kolodnik muttered to himself of the cell phone, and began walking more quickly. Behr, in turn, stepped up his pace.

Executive protection. It wasn't an area in which Behr was expert. He was pinch-hitting for Pat Teague, who had approached his desk at 6:15, when he'd been about done for the day, and asked him to fill in. Teague was an involved father apparently, and had a few kids playing several sports or vice versa. Either way, there were a lot of games for him to go to, as Behr had gotten similar requests a few other times over the past six months he'd been at the Caro Group, the private investigation and security company that was as close as it got to a white-shoe firm in the field.

The job was an uneasy fit for Behr. Working for someone else—along with the starched collars, the suits and ties, and the stiff and shiny black Florsheim wingtips he was required to wear—rubbed him the wrong way. In fact, the outfit chafed his feet and neck raw for the first couple of weeks. But with Susan near nine months pregnant he found himself doing what he had to to earn a living, and trying to make his peace with it.

Behr had been reluctant about filling in for Teague the first time he was asked, not being professionally trained as a body man. But Teague assured him he was up to it without any advance preparation, that Kolodnik was a low-maintenance client who just wanted someone to organize his table at restaurants and to keep away "wakeboppers"—his term for business aspirants hoping to make contact and gain by the association. There was nothing against the switch in company policy, so Behr had asked a few questions, read some tactical guidance in the archives, and gone ahead in order to collect the extra money. He soon learned he was basically meant to be a hybrid of chauffeur and babysitter.

All sound besides their footsteps dropped away as they neared the P3 level. The elevator wouldn't take them lower than P1. It was broken, or perhaps they needed a key card this late in the evening. Though Behr wasn't an experienced bodyguard, even he could see that this should have been a two-man detail, minimum, had they been going by the book: one man to accompany the client to his meeting and a driver to stay with the vehicle and pull up to a rear or side entrance of the building when it was done.

Three men, with a backup for the walk, would've been even better. But in the current economic climate the "book" was out the window, and no one who earned his own money, even a guy like Kolodnik, was springing for multiman teams unless there was real reason. That was Behr's guess anyway.

So when Kolodnik had asked him to come inside, to wait while he took his meeting, and to help him carry some stuff out, Behr had done so. He'd parked the Suburban on a low floor in the visitor spaces because the garage had been full at that time, rode the elevator upstairs with Kolodnik, and waited outside the glass-walled conference room while a nearly three-hour meeting took place between Kolodnik, a redheaded woman, and a pair of gray-haired men, all dressed in sober blue business suits. Now Behr toted two bankers' boxes full of files back to the vehicle.

They turned the corner and reached the head of the row where the Suburban and a few other cars were parked, when Behr felt a blip on his mental radar. He transferred the boxes to one hand and was fishing in his pocket for the Suburban's key fob when it caught his eye. There was an aberration in the lighting pattern. A black gap, like a missing tooth, in the otherwise uniform yellow light grid of the garage, and then it was too late.

The gunshots punched through the air in a broken chain of crackle and thunder. A stripe of rounds tore into a Toyota Camry near them as Behr dropped the bankers' boxes and jammed Kolodnik to the ground beneath him. The air went out of Kolodnik upon impact. A breathless "fuck" was all Behr heard before more rounds wanged off the concrete behind them and started getting closer.

Behr had never been fired upon by an automatic weapon before, and he instantly found he was not a fan. The buzz-saw sound scrambled his mind, and he felt the urge to make his six and a half feet and two hundred forty pounds as small as he possibly could, but that urge competed with the instinct to cover Kolodnik. He stayed over the businessman and scramble-crawled them toward the Suburban, shredding the knees of his suit pants as he went.

He scanned the darkness for a target, but between bursts, the area the gunman fired from was pitch-black. Another stripe of rounds ripped past them on the ground, and Behr was sure he was killed as he pressed the key fob. The Suburban unlocked with a chirping sound that joined the ringing in his ears. The fob tumbled from his hand and fell to the pavement as he reached up and jerked the door open between them and the shooter. There was little chance they'd be driving out anyway, as the shooter let off another burst.

Dead, Behr thought, with just a piece of flimsy Detroit steel between him and what were undoubtedly full-metal-jacketed .223 or 7.65mm shells coming their way.

The door shuddered with the impact, and Behr expected he and Kolodnik to be covered with shattered glass and worse. But there was merely spalling, and the window held. The door shook and absorbed the live rounds with a dull whump.

Armored. The realization echoed in Behr's head. But getting the principal up and inside the vehicle would be more dangerous than leaving him down right now.

"Oh, Jesus," he heard Kolodnik grunt from behind him, and Behr realized this wasn't going to end on its own.

Return fire, Behr exhorted himself. His hand, slick with sweat, found the holstered Glock 22 .40 caliber that Caro required him to carry on his hip. He didn't generally favor the gun, the squared look and plastic feel of it, but he loved it at the moment.

When firing in low-light or no-light conditions, the idea is to keep the shots within an imagined two-foot box, centered on the opponent's muzzle flash. Another burst erupted at them. There was some muted flare coming from the weapon across the garage, but not the three-foot stream of flame he expected.

Flash suppressor. Nice information but not that helpful at the moment. Behr sprawled out beneath the bottom edge of the door and put the tritium dot of his front sight where he'd last seen a muzzle burst, hoping the shooter didn't know enough to fire and move, and emptied a mag. Ten rounds pitched worthlessly into the darkness. Behr tried to determine if he'd made any hits as he dropped the clip and reloaded. At least he'd stopped the incoming fire for a moment. Then Behr's desperation to survive fed him an idea. He rolled onto his back, accidentally kicking Kolodnik along the side of the head as he did, and shot out all the nearby lights along the ceiling. Plastic and glass sprinkled down on them along with a thick blanket of darkness.

Behr had gone through his reserve mag now, but he hadn't quite shot himself empty. He grabbed at his ankle where he wore his Bulldog .44 as a backup gun, strictly against company policy. He had the five rounds in it and then they'd be done.

He tried to listen as he held fire, but there was only a hollowed-out buzzing in his ears after all the shooting. Behr perceived Kolodnik's racked and panicked breathing nearby. Then he got the impression there were footsteps across the way in the dark. There was a broken rhythm to them, perhaps a limping gait, and Behr wondered if the shooter was actually hit, or if he was coming toward them. But then the steps grew fainter. Behr's heart surged at the idea he was giving up and leaving. There was the sound of a car engine, just around the corner; that came through clear enough.

Get up after him, Behr urged himself. But he didn't move an inch.

2

Behr felt Kolodnik lying still under his hand. He was sure the man had been hit and he wondered how badly.

"Is it over?" Kolodnik asked, then started to stir.

"Believe so," Behr said, hardly recognizing his own voice. A set of high beams had striped the wall opposite them, followed by a screech of tires, and then they'd been left alone.

Kolodnik's knee and elbow had gotten thumped when he'd fallen to the concrete, and his jaw was sore from the kick, but otherwise he was unshot and unhurt. Behr, for his part, felt giddy to be alive.

"Get in the car," he ordered Kolodnik. They climbed in, Kolodnik in the front passenger seat, Behr behind the wheel.

"I got nothing," Kolodnik said of his cell phone.

"One bar," Behr said of his, and dialed 911. He gave the particulars to the dispatcher and they waited in shocked silence for about two minutes before the first police cars responded.

Vehicles and voices and activity quickly filled the parking garage, along with lights—the red and blue of the cruisers' flashers, the xenon white of headlights, and the hard carbon glare of the driver's side spots—that chased away the darkness in which the danger had been hiding.

A young/old pair of patrolmen was first. Then another. Behr stepped out and identified himself and showed them his Caro credentials. He found the key to the Suburban. Then a dark Crown

Vic tooled into the area and a solid man, who was dressed in a suit, climbed out.

"Lieutenant," one of the patrolmen greeted him.

"I'm Breslau," the new arrival said in a husky voice, and shook Behr's hand.

Behr ran him through what had happened, beat by beat. Breslau's muscled jaw worked a piece of gum feverishly around his downturned mouth, his eyes cutting about the garage, landing on the Suburban, the place where the shots had come from, Kolodnik, and finally back on Behr.

"Uh-huh, uh-huh, uh-huh," he said as he processed each piece of information.

Kolodnik, meanwhile, had removed his jacket and stood off to the side, talking with a tall, lanky officer. Behr heard the muttered particulars of his statement.

"On recommendation of several executives at my company," is what Kolodnik said when the cop asked why he had security with him, and "no" was the answer to whether there had been any specific threats made on his person recently.

"Yes, of course," Kolodnik said to the follow-up question: "Are you known to carry lots of cash?"

A paramedic arrived on the scene and sat Kolodnik against a nearby car to look him over.

"So, Caro . . . I know plenty of those boys—how come I haven't met you?" Breslau said to Behr, half question half accusation.

"I'm fairly new," Behr answered.

"You just a meat shield? Or are you an investigator or case manager?" he wondered.

The question wasn't a simple one. It got to the heart of what Behr didn't like about the Caro job. When the company had come to him the first time, he'd suspected it was to do the dirty work, to be the "radioactive man" for the company, so the rest of them, a tight clique of mostly ex-FBI and ex-Treasury guys who'd gone private, could keep their hands clean. He'd turned them down because of that, but they'd come back two months later, and he surveyed the paucity of clients out there for him on his own. Ten million people were looking for jobs and here was one. A good one. He signed on.

After a short honeymoon of polite respect around the office, he'd seen his concerns bear out. Caro was on retainer to an insurance conglomerate, and they started by asking him to videotape a waitress pulling some disability fraud. It was easy enough, even if she was a single mother who got arrested because of it. Then it was on to placing GPS units on subjects' cars. They requested he break into a few vehicles next, to plant voice-activated recorders. He tried to put them off, saying, "I look like the Pelican to you?" referencing the dirty tricks P.I. who was currently serving a long jail sentence. He'd gotten a laugh, but they'd pressed him and he'd done it; and after that they wanted him to illegally enter an office after hours in order to retrieve certain documents. He'd balked at the office job, and found a work-around, getting the papers while the place was open, but he knew it wasn't the last time they'd be asking for a B and E.

"I guess you could say I'm a floater," Behr finally answered. Breslau just looked at him.

"Gonna need to borrow that for a bit," Breslau said, pointing a forefinger at Behr's hip.

"Sure," Behr said, easing the empty Glock out of its holster and dropping it into a plastic evidence bag held out by a jowly sergeant who appeared next to Breslau. The police would run a serial number check, make sure it matched the company's paperwork. Behr added the first magazine, which he'd collected from the ground, and wished he'd been wearing his gold ring with the diamond-studded letters "IMPD." It was commemorative of a special relationship with the department, and only given by the brass, which was how Behr had gotten it. But it was sitting at home in a drawer as usual.

"We'll return the Glock to you asap," Breslau said curtly.

Behr nodded and watched as Breslau went on a little walking tour of the scene, shining a small flashlight at a few particular spots, taking it all in. He kept the gum moving all the while as he walked, like he was training for an Olympic chewing event; and

Behr found himself standing next to Kolodnik, who was finished with the medic.

"How you doing?" Behr asked.

"Good. I'm all right," Kolodnik said.

"So, an armored SUV . . ." Behr said, leaving it out there.

"We have a project coming up, a big development in Mexico. Between the drug wars and the kidnappings down there, we thought we might need a half dozen for the executives and the project managers. The company in New York we ordered them from sent us this one to try, to see how it performed."

"Performs pretty good, I'd say," Behr remarked, and they shared a jagged laugh. Then there was a moment's quiet rippled only by radio calls as the cops all looked at the ground or crawled around on it. They'd found eighteen of Behr's shell casings but were having a heck of a time locating the other two, as the things had a tendency to roll.

"Thank you, Frank," Kolodnik said, clearing his throat. "I mean it. What you did . . . That was . . . I really don't know what to . . ."

"Just glad how it came out," Behr said. "Believe me."

Kolodnik handed Behr a business card, just his name and a telephone number engraved on heavy ivory stock. "That's my personal number. You call me if you ever need anything."

Behr nodded and went back to watching the cops work, when the squealing of tires on the cement announced the arrival of another vehicle. It was a blue Cadillac STS adding its headlights to the party. Behr recognized the car as belonging to Karl Potempa, the head of Caro's Indianapolis office. The Caddy jerked to a stop, and out jumped Potempa, looking oddly casual in a velour tracksuit with an FBI crest on the left breast. Behr had never seen the man without a necktie, but the absence of a business suit didn't diminish his authority any, and his silver gray hair was perfectly combed. After just a handful of months on the job and no real interaction, Behr wasn't close with Karl Potempa but knew him well enough to see he was shaken.

"Karl," Kolodnik said.

"Bernie, Jesus H." Potempa crossed to Kolodnik and wrapped him in a brief but intense embrace. "I've got a team reporting here, and another on your house right now. Cops were already there—all's quiet."

"Good, good," Kolodnik murmured.

"Why don't you wait in my car," Potempa suggested, and Kolodnik made his way toward the Cadillac. "I'll drive you home myself."

"Find any blood trail over there?" Behr asked Breslau as the lieutenant rejoined him.

"Nope," Breslau answered. "So twenty rounds, no confirmed hits." It hung in the air like an allegation.

"You notice there were none on our side either," Behr said, indicating that he and Kolodnik were standing there, healthy as hogs, "dumb ass," Behr finished, half under his breath. Even as it came out of his mouth, he wished he hadn't spoken.

"What'd you say?" Breslau demanded, his gum finally stopping for a moment.

Behr quartered toward him. "I guess you heard me or you wouldn't be asking."

"It wasn't ducks on a pond here, Gary," Potempa jumped in, using his command voice, a varnished baritone, as he strode closer to Breslau.

"I know, I know," the lieutenant said. Potempa shook Breslau's hand in greeting, then he turned to Behr and pumped his hand with vigor.

"Congratulations, Frank. Hell of a job tonight."

Behr just nodded.

Breslau, brow knit, was already on to the next topic on his mind. "No casings on the shooter's side. What do you make of that?"

"Brass catcher," Behr said flatly.

Breslau nodded quickly. He'd either had the same thought or was quick at looking like he had.

"Brass catcher *and* a flash suppressor. That's a tactical weapon. Military," Behr added.

"Well . . ." Breslau said, "let's not get too excited. It might be. Might be something jerry-rigged at home, too."

"Is that right?" Behr said.

"I'm looking at the shot patterns here, and I'm not reading 'professional.' " Behr glanced at the Toyota and the door of the Suburban and the wall behind it. Breslau wasn't wrong: it had been some messy shooting, and he was alive thanks to it. Breslau put a hand on Potempa's shoulder and steered him away into the police activity. "We're pulling up security tapes and entry tickets on the garage . . ."

Behr remained standing there, alone.

3

The bloody cunts in America had bollixed it. One of 'em was even sicked up and crying over there now.

The Welshman, Wadsworth Dwyer, circled with his training partner, his mind far away from what he was doing. But he didn't need to think in order to grapple. He'd been doing it for too long. He held black belts in judo and Japanese jujitsu—the kind the samurai had invented to use when the battle was to the death and the sword had been lost—and that's how Waddy Dwyer used it. But that was just the beginning of his schooling. He'd been a striker growing up in the pubs in Merthyr and had learned military hand-to-hand at Hereford, before practicing it in piss-smelling beer holes the world over. He'd studied sambo when he was "working" in Russia just after the wall came down and liked it for its similarities to legitimate grappling. He'd quickly moved in and out of *systema specnaz*—the mystical and suppos-edly deadly art they taught to Russian Special Forces—when he'd choked out the teacher with a simple guillotine. He tried Krav Maga when he was on loan to Israeli intelligence, and liked it for its aggressive mind-set, but realized he didn't need it much after he broke the instructor's jaw the third day when he'd been feeling mean and homesick. That's when he knew it was time to get out and come back to Wales.

Wales. He must be some kind of arsehole, because he loved the weather here, cold and rainy most of the time, even in the summer, up on the top of the mountain in the Cambrians where he lived now.

His training partner shot for a single leg takedown, and the Welshman sprawled, leaving a knee behind to clock the boy on the top of his head for his trouble. He couldn't remember the last time he'd been taken down. At five foot seven, fourteen stone, it was like toppling over a fireplug. His training partner got back up a bit slowly after the knee to the head, so Dwyer took his own shot. His was a double, and he wrapped his arms around both his training partner's thighs and cranked to the side like he was turning a lorry's steering wheel, dumping the boy on his head onto the hard mats.

Bloody fucking 'ell, he thought as he leaped on top of his training partner and worked a crucifix, catching one of the boy's arms between his legs and hyperextending it, and doing the same to the other using his hands. *I'm gonna have to go to America.*

The training partner was stretched out and helpless but didn't say "tap," so the Welshman gave him a rap across the mouth, causing blood to run red over the boy's teeth.

"Fuck's sake, Waddy!" the training partner said.

Wadsworth Dwyer got up, certain as fuckall he hated leaving his mountaintop.

4

Behr sat down at the kitchen table before 7:00 A.M. and appreciated the morning light coming through the window in a slanted shaft. He hadn't gone to bed until near 4:00, and hadn't slept much before waking unrested but automatically around 6:00 to a day that could easily have never come for him. He couldn't help but savor his coffee, the sweet sugar underneath the slight bitterness of the roast.

It hadn't been a single team that had arrived in the garage late the night before but a wave of Caro boys who flooded in after the call had gone out and word spread.

To do what? Behr wondered. It wasn't clear. To help with the investigation, perhaps. To herd up and feel the numbers of the organization standing strong against an outside threat. Or maybe it was simply to tack man-hours onto Kolodnik's bill. Behr had caught a ride with one of them to his car, which was parked back at Kolodnik's office, and had then driven home.

"Hi," Susan had said when he'd walked in, looking up from the body pillow she hugged, aware of how late it was. The television was on in the bedroom.

"What's this?" he asked. She often fell asleep to the TV, and she'd been sleeping not watching, but a glance gave her the answer.

"*Women Behind Bars.* Mostly wives who killed their husbands."

Susan was a fan of true crime and reality shows. "You thinking about bumping me off?" Behr asked. "Studying where they slipped up?"

"We'd have to be married first for that," she said.

"Right."

"Why are you so late?" she asked.

He'd sat down on the edge of the bed and after catching a look at the large swell of her belly beneath the bedsheets, told her everything, trying to make it sound as routine as possible, which it wasn't, and she knew it.

Behr went for his second cup of coffee. His shoulders and neck and his knees and wrists felt raw this morning. It wasn't a question of injury, but as if all the adrenaline that had fired through his system, the absolute tensing of every muscle, had an effect similar to a full body workout. He didn't mind it. He didn't have a problem with anything that reminded him he wasn't dead right about now.

He looked down at the morning paper to find they had the story. But they'd missed most of the details due to how late the deal had gone down. No names of the players were mentioned, just that two men had been fired upon in a downtown parking garage, that the shooter or shooters had gotten away, that no one had been killed.

Susan entered the kitchen and looked at him, noticing his shirt and tie, and the suit jacket hanging over the back of his chair.

"You're going in to the office?" she asked, surprised.

"Yeah, sure," he said. "What else am I gonna do?"

"No workout today?" she wondered. Almost every morning around 5:30 or so he'd be at it—running or weights, various other types of strength training, hitting the heavy bag or rolling Brazilian jujitsu. Not today though. After last night, there was something about it that seemed superfluous.

"I took a holiday on account of being alive," he said, smiling, trying to sound light.

"Seems like a good reason," she said, going to get a mug for the one cup of coffee a day her obstetrician allowed. "I didn't even hear you get up. I'm sleeping like someone dropped a cinder block on my head these days." Susan was complaining a lot about how tired she was, which was unusual for her—both the complaining and the fatigue. Her customary state was one of vivacious energy. "Have I mentioned that being pregnant isn't much fun?"

"You might've, once or twice," he said. "A couple more weeks, then it's lounging around and bonbon time," he said, alluding to the start of her upcoming maternity leave.

"Yeah, I've heard newborns are easy," she said. "You want to go look at that place over on Guilford after work?" They'd given up Susan's apartment three months back. It was nicer than his but small, while his had the extra bedroom that, though currently serving as a storage space, could be set up for the baby. But since his steady Caro money had been rolling in, they'd been seriously considering moving somewhere nicer. There were some new town houses over in Broad Ripple that would be a clean, fresh place to raise a child.

"Sure," he said, "shouldn't be a problem. I'll let you know if they're going to keep me late."

5

Morning had stolen in like a secret, and the big house was still and empty and quiet around Lowell Gantcher. Nancy and the kids were away in lake country for the month and he wasn't doing well alone. He'd spent the night checking the paper's Web page every minute for updates and had quickly begun to feel like he was playing the starring role in an unfolding nightmare. At first there'd been no information. Then there'd been a brief bulletin at around 4:30 A.M. He had kept checking incessantly, waiting for further details, but they didn't come. The starkly worded initial report was all there was for hours.

He'd taken to pacing around the house. Ten thousand square feet of living space, plus three thousand more in the finished basement that included screening, workout, and poker rooms, probably was a bit much. It hadn't seemed so when he and Nancy had been buying it and tricking it out, but it was a real bull market house. That was only two and a half, three years ago, but it seemed a lot longer. Hell, they hadn't even gotten the place fully furnished yet.

He sat in the study, which was dark and silent, and wrapped in oak paneling. The only light in the room was the early sunlight bleeding through the closed slats of the horizontal blinds, which were also made of oak. This room was furnished. It was done up to the nines. His hands rested on a massive mahogany partners desk. There were matching leather couches and armchairs in a lustrous tobacco color, silver frames and leather-bound books on the shelves around a wet bar. Over the marble fireplace hung a plasma television that was so large it could serve as the scoreboard in a minor-league baseball park. It was the first room that had been done once the master and the kids' bedrooms had been made livable. When they'd been walking around the newly built house, it was the study that had practically sold the place. The Realtor drifted away, leaving them alone, and Nancy had turned to him and said, "Let's buy it. You'll be like Don Corleone in here."

"Yeah?" he said, hesitating for a moment.

"Yes, Lo. Every man needs a *Godfather* room." And she gave him that smile that inspired him to greatness, that made him feel he was able to do anything, and they'd bought the place. But Don Corleone was a grave and powerful man, restrained and effective. Lowell was an aspirational real estate developer who had fed on times of easy credit until he'd practically turned into white dough. He even *felt* pale and washed out sitting there. The phrase "nouveau riche" was one he'd just recently learned.

It seemed simple once, to sit at the brand-new partners desk, going over statements that outlined the take of each machine and table and the casino's total. *How could there be trouble in the world*? he'd wondered back then.

But now he was staring at a B rating on his venture. B. When he was in college a B would've been a welcome sight on his transcript. But now, because ratings started at AAA, a single, measly B was six classes down the quality scale; and once an investment had ticked south out of the A's, it started to stink worse than a road-killed skunk. With a tumble from even BBB, there was no chance of rescue investors coming in now. No chance at all.

A report had recently landed on his desktop full of projections that intimated the state's casino business had hit a high-water mark. That was more bad news. Adding to the gloomy forecast was out-of-state competition, the specter of those sausage eaters in Chicago passing gaming downtown, and the god-blessed Indians opening up all over the place with their tax-sheltered free rolls. A housing slump, a credit crunch, and record unemployment sucking disposable income out the customers' pockets were the final grim strokes to the ugly picture. There was only one hope, and that was abatement by the state on the 75-million-dollar-per-year gaming license tax.

He heard tires on gravel. It was the sound he'd been waiting for. He hurried to the door to see a battered Honda Civic driving away, and the morning paper resting in its pink plastic sleeve at the end of the driveway. He hurried barefoot to get it, the sharp gravel digging into the soles of his feet. He bent and picked up the paper, tearing the plastic away, and scanned with his eyes while he hop-ran back to the house. What he read confirmed what he'd seen online. He didn't make it back to the house. He collapsed to his knees on the pebbled ground, as if he'd been hit in the gut with an ax handle. Powerful, ungodly, tearless sobs shook his chest. It was all going to end.

6

Behr walked through the walnut doors into the Caro Group office well before 9:00, but there were nearly a dozen investigators and clerical staff already there, and when they saw him they started clapping. He didn't know what to do with himself, so he stood there dumbly for a moment, until the applause and a single whistle subsided.

When he headed for his desk, Joanne, the new receptionist, smiled and wished him good morning as if he were the mayor.

"Frank Behr in . . . *Bulletproof*!" a mock announcer's voice rang out as Behr put his stuff down. It was a pair of investigators, Reidy and Malick, who pumped his hand and gave him a few whacks on the shoulder.

"You get a look at the shooter?" Reidy wondered.

"Didn't get a look at anything," Behr said.

"You put any in him, you think?" Malick asked.

"Don't know. Doubt it," Behr answered. "They didn't find any blood."

"Don't mean he wasn't hit," Reidy opined.

"It was dark." Behr shrugged and after a moment the investigators drifted on and Behr went to pour himself a coffee.

He was in the break room filling up, when Pat Teague walked in looking rumpled around the edges as usual.

"Holy Christ, Frank, I *knew* that was a shit detail when I asked you to switch," he set in, forcing a laugh.

"Sure was," Behr said, giving him back a smile.

"How the hell are you?" Teague asked and didn't wait for an answer. "When my BlackBerry binged and I saw the e-mail that went around, I almost crapped myself. Couldn't sleep the rest of the night. I e-mailed you, did you get it?"

Behr nodded. An e-mail from Teague inquiring about his health had come through, but he hadn't bothered responding.

"I would've called too, if it wasn't so late," Teague continued. "I mean, shit, Frank, it should've been me out there . . ."

"Don't worry about it, Pat, luck of the draw," Behr said. "How was the game, anyway?"

"Oh, it was fine. Forget that—I'm just glad everyone's still using up some air here."

"You and me both," Frank said.

"Some shit detail," Teague said again. That's when Karl Potempa, hair locked down, and razor sharp in a blue pinstripe, appeared in the doorway.

"Teague. In here now," he called out, then regarded Behr. "Hcy, Frank, how you doing? No day off, not even the morning, huh?"

"I don't golf. Not well anyway," Behr said. The truth was he hadn't even thought of taking time.

"I want to talk to you in a minute," Potempa said. Behr nodded and continued to his desk as Teague headed into Potempa's office.

Behr found himself less than interested in work—which at the moment meant finishing a forensic financial background check on a corporate executive. He'd only managed to tap out a few sentences on his computer. He'd write up his report on last night's incident once he'd talked to Potempa. A quarter of his life now was reports. Another quarter was answering e-mails, texts, and calls on the BlackBerry that Caro had issued him. He may as well have had the thing surgically mounted to his hip he was such a slave to it. He recognized he was part of an organization now, and as such he wasn't alone. There were upsides, like the health insurance and the squad of colleagues appearing in the parking garage and the whole office showing up at his desk this morning, one of them with a flyer advertising a combat shooting school in the Nevada desert that had been printed off the Internet and waved around with much hilarity. There were the steady paychecks of course, but there was a price that came with the belonging, too, like being told what to do and when to do it and remaining reachable and accountable—always. He swallowed it down and dealt with it. That's what being a father, even an expectant one, was about.

By 9:45 the newspaper's Web site had begun to fill in the gaps. Prominent citizen Bernard Kolodnik was mentioned, as well as his unidentified "private security who had returned fire." That suited Behr just fine. Lieutenant Gary Breslau was quoted as saying police weren't sure whether "it was attempted robbery, carjacking, or other motive behind the shooting." That "other" glowed in Behr's mind for a moment, but before long Ms. Swanton, Karl Potempa's helmet-haired secretary, appeared at his desk.

"He's ready for you now, Mr. Behr."

Behr took a seat across from Karl Potempa, who was ringed by plaques on the wall commemorating his civil and law enforcement service, including his stint in the FBI. Potempa had his feet up on the desk and was shaking his head at the departing Teague.

"How are you doing this morning, Frank?" Potempa began.

"Pretty good, considering," Behr said, hoping now that everyone in the office had had a chance to check in with him, and Potempa had even taken two bites at the apple, that the solicitous questions would abate sometime soon.

"Bernie Kolodnik was more than pleased at the way things resolved. I don't know if one's on the way, but if a bonus comes in, it'll be passed on to you."

"Okay." Behr's eye found a series of family photos on the credenza behind his boss. It was Potempa and his handsome auburn-haired wife, along with photos of a son and a beautiful daughter. There were several pictures—slices of life—a cheerleading shot, the son in football pads, all of them dressed for a formal occasion—taken a few years apart, that tracked the kids from youth to young adulthood. In the last one of the whole family, the son looked to be around twenty-one, the daughter eighteen. Then there were a few more, from which the daughter was absent, including a wedding photo of the boy at around age twenty-four. Maybe the daughter was studying overseas, Behr considered.

"Now as far as press goes, it's zero-sum here. You haven't spoken to anyone yet, have you?" Potempa asked.

"Nope," Behr said. He remembered reading in the company's introductory materials that Caro's stance was that no individuals were to be named in news stories or press releases. "Security by the Caro Group" or "Investigative services provided by the Caro Group" was all the information that was supposed to be given.

"That's company policy, organization-wide." Potempa spread his arms, indicating, no doubt, the dozen Caro Group offices out there dotted across the nation. "We stay behind the scenes, not out front. If anyone contacts you, refer them to Curt Lundquist."

Behr nodded. Lundquist was house counsel for Caro's Indianapolis office and its mouthpiece in matters such as these.

"What the hell happened between you and Breslau last night?" Potempa wondered.

"You saw it. Guy's got a way about him," Behr said.

"Uh-huh. He's a cop with a real upward trajectory."

"Of course he is," Behr said, and Potempa looked at him for a moment.

"So, how long before your report on last night is done? It's got to go to corporate."

"I was wondering if you wanted anything in particular left in or out," Behr said. He was aware of how blunt the question might have sounded. He was also aware, painfully so, of how short his political skills landed when it came to things like this.

"Smart question. Just write it the way it happened," Potempa replied, in a way that gave Behr no real insight.

"End of day then, on account of all the details."

"Get it done," Potempa said, and Behr bit down. A handful of months wasn't enough time to get used to taking orders after the years of doing it all his way. "I got something I need you on. If you're up to it." The challenge was out there. Behr stood.

"Sure, Karl, whatever you need," Behr said.

"Oh yeah, here you go," Potempa said, going into a desk drawer and coming out with Behr's Glock .40 and magazines in a police evidence bag. "They just sent it over."

Behr nodded, took the bag, and headed for the door, where he paused. "The cops get anything, by the way? Wits? Security cameras?"

"I haven't heard yet, but don't worry, they're all over it like white on snow."

7

"Purpose of your visit, business or pleasure?" the customs agent, a broad-faced, chesty Midwestern man, asked.

"Vacation and sightseeing," answered Waddy Dwyer, who stood in the hall for arriving international passengers at O'Hare Airport. Despite his answer, he was thinking about his business, which consisted of nipping a loose thread and finishing the Kolodnik job before it could be pulled at and unravel the whole bit of knitting. "Since the wife isn't along, it might actually be pleasure."

The customs agent looked up with bored, heavy-lidded eyes from the mostly blank pages of Dwyer's dummy passport. If the man had been looking at a real document, and Dwyer had made a habit of going in legally, he'd be thumbing through page after page of entry stamps from the Czech Republic, Hungary, Bosnia, Russia, Congo, Tanzania and three quarters of the rest of Africa, Java, Pakistan, the Middle East, and basically anywhere else there'd been a shitstorm of trouble. And the Maldives, too, but that was just for the scuba diving.

"Have you been to a farm or agriculture site? Are you carrying any food, specifically fresh fruit or vegetables?" the agent asked in a bureaucratic monotone that could only lull an absolute imbecile into divulging anything important.

"No," Dwyer said.

"Are you carrying more than ten thousand dollars' worth of any currency?"

"I wish," Dwyer answered, although he was carrying twenty-five grand in four different packets that he'd taped to his abdomen and thighs in the lavatory during the last hour of the flight. Buying the clean weapons he'd need didn't come cheap, and the sellers didn't take Visa.

The customs agent roused himself into a moment's vigorous action as he abused Dwyer's passport with a rubber entry stamp. The sound reminded Dwyer of the fishermen braining mackerel with wooden billy clubs down by the docks of Trefor. "Enjoy your trip," the agent said, handing back the passport.

Duly welcomed, Dwyer walked out of the customs hall and into the Chicago afternoon.

8

Behr's write-up of events was a composite in style of a law enforcement incident report and the more detailed prose format that Caro expected. It took him several hours to complete, and he didn't even bother hurrying. He started with Teague's approach to him to handle the shift and continued all the way through to leaving the garage. He broke off from his work at lunchtime for half an hour and went to Shapiro's for a sandwich. When it was time to pay, Behr found his check had been taken care of by a trio of Caro case managers who were eating in the corner. He gave them a salute of thanks as he left, which they returned, fists and thumbs in the air. By the time he got back to his desk and finished the report, printed one out for the files, and e-mailed digital copies to Potempa and Curt Lundquist, the brief stretched to more than eight typewritten pages.

As for the thing Potempa had mentioned, Behr received it right before the end of the day. Moments after his report hit Potempa's in-box, Ms. Swanton delivered to his desk a CD-ROM containing a case file on a string of unarmed robberies, thefts really, of a check cashing/money wiring business called Payroll Place. Payroll Place had sixteen locations throughout Indiana, southern Illinois, and northern Missouri. Canvas cash bags and strongboxes had been taken out of a half dozen armored cars and safe rooms over the past few months.

As Behr looked over the file, it seemed possible an outside ring might have identified a weakness in the company's security plan and was having a field day. But there was a company personnel list included, almost one hundred and fifty names, and Behr knew it was much more likely to be an inside job. That would account for the company's avoiding the police and coming to Caro in the first place. The background checks on the employees who had access to cash and codes were standard surface-level time-of-hiring reports, but deeper p-checks were needed, and the police weren't going to bother with something like that. Especially when the thefts were only netting between five and ten thousand dollars apiece and had been free of violence so far. Behr rubbed his temples, realizing he'd be chained to the computer and the courthouse, searching databases, until his coming child was in preschool. And when he'd finally narrowed the pool to a few dozen likely candidates, *then* the interviews would start . . .

The end of the day was close enough at hand and the case represented far too much work to start now. Behr closed the file and glanced at his computer to see that Kolodnik had become the headline on the local news sites, but not, Behr noted with muted surprise, for what had transpired in the garage last night. That had been referenced in some short, linked articles, which chalked up the shooting to random violence, inner-city crime, and the glut of guns on the streets; but Kolodnik had made an announcement that was much bigger news.

A press conference had been held—the one that Kolodnik had mentioned on his call before the shooting—to announce that the state's senior senator had just resigned his seat to fight advanced prostate cancer, the junior senator was now senior, and there was an opening. In cases like this in Indiana, a special election wasn't held. Instead, it became a gubernatorial appointment, and Kolodnik had been handpicked by the governor as the replacement to serve in the Senate until the next regular election four years out. The governor had tapped Kolodnik, saying, "His business and community leadership is unparalleled."

"I look forward to taking a leave of absence from the day-to-day operations of my company to act upon a long-held goal of mine: to enter into public service," Kolodnik said, "to work to curb crime and increase prosperity for all Indiana citizens." His stake in his company would be moved into a blind trust to be managed by a third party until such time as he left government. Barring any confirmation problems, Bernie Cool was going to Washington.

He must have one hell of a PR machine, Behr mused, seeing how the shooting had been tucked away into obscurity behind the announcement. Then another thought lodged itself in Behr's head, considering what little he had gotten done on his own day after: *that's one single-minded son of a bitch.*

There was a photo of the press event held in the glare of the sun on the statehouse steps right by the statue of old Oliver Morton, the governor during the Civil War. Behr made out a few of his counterparts behind Kolodnik, his neatly bobbed wife, and the governor up on the podium. He didn't recognize them as Caro boys, at least not from the Indianapolis office, but he could spot the breed. They were professional body men, perhaps hired from Kroll, Executive Solutions, or Securitas—which was what Pinkerton was called these days—or maybe some other outfit. They looked like they were sweating up there in their blue suits and dark sunglasses. But Kolodnik didn't look overheated. Of course he didn't, he was Bernie Cool.

Behr sat there, staring at the computer screen for a long, long time, wondering what else he thought. Then the tone of an incoming e-mail sounded. Behr clicked it open. It was a company-wide humor post from Pat Teague, a list entitled "Ten Reasons Guns Are Better Than Women." Number ten was: "You can trade in a .44 for a .22," and number one was "You can buy a silencer for a gun." Behr put the computer to sleep, stood, and left for the day.

9

"What about that one?" Susan said, pointing to a girl in a plaid skirt and white blouse sitting momentarily alone at the bar. "Strawberry blonde. Pretty face."

"The hair works . . ." Chad Quell, her coworker agreed.

"You'd know," Susan laughed. "You probably spend more time on yours."

"Very funny. But I'm gonna pass. Too much makeup and I don't do cankles," Chad said.

"Cankles?"

"Calf and ankles with no delineation in between."

" 'Ey, don't harsh on the cankles, young man," Susan said.

"C'mon, you've got special dispensation. A pregnancy pass." Chad smiled.

"Thanks a lot," Susan said. There were moments when she saw the beauty in it—the round belly, the glow of incipient motherhood, nature's majesty. There were other times when she just felt big and sloppy and with her youth behind her.

"Can't believe it—little Suzy Q., having a little one of her own."

"Better believe it," Susan said, even though she still had trouble doing so herself most of the time. She surveyed the big table, nine or ten chairs now empty, the detritus of plates of buffalo wings, timber fries, beer bottles, and hurricane glasses with the pink swill of strawberry margaritas in the bottoms. The Wild Beaver wasn't her choice, but some of the guys from the office liked it because of the sassy female bartenders, and the girls were happy to come along; so even though it was her good-bye to the office before maternity leave, she didn't protest.

"What about one of those bartenders? You can fight through the competition."

"Maybe. Not sure assless chaps and dancing on the bar are good credentials for my next girl," Chad said, scanning the sexy pair pouring drinks for a few rows of guys.

"Don't try and act like a grown-up for my benefit—it doesn't wash. You'd love a girl in assless chaps."

"Speaking of grown-ups, wasn't Grandpa Behr supposed to be meeting you?"

"He is."

A pause ensued, during which Chad seemed to wrestle with himself over something he had to say.

"Suzy . . ." he began.

"Yeah?"

"Nothing."

"What?"

"It's just . . . what are you getting out of this?" Chad didn't wrestle very hard or for very long. "I just don't see it . . . I mean, how many divorces does this guy have rattling along behind him?"

"One, for god's sake, Chad," Susan said.

"And that other stuff. All that other *stuff*. This guy's got *baggage*. He's got a frigging luggage carousel spinning around his waist. And now with the kid on the way . . . I just don't see it."

"I do. And luckily you don't need to."

"All right, all right." Chad retreated. "You want another drink?"

"No, I've had my one beer," she said.

"You're some kind of saint, Suzy."

Behr made his way through the faux-log-cabin-themed bar toward the tables in the back. The crowd he waded through had made good use of their happy hour and were well on their way to being juiced. It was still early, but the music was loud. The place was a long way from the lodge it was trying to resemble. As he cleared a column, he saw her sitting there, pregnant, looking like she was ready to leave. And her little buddy Chad was there next to her, like a dog waiting underneath the table for a scrap to fall. He walked over to them, ran his hand over her blond hair.

"Hey, Suze," he said. "Some place you picked."

"Guys from the office picked it," she said, smiling up at him.

"I feel ten years too old to be here." Behr shook his head.

"Fifteen," Chad said, "and overdressed too. How you doing, Franklin?"

"Chadwick," Behr said. "Still trying to develop that personality, I see."

"And that's coming from the master. Well . . ." Chad said, pushing away from the table, "duty calls." He gave Susan a half hug, stood, and made for the bar, where a gaggle of young professional females were sizing up a row of shot glasses along a six-foot-long wooden beaver tail.

"Be careful out there, player," Susan called after him, then turned to Behr.

He didn't know if her little party was done or if some of her coworkers were at the bar. He meant to offer her the chance to stay, but "You ready to go?" is what he said.

The units at Broad Ripple Arbor were clean and neat and spacious, with brand-new stainless steel appliances, cream-colored walls, and spongy gray carpet. There was a pool, a common room with a big-screen television, a fitness center, and an outdoor barbecue. The residents were mostly young professional couples, and more and more of them were having babies, which was giving the complex a family feel. It was near the Monon Trail, which was good for jogging, rollerblading, strollering.

Behr's feelings were mixed. He didn't feel at home in the well-scrubbed, almost cookie-cutter complex. *We should have a house*, he thought, as he followed Susan, a car length back, but the town house was a big step up from their current situation. There was no denying that. A three bedroom had just come available at the Arbor. It needed to be painted and cleaned and they could take it in about five days. All *they* needed to do was give a check for first, last, and security—forty-five hundred dollars—and pass the credit check.

Behr parked and made his way up the steps of their place. He knew Susan liked the town house. If they moved quickly, they could be in and settled before the baby came. He reached the door, where Susan waited. There was a wooden crate with his name on it blocking their way. Behr bent and saw a Laurel Ridge return address. Laurel Ridge was one of the highest-end neighborhoods in Carmel, which was about the highest-end suburb of the city. Behr bent, lifted the box, and carried it inside.

Once in the kitchen, he used a flathead screwdriver to pry the lid off.

"What's that?" Susan asked.

"Don't know," Behr said. He pushed back packing straw to find smooth green wine bottles lined up, torpedo-like, in rows. The labels read: Harlan Estate, the Maiden, Napa Valley Oakville Cabernet Sauvignon.

"Who sent it?"

"Not sure."

"So you want to take the town house?"

"Maybe."

"I know it's kind of expensive for a rental." It was true, fifteen hundred a month was a much bigger monthly nut than Behr was used to, but that's the way things were headed.

"Yeah, it's not that—"

"And it's not as private as we were hoping for . . ."

"Right."

"We could—"

"Just let me breathe on it for a minute." He said it quiet and calm, but the words themselves were strong and certainly didn't invite further conversation on the topic.

Down between some of the bottles Behr found an envelope and opened it. Inside was a card with the letters "BK" embossed at the top that bore the handwritten message: *With my deep thanks, Bernie.*

"It's from Kolodnik."

"That's nice," Susan said, knowing enough not to dwell on the apartment question for the moment.

"Yeah," Behr said, pulled a bottle out of the case and took it to the computer. He sat down and punched the wine's name into Google and quickly learned that it scored in the high 90s in all the major ratings.

"Retails for two-fifty a bottle, case price twenty-two hundred," he said.

"That's an expensive gift, Frank," Susan said.

"Technically I should declare it to the company," he said, turning the bottle in his hands.

"What are you going to do, O ye of fancy friends?" she wondered.

"I'm gonna drink it," he said, rummaging in the drawer for a corkscrew.

"Aren't you supposed to wait a few weeks after shipping for it to settle?"

Behr just looked at her and pulled the cork.

10

A bright orange wind sock, luffing in the breeze.

It was the first conscious memory Shugie Saunders had. He was five years old, standing out on the tarmac at Hendricks County Airport, waiting to fly to Cincinnati with his parents. He had seen the sock filling and turning and instinctively understood why the airplanes were taxiing around, taking off, and landing according to which way the wind blew. It made sense to him, young as he was.

It was something he had taken with him all the way through his school years and into politics. Some called him a campaign manager, others an adviser, still others a fixer, but thirteen state senators, a dozen mayors, and the last three governors would all agree that when it came to the Indy political scene, Shugie Saunders was a necessity. But that day of clarity on the runway was forty-three years ago. Things weren't so clearly indicated now. The wind sock was either hanging limp or blowing around in all different directions these days.

How the hell did I end up here? he wondered.

He glanced at the envelope on the edge of the desk, holding three thousand dollars he couldn't really afford. Melting ice clinked in his glass and he took a sip of the sour-tasting small batch bourbon that was supposed to be so smooth and looked out over the city. Twinkling lights and the occasional monorail-like movement of a car along St. Clair were the only indications of life out there.

The musical ringing of his cell phone startled him and made him angry all at once. It was going to rouse Lori, and she was going to leave. He crossed quickly to his desk to answer, and his anger grew when he saw the name of the incoming caller: Lowell Gantcher. He would have loved to have let the call go to voice mail, but that would be four more rings, four more times through the brassy samba figure that was his ringtone, and Lori would certainly be gone by then. He snatched the phone off the desk.

"What is it?" he said by way of greeting.

"I want to talk to him," Lowell Gantcher said on the other end of the phone. The connection was so clean it was as if he were in the room.

"No," Shugie Saunders said.

"What do you mean, no?" Gantcher asked.

Shugie let silence reinforce his answer, and heard the regretful sound of rustling in the bed behind him. He glanced back and caught a profile view of Lori's rounded breast, the curve of her back, as she reached for a piece of clothing in the near darkness.

"Come on, Shugie, don't gate-keeper me. You're standing in between Bernie and me, and I'm reduced to leaving messages like some kind of jerk off."

"Then stop leaving messages."

"I just want to talk to him."

"Not now." It was a conversation they'd had a dozen variations of over the past few months, as things had tightened to the strangle point on the business front and as the political picture grew more clear for Kolodnik. Lowell Gantcher was an important builder who held some sway in certain business matters around the city, but for him to call Shugie, insisting on a conversation with Kolodnik *now,* revealed thinking that verged on the delusional.

"He's my partner, for god's sake," Gantcher insisted.

"*Was,*" Shugie corrected. "He doesn't touch that investment anymore." Then he felt a tap on his shoulder, a few fingernail tips dancing like ballerinas along his clavicle. Shugie turned to see Lori standing there, dressed, her sandy blond hair bed-ruffled, and her eye makeup gone slightly raccoon. He loved seeing her this way. She looked five years younger than her already youthful twenty-three, and it also meant that they'd been together, that he'd had her. He raised a single, feeble finger for her to wait one minute.

"He's in public service now. He considers you a friend, but that's all. He's got to weigh the public good and many other interests against those of the gaming industry. Perhaps you can talk to the trustee overseeing the blind trust—"

"Fuck you, Shugie," Gantcher said.

"I'm going," Lori mouthed to him.

Disappointment and fury met in Shugie's chest and he vented it on Gantcher. "This conversation is over," he said icily and hung up.

Lori already had the envelope in her hand as he tossed the phone down on the desk. Her hand crushed the paper softly, and she let him wrap her in an embrace that had a similar effect. He breathed in the scent of her hair—a synthetic fruit smell—that delighted him to his core. She stepped back.

"When am I going to see you again?" he asked.

"Just call me." She smiled. Of course.

"Better question: when are we going to take this to the next level?" he said, as lightly as he could.

"Same old question." She sighed. "You know the deal, Shugie: overnight is no problem if you tell me in advance and you're willing to spend the eight. And you can book a weekend."

"Sure, just go on the Web site, and you'll need your own room. Right?"

"Just for a few hours a day. It'll still be a great time. And *you* don't have to go on the site, you can text me," she corrected.

"You know that's not what I meant," he said, hating how it sounded.

"I know," she answered, and he swore he recognized real feeling under her words. He embraced her again, nuzzled her neck, and then she was gone as if he'd been holding a ghost.

He knew exactly how he'd ended up here.

11

C'mon, Frank, Behr urged himself, *get up.*

When he had woken, he hadn't felt much like working out, but the idea of skipping two days in a row didn't sit well with him either. He pictured the two turning into a hundred and saw himself fat and logy and permanently planted in a rocking chair or, worse, a desk chair. So he'd put on T-shirt and shorts, drank some water, and got his ass out there. Now he had a kettlebell, a cold black chunk of iron that resembled a cannonball with a handle and weighed fifty-six pounds, in his right hand and was in the middle of a set of Turkish get-ups. The exercise consisted of lying on his back, arm locked out straight overhead, and then climbing to his feet, arm still straight up, and dropping into a lunge before rolling onto his back again. And then, of course, it was rinse and repeat for twelve reps each arm. It was full-body torture that involved pushing the muscular, ligamentous, lactic acid, and cardiovascular systems to their limits. Arms, legs, core, and wind—there was nowhere to hide and there was just no way to do them fast enough so that he wasn't doubled over and panting by the end. The bottle of expensive grape juice he'd drunk that was now rolling around in his gut didn't help much either.

Behr tried to distance his mind from the exertion, to take the focus off the pain of what he was doing, and to think about what he always did these days: the moment in less than four weeks when his soon-to-arrive son would be born. He and Suze had found out it was going to be a boy a few months back at an ultrasound.

"There it is," the technician said. "You want to know?"

"No, we just want *you* to know," Behr had answered.

"Yes, tell us please." Susan laughed. She was generally amused at the semirude utterances he inadvertently dropped. But that didn't stop her from spreading some diplomacy around.

So, his second son was on the way. The one he'd be able to hold, to feed, to take places, teach, and to support. *To support.* It stopped him. It was *the* question that weighed heavy on him now, and it always would. He remembered that much from the first time around. It was what pushed him to go ahead and give up his own business and take the Caro job. *A fallow period is one thing when you're the only one eating spaghetti at home three weeks in a row,* Behr thought. But with mommy and baby, that kind of struggle just wasn't acceptable. And he couldn't forget the fact that in three and a half years' time he was looking at preschool and private school bills, which was going to be required barring a miraculous turnaround by the city's abysmal public system. At times like this the steady paycheck was mighty welcome. Which was why it was of no use to him for his thoughts to keep drifting back to the night in the parking garage. The sledgehammer pounding of the rounds hitting cars had a physical quality as he remembered it. The air around him had been so disturbed it was like being in the wake of scores of tiny fighter jets buzzing by.

Behr stood between sets, and paced around the small patch of grass, getting his wind back. The attempt was made on Kolodnik the night before he was announced as the governor's choice for the vacant Senate seat. Political assassinations didn't happen in America more than about twice a century, and more often than not they concerned a psychopath working out some inner drama on a public stage. They sure as hell didn't happen in Indianapolis, aka Nap Town, the city that never wakes. But the cops would have to be blind not to see it as such. As an investigator, Behr needed to not leap at the obvious, and as a Caro investigator he needed to not worry about it at all and instead focus on his cases, which meant the Payroll Place robberies.

Then there was the wine. He hadn't been very communicative with Susan the night before about receiving the gift—if that's what it was. The reason for that was it had made him *uncomfortable*. A few thousand bucks' worth of cabernet—on one hand it was uncalled for. It was more than was necessary. Behr had been doing his job, what he was paid to do, and he'd been protecting his own ass too. On the other hand, what kind of gesture was it from a rich man such as Kolodnik? Did a man like Bernie Cool think the value would be lost on someone like him, or that he'd be overwhelmed by it? It seemed the case of wine and the note was supposed to put final punctuation on the matter. But was it a thank-you or was it grease?

Behr picked up his kettlebell and retook his starting position on the ground, lifting the weight overhead. He sucked in a deep breath and climbed to his feet. He didn't know much about the Turks, or what had pissed them off enough to create something as nasty as their get-ups, but by the end of the set there'd be nothing in his head except blinding white pain. He lunged and rolled back to the ground and tried not to extend the pause.

Get the hell up, Frank, Behr told himself again, and he did. He kept on getting back to his feet.

12

Altgeld Gardens—Alligator Garden as the locals called it—was a place that struck fear into the hearts of white Chicagoans. Waddy Dwyer knew that, and it followed naturally that that's where he was. He needed weaps, and he couldn't be buying them from the Walmart. That's why he'd called his contact and had come here. Besides, he'd been outside the Green Zone in Baghdad after dark. He'd walked the streets of Al Mazraa in Beirut. He'd done solo night ops in Grozny, Chechnya, so the pair of blackies in front of him was hardly going to make his knees quake.

"Have you got H and K? Or SIG?" Dwyer asked.

"Nah, man," the kid answered. The kid was lean, maybe eighteen years old, and was named Blaze. That's whom he was supposed to ask for, anyway, according to his contact. He'd approached the kid in front of the cluster of decrepit government-built row houses.

"Are you him?" Dwyer had asked.

"I'm Blaze, as in Johnny Blaze," the kid had said, whatever the fuck that meant. "You the English guy?"

"I'm a *Welshman*," Dwyer corrected pointlessly.

The kid had shrugged and started walking toward one of the buildings. Dwyer followed and another kid, a big one with a black nylon stocking on his head, had fallen in behind.

Now they were all crammed into a small, airless storage room that smelled of old marijuana and was filled with pressboard desks and other cheap furniture.

"Look, look, look, we don't got no high-end SIGs and shit. We got Taurus. We got these Colts . . ."

Dwyer shook his head. He didn't love his choices.

"We also got this AK . . ." Blaze pointed to a battered weapon that looked as if it'd been recovered from a cave in Waziristan.

Dwyer shook his head. Tempting though it was to wrap his hands around the familiar wood grips of a Kalashnikov, he couldn't see himself waltzing around U.S. cities with an assault rifle.

"What's your personal gun, then?" Dwyer wondered.

"My personal gun?" Blaze asked back.

"That's right. You're armed, aren't you?"

"Yeah, I's motherfucking armed."

Blaze lifted the basketball T-shirt that went down to his knees and showed the butt of some kind of chromed-out heavy-caliber automatic. It was exactly the kind of flashy nonsense Dwyer didn't need. At least now he knew what the kid was holding when it came time for them to try and rob him.

"Lovely," he said. "Let me look at the Colt." Blaze handed it over and Dwyer was pleased to see that it was a .45 ACP, but that the make was actually Česká Zbrojovka. The CZ 97 B was a good gun, not off the Springfield production line, and had a smoother action and better balance than those did. Dwyer didn't bother asking how they'd come up with a Czech-made gun, as he quickly racked the slide, removed the slide stop pin, and broke down the automatic. He inspected the recoil spring, barrel, and trigger action. The weapon was sound. "Okay, this'll do. I'll have it with four magazines."

For a moment Blaze's shrewd look went blank.

"Clips, man," Dwyer said. "Four of 'em."

"I got two," was the answer. It wasn't ideal, but it was the way it was. Then a dull black object that was leaning against the wall in a dark corner of the room caught Dwyer's eye. "Is that for sale?"

Blaze looked at his hulking companion and they laughed. "Homeboy likes the shotty," Blaze said. He went and picked it up, then crossed the room and rested it on a desk. It was a short-barreled Saiga 12-gauge automatic shotgun. An impressive close-quarters weapon designed for leveling men in enclosed spaces. And if things went poorly, it was equally useful for getting out of the same spaces—three or four rounds fired into a wall and there would no longer be a wall, and escape could be made. Dwyer inspected the shotgun and saw it was in working order and that it was loaded with 00 buckshot.

"I'll have both," Dwyer told them, putting the shotgun back on the desk.

"Wasn't gonna sell the Saiga," Blaze said, "but a'ight. I'll do both for twenny-fi' hunned." The price was too high by half, but Dwyer didn't waste time.

"Done," he said. Then he pulled one of the packets of American cash off his abdomen. Proper tradecraft would have had him secreting the money in five hundred or thousand dollar increments all over his body. But he came in here recommended and hadn't wanted to waste time. His mistake became clear the minute the two salesmen saw the five-thousand-dollar brick he had started peeling bills from.

"You want something else?" Blaze asked. "Can't let you be leaving with all that cash."

"No, just the CZ and the Saiga," Dwyer said.

"Go on, buy a Taurus."

"I don't want a mingy Taurus."

"Well, likes I said, we can't let you be leaving with all that cash." Blaze's voice had changed when he said the last. Dwyer felt it and had looked up from counting money in time to see the big fellow reaching for the Saiga on the desk. Dwyer bunched the cash in his left hand into a fist and swung a thousand-dollar hook that drilled the big man in the throat. The man's face registered surprise, then crumpled into pain, and he went off his feet sideways. He landed, gurgling, on the floor. Dwyer lunged across the space between him and Blaze and grabbed the wiry young man's wrist, which had been diving for the heavy chrome auto at his waist. Dwyer yanked the wrist down and held it firmly in place against the kid's body. The other hand caught him by the neck. He stared into Blaze's eyes and let the kid feel his superior strength.

"I was wondering whether you was gonna be twats, and now you've gone and done it." For a moment the only sounds in the room were Dwyer and Blaze breathing through their noses, and the big fellow gasping wetly on the floor. "Now, do you scruts want *two grand* for the guns, or do you want to fucking die?"

Moments later Dwyer stood at the trunk of his rented Lincoln Town Car with the .45 tucked in his waistband at his lower back, and put the shotgun, now wrapped in an old towel, in the spare tire well under a piece of carpet. He closed the trunk and saw Blaze and his friend framed in the doorway of the building he'd just left. They paused when they saw him there. Blaze raised his thumb and forefinger at Dwyer and mimed firing a single shot. Dwyer ignored the gesture, got in the car and on the road for Indianapolis.

13

Behr's bag clinked softly as he walked through the Caro offices. He sat at the desk and set five bottles of fine wine on the corner. Half the case, minus the one he'd drunk the night before. He figured that was fair, considering what he'd done to get it. The other half case was at home, lying sideways, waiting for another day.

"What's this?" his coworkers asked of the bottles as they passed by his desk.

"Client gift. Grab one," Behr answered. There were only a few takers, a few more raised eyebrows, and by the end of the day there was still one bottle left. Maybe when it got down to one, it didn't look like much of a display. Or maybe the office preferred drinking harder stuff.

In between those visits Behr cranked away on his Payroll Place file. It was click, jot, scroll, and cut and paste as he got through four background checks, going alphabetically, searching databases in order to view past employment history; former residences; and credit, motor-vehicle, and criminal records. He went as fast as he could, but it took hours by the time the searches were done and the reports were written up. The last one was a killer because the employee's name, Edward Charles, was a common one, and dozens of hits came up that had to be combed through and canceled out against his social security number. There were some speeding tickets, a DUI, a personal bankruptcy in the pool. The checks sketched in a bland picture of an employee base that didn't tell him very much. He had dozens more to do. He was feeling buried. Each time he looked up from his work that last bottle of Harlan Estates caught his eye. And each time he tried to go back to what he was doing, it took him longer and longer. Finally he acknowledged why, picked up his desk phone, and dialed a familiar number.

"Downtown District," an assistant answered.

"Lieutenant Breslau, please," Behr said and his call was put through.

"Breslau," came the voice over the line. Behr was surprised he didn't have an assistant, or maybe he or she had stepped away.

"Frank Behr," he said. There was a pause and some rustling of papers.

"What can I do for you, Behr?" Breslau said in a low-effort attempt at cordiality.

"Just wondering what's turned up on that shoot."

"Well, I told you I'd let you know when something had, so obviously not much."

"You told me that?" Behr asked.

"Told your boss." Breslau sighed.

"I see," Behr said, about two dozen more questions rattling around in his head.

"Love to sit and chat, but I've gotta—" Breslau began his sign-off.

"Uh-huh," Behr said, cutting him off, as he felt a kernel of anger glow to life in the pit of his stomach.

"I'll ring you when we have something."

The line went dead. Behr slowly hung up the receiver, willing himself not to smash it.

"Happy hour?" Behr heard, and looked up to see Pat Teague standing there, a finger tapping on the remaining bottle.

"Sweepstakes giveaway," Behr said.

"So I heard," Teague said.

"Help yourself," Behr offered.

"Don't mind if I do. Thanks," Teague said and walked away with a rolling, bandy-legged gait, cradling the last bottle, like a football, in the crook of his arm.

Just keep collecting your check and don't think so hard, Behr told himself. But then he picked up the phone again.

Behr walked toward the Lutheran Church on Kitley, where there was a small group clustered a few steps away from the side door taking a nicotine break. Behr recognized the tall, thin figure and salt-and-pepper hair of Neil Ratay, crime reporter for the *Indy Star,* getting ready for his regular meeting. Behr approached and they shook hands and moved away from the other smokers.

"So what's up, Frank?" Ratay asked, waving away a cloud of cigarette smoke that wafted between them. Behr hadn't known him for long—and couldn't call the man a friend, exactly—but the bond had been immediate when they'd met about a year back. He'd quickly identified a sense of code in Ratay, perhaps springing from the time-honored practice of reporters protecting their sources, which had led him to believe he could trust the man. And he hadn't been proven wrong.

"That shoot in the garage on Pierson the other night," Behr began.

"Kolodnik thing," Ratay said.

"*My* thing too," Behr said.

"That was you?"

Behr nodded and told him how it fell, even including the bit about the wine. The reporter's eyes grew a bit in circumference from their normal knowing slits when he heard Behr tell it.

"The story got a single coat in your paper, barely covered the primer. My office isn't looking into it, and whether or not the cops have anything, this hump Breslau got handed the package and won't be sharing anything with me," Behr said.

"Breslau . . ." Ratay murmured.

"What's his deal?" Behr asked.

"New breed. Got a master's degree. Camera-ready."

"Started grooming him for captain before he drove his first patrol?"

"Pretty much. So, can I take a run at it?" Ratay asked as they watched the few other smokers finish up and drift inside.

"Yeah, give it a shot," Behr said, "and let me know if you find out anything interesting, would ya?"

Ratay nodded slowly three times and then glanced to the church door. "My meeting's about to start." They shook hands and Behr left.

Even though he'd started his day with a brutal workout, Behr had something in him—that kernel—he still needed to burn off. He drove home, parked on the street but didn't go inside. Instead, he pulled running gear out of his trunk, changed right there in the front seat, and set out. He looped around the neighborhood streets until he'd covered about three quarters of a mile and then set off toward Saddle Hill.

He didn't have his weighted vest in the trunk, so Behr focused on explosive speed as he churned up the hill. His knees kicked high and his feet pounded down on the asphalt as sweat bounced off the sides of his head.

Why aren't the police killing themselves following this up? he asked himself on one trip up.

They are, they just don't seem to have much, Behr told himself on the way down.

Be glad it's not your problem, he told himself the next time up.

He jogged down the hill, filling his lungs. He'd been guarding a multimillionaire businessman who was about to become a senator.

Money or politics, or the place the two intersected, he told himself as he raced up with chopping strides. *The only question was why?*

Or was it a woman, a deal gone bad, a personal slight, or a hundred other things? he reminded himself as he made his descent.

Just don't ask, Frank, he urged himself as he charged up the hill three more times.

But coming down the hill that final time, he knew he was going to.

"You fall into a pool?" Susan asked him and laughed when Behr entered his place. "You're soaked." She wasn't alone on the couch, and another gentle peal of laughter joined hers. Sitting next to Susan was a pretty girl with well-dyed blond hair who couldn't have been twenty-five years old and looked ready to pop out a kid within a month of Susan.

"Just took a run," he said.

"We can tell by the running shoes," the young lady said, as she and Susan stifled more laughs.

"You two been drinking?" Behr wondered.

"Just high on pregnancy," Susan said, and they laughed again, though this time it was closer to a howl and the girls even shared a high five.

"All right, what's going on?"

"We were down at baby care class, learning about swaddling and umbilical cords and filing tiny fingernails, and gabbing it up, I guess, when this *woman* in the class—"

"This dowdy bitch," the younger blonde volunteered, "barely seemed fertile."

"Says to me," Susan continued, " 'Could you two keep it down? I'd like to hear what the nurse has to say about ointment,' all snooty, but then she shifts in her seat and lets out this blast of a fart. So Gina says"—Susan pointed to her little friend— " 'I thought you said you wanted quiet.' " This brought on another high five and paroxysm of laughter. Behr could only shake his head and wait for them to finish.

Finally, Susan's friend said, "Sorry, Frank. I'm Gina Decker. And you know you just can't cross a heavily pregnant woman."

"Nice to meet you," he said.

He made small talk with the women for a few minutes, and then went off to shower. When he was finished, he came out to find Gina had left. He headed into the kitchen for some water and Susan followed him in.

"Frank, can I ask you something? It's for Gina," she said.

"Sure. She seems like lots of laughs," he said.

"Not all fun and games."

"No?"

"No. Her husband, Eddie, he's . . . got issues."

"I see."

"He was in the marines. For a long time. He did a few tours— Iraq and Afghanistan, I think she said. And other places."

Behr said nothing.

"Anyway, he's been back for like a year, and he's a cop," Susan continued.

"Indy?" he asked.

"Yeah." Susan nodded. "But it's not going that well. He caught a thirty-day rip for beating the living shit out of some suspect who resisted."

"The living shit," Behr said.

"Gina's words," Susan said. "And it wasn't his first. Anyway, she's freaking out that the suspensions are gonna kill his career."

"They will."

"So we were—I—was wondering: Would you go talk to him, give him some advice?"

"On how to make it permanent?" Behr asked.

"Funny. Will you?" Susan looked up at him with wide, innocent eyes. He hoped their son would have those eyes. "For me?"

There was nothing that seemed more miserable to him than sitting down with some angry young cop. "For you," Behr said, "anything." Then they started talking about dinner.

14

"Don't say my name."

The words came through the phone low and gravelly. The accent, the tone of voice, the cheap cell connection, brought a cold bolt of surprise directly to Lowell Gantcher's stomach. *Dwyer*.

"Why would I do that?" Gantcher finally managed to answer, groping for the breezy tone of the successful real estate developer he'd once been.

"Fuck if I know—just don't," the voice came back through the line. "We need to meet. About the situation."

Gantcher's head dropped into his hand. He was in his godfather office, but he was no godfather. He'd just sent an e-mail to the accountant, to tap a final line of credit in order to cover operating expenses and a partial payroll down at the company. It didn't get less godfather than that.

"You're in the States, then?" Gantcher asked.

"Not only."

The surprise became fear. "You're *here*?" Gantcher said. "In Indy?"

"Fuckin' 'ell."

"Well, where are you staying?"

"Stand by. I'll give you a location to meet when I decide it."

"Okay," Gantcher said. His gut instinct suddenly told him not to meet. Some inner voice he didn't hear from very often was screaming it, in fact. He didn't know whether he should try to run, hire a bodyguard, or lawyer up and go to the police. Maybe all three.

"When?" he asked.

"Tomorrow night," the voice said.

"Tomorrow," Gantcher said. He clicked on his calendar, having suddenly become a method actor, and saw it completely empty. "I don't think tomorrow's going to be possible—"

"Tomorrow night," the voice repeated, and the line went dead.

15

"John Lutz, please. Frank Behr calling," he said into his cell phone. After a moment's wait, a warm voice came on the line.

"Y'ello?"

"Mr. Lutz?"

"Call me John," the man said.

"All right, John," Behr gave him his way. Lutz was the president of Payroll Place, and at the moment, his client.

"We're expecting to see you in about a half hour, aren't we?" Lutz asked. Behr couldn't tell if others were supposed to be in the meeting or if Lutz was just a "we" kind of guy.

"That's what I'm calling about, sir," Behr said. "I wanted to let you know I wasn't going to be able to make it down today."

"Oh," Lutz said, disappointment creeping into his tone.

"I am working on your case. I'm hip-deep in background checks on your employees, as a matter of fact."

"I see," Lutz said, brightening to the information. "Anything good? You have any thoughts? Any ideas?"

"Still in the preliminary stages. I'm going to get back to you about setting up some employee interviews shortly."

"Okay," Lutz said, not sounding too sure.

"Now I'm gonna just pop into the courthouse here and get back to work on these checks. I'll be in touch, so . . . Take care," Behr said, hanging up.

He stepped inside, but not into a courthouse. Rather, he left the sunlight behind and entered the artificially lit concrete confines of the parking garage of the office building on Pierson Street.

The place had nearly become his crypt a few days back, but it was the start of a workday and now it was full of parked cars and slowly trolling ones looking for spaces. He walked down, deeper underground, past P2, to the P3 level where it had happened. He turned the corner and got a view of the row where the Suburban had been parked. There was no crime scene tape. No indication that anything had happened there—certainly not from a distance, anyway. The shot-up cars had been towed or otherwise moved. The light fixtures that the shooter had disabled had been repaired. The lights he had shot out had been replaced. The area was once again bathed in a symmetrical amber pattern. It was business as usual, as it would have been had he caught some of the lead. Only when Behr drew close did he see signs of the encounter: small pockmarks along the concrete wall where the shooter's rounds had chipped away at the smooth uniformity.

Behr squeezed in between a Toyota RAV4 and a Chrysler Pacifica and went to the wall. He ran his hand along the pattern of shots. It felt rough, like chips from a chisel point. It felt like nothing. He looked down to where he had dropped and fired, then he crossed toward where he'd tried to acquire his target. Fifty or sixty feet across the lanes where cars traveled to the next set of parked vehicles. It took him a minute, but he found his own shot pattern. His were lower, what would be right around the shooter's midsection if he'd had any hits. His grouping wasn't that spread out, all things considered, especially compared to his counterpart's. But Behr had only been firing on semi, while the other guy was spraying and praying on full auto.

After a moment Behr walked down to both ends of the garage and found doors opening onto stairwells. One smelled like urine, the other was relatively clean. Neither held shell casings or any other evidence of the shooter's presence. As he left and made his way back toward the shooter's route of escape, he considered whether there was a driver, or if the shooter drove himself, and whether he had left the car running, or the key in the ignition at the very least. Then Behr stopped and looked up. Placed at the ramp where the rows of parking jogged back to create another level was the black glass hemisphere of a security camera.

Behr went to the booth by the exit, where monthly parkers waved a magnetic card that caused a wooden arm to rise and let them out and where visitors had to stop and pay for their time. There was an attendant in the booth, a heavyset woman who appeared to be from India or Pakistan. Behr approached her.

"Hello," he said.

"Lost ticket, pay maximum," she responded. Her English was rough, the phrase rehearsed.

"I didn't lose my ticket," he said.

"Lose ticket?" she asked.

"No ticket," he said, attempting to wave away the topic. "Do you know about the shooting?" He made a gun out of his thumb and forefinger and mimed firing. It seemed to register and she began to nod. "Were you here? The night of the shooting?" he asked, speaking slowly but checking a pointless urge to raise his volume.

She processed for a moment, then shook her head. "Me, night, eight o'clock . . ." she said, and used a hand gesture to indicate her going away.

"Okay," Behr said, remembering that he had had to pay in advance that night and had received an exit ticket to feed into the machine since the booth would be closed and the attendant off duty. "Security?" Behr asked, pointing to the ceiling. "Cameras," he added. But she just shook her head. "Security? Guard?" he continued.

"Guard. Yes." Now she was nodding. "P one, P one."

Behr found the garage security office, an offshoot of the building's main security center, through a battered metal door near the elevator bank. He knocked and entered a cramped space that was dominated by a desk, which was crowded with black and white monitors blinking views from one area of garage to the next.

"Help you with something?" Sitting behind the desk was a middle-aged square badge in a rent-a-cop uniform. His glasses sat loosely on his face, the arms bent wide from being removed too often.

"Yeah, it's about that incident the other night," Behr began. In his experience security guards were either buffs, who could be induced into enthusiastically sharing all their information, or scared bureaucrats, who wielded their scrap of power like a truncheon. He wasn't sure which he had in front of him.

"What about it?" square badge asked.

"Were you on duty?"

"Go ask your buddies," the guard said. "Buddies" implied the cops, and Behr smelled some resentment there.

"I'm not with the cops," Behr bit out. Instead of this information opening the man up, it closed him down.

"Then why would I tell you anything about our system?" the man said with some edge, crossing his arms.

"Not asking you for state secrets," Behr said, "just wondering if you were around."

"Are you suggesting some failure on the part of building security or garage security in specific?" the man said, his voice thinning to an almost aggressive whine.

Great, Behr thought, *shut down, self-important, and paranoid—the perfect subject.* There was a time when Behr would've grabbed the geek by the neck and shaken him until the information fell out, but nowadays, as a Caro boy, Behr was doing things differently. He was trying to, anyway. So he spread his feet and settled, as if he had no plans to leave anytime soon.

"But for your information, no, I wasn't on. I'm the day man. I punch out and another guy handles the afternoon and early evening. There used to be an overnight shift, but that got trimmed because of budget. So, you know, what does management expect if they don't pay for coverage?"

Behr pictured the guard, had he been on duty, armed with a

flashlight, rounding the corner into the firefight. That would've done a lot of good.

"So it was just the cameras, then. They get a pretty good look at the whole thing? What's the storage length on the footage?" Behr asked as lightly as he could.

A cagey look came to the guard's eyes. "Why're you so interested?"

"I know the guy involved."

"You work for him?"

Behr just shrugged.

"I was in charge of burning copies to a disk for the police," the guard said. "You can ask them what was on the tape. As for storage, we used to run thirty days—probably would've had footage of guys casing the garage. But now it's seventy-two hours, because they took a bunch of our hard drives for the lobby. Lobby guys get it all. New cappuccino makers, new chairs, extra hard drives . . ."

Behr cut a glance at the bank of monitors, wondering what he'd be able to pick up if he saw the footage from the shoot.

The guard leaned forward. "I think we're done here," he said.

Behr was headed back to his car when he saw a janitor, a Hispanic kid wearing earbuds and pushing a rolling garbage can.

"Hey, man," Behr said loudly, tapping his own ear. The kid stopped and pulled out the left earbud, allowing the tinny sound of congas and trumpets to spill into the garage.

"Yo," the janitor said.

"What happened here the other night?" Behr asked.

"That throw down? Some Bs flew." The kid shifted his weight and a thick ring of keys clinked.

"You think it's on the security tapes?" Behr asked.

"How much?" the kid responded.

"How much what?"

"How much you got?"

A hundred bucks. It was more than he could afford, but it was still the standard unit of measure for bribery in matters of any import on the street, and that's what Behr paid him. The kid thought the security guard was a prick, and knew he was headed to lunch in an hour. He told Behr to go get a cup of coffee and meet him back at the security office in an hour and ten exactly, so that's what Behr did.

When he returned, it was in time to see the kid leave the security office with a wastebasket, dump it into his rolling garbage can, and replace the basket in the office. When he exited, however, he left the door slightly ajar and rolled off into the recesses of the garage. Behr knew the area was probably on camera, but the kid's actions would look like a mistake, some youthful, sloppy work. *His* entry, on the other hand, would not. Behr tipped his chin down and walked briskly inside.

He locked the door behind him. Not that it mattered. The cramped, hot space had no other way out. If square badge returned, Behr would be discovered. So he worked quickly, sitting down at the desk, and keyboarding in to the security archives. It took him a few minutes, but the log was fairly straightforward and clearly dated, and he soon found the time and angle he was looking for. Behr scrolled to 10:55 of the night in question. He estimated the shooting started within a few minutes of that time. The video ran, showing no movement, but at 10:57 it blinked forward to 12:31. This footage showed the police in the final stages of their investigation and cleanup.

Confused, Behr scrolled back, thinking he'd perhaps hit a key commanding the system to skip. But he hadn't. Behr assumed a copy had been made for the police. That's what square badge had said. In the days of videotape it would've been conceivable that they'd handed over the original, but now everything was digital. While a CD may have been burned and given to the police, after that, either accidentally or intentionally, the material had been deleted. Behr knew enough about computers to understand that unless an elaborate scrubbing process had been followed, the footage was actually in the hard drive somewhere, because delete usually meant a repurposing of the memory space. But it would take him hours and a call to his computer guy to figure out how to pull it up, and he didn't have that kind of time. At the moment he didn't have much of anything.

Behr drove out of the garage into daylight and a ringing cell phone. "Behr," he said.

"Frank, Neil Ratay here." The reporter's voice came back to him through the phone.

"What's up, Neil?"

"Not much. Listen, about that story, my editor doesn't have any appetite for it."

"I see," Behr said. He needed to make a right onto Delaware to head back to the office, but he found himself turning left onto Capitol. "Did someone tell him not to, or is he just not hungry?"

"Don't know," Ratay said, "but with the state of the news-paper business, it means the same thing to me. Sorry I can't help you."

"Got it," Behr said, "and thanks, Neil." Behr hung up. He was on North Meridian now, the big dividing road that bisected the city. He passed stately homes behind wrought iron gates, includ-ing the ceremonial governor's mansion. As he continued north and out of town, the city quickly released its grasp and gave way to thick trees that spread into a more open sky. He was headed toward Carmel, the well-to-do suburb that was Bernie Cool's domain.

16

It shouldn't be long, if what the prim, attractive secretary told him about the twenty-minute wait was true. Behr sat on a leather couch in a plush waiting area in Bernie Kolodnik's office. There was an array of thick, glossy magazines on a well-waxed coffee table in front of him, but he was staring toward the opposite wall at a large photo of Kolodnik, dressed in golf togs, standing with Phil Mickelson in a tee box.

Behr had found the business card Kolodnik had given him in his wallet as he walked back to his car. He hadn't called that personal number, but it had inspired him to call Kolodnik's company and ask for a brief appointment even though he was due back at the Caro office for a marketing and client service meeting. He wasn't too busted up over missing it, though his bosses might be if word trickled back to them that he was absent. It turned out that Kolodnik wasn't at his downtown location but was at the company's satellite office in the tony suburbs, so he was headed in the right direction.

Driving out, Behr had crossed a development of new town houses at 86th and North Meridian, which functioned as a border of sorts to a sleek, high-priced world of glassy business parks that seemed to house the medical practices of half the doctors in the state. Then he had passed under an arch announcing the Arts & Design District of Carmel, and he entered the picturesque town of low brick buildings, cobblestone crossings, and lifelike Seward

Johnson–style statues of people on the sidewalks. On several corners were large churches that represented a range of Christian denominations. The surrounding thoroughfares of South Range Line and Carmel Drive were thick with chain restaurants—but the nice ones—and country clubs filled in the spaces between neighborhoods.

The town represented the good life, and he had a momentary pang when he thought of Susan and pictured her and the coming baby eating at the restaurants, shopping at the many kids' shoe stores, going to Nordstrom's. The place was a little sterile. That's what she would probably say. She didn't care much about money or material things, but he knew the life they were leading wasn't a result of choice but of limits. He wouldn't mind giving her the alternative. He just didn't see how that was going to happen. Maybe after five or ten years with Caro, after moving up into the supervisory ranks and partnership, there would be a possibility. He'd be in his fifties by then . . . but not now.

There were plenty of big buildings going up around town, Behr noticed on his way to his destination: The Kolodnik Company, which was housed in yet another brand-new, sparkling limestone and glass pod. New developments. Ground broken. Foundations dug. Girder skeletons erected. Crane arms topping off roof pieces. The town must not have heard of the real estate crash or the wave of unemployment or the recession that had howled over the country like a tornado. Perhaps Kolodnik was responsible for all the work here. Maybe his company, with a fleet of bulldozers, was trying to turn the whole thing around single-handedly.

The left-hander of a pair of mahogany double doors swung open, and there he was, Bernie Cool himself, in crisp white shirtsleeves and silk tie. His burnished custom-made shoes shone from what looked like three thousand coats of polish in an altogether different way than Behr's Florsheims.

"Frank, how the heck are you?" Kolodnik said, crossing to him.

Behr jumped up, they shook hands, and he saw the energetic and intelligent gleam in the man's eyes.

"I'm under water today, but I'm really glad to have this chance to at least say hello," Kolodnik went on.

"I'm fine, Mr. Kolodnik," Behr said. "How are you?"

"Call me Bernie. Did you get that Harlan Estates?"

"I did and I thank you. It was unnecessary."

"Did you try it? What did you think?"

"Good stuff."

"They say you should lay up good wine for a while after it arrives. But I never do . . ." Kolodnik offered with a smile.

"I didn't happen to wait either."

As Behr traded the pleasantries he wondered if he was going to get invited into Kolodnik's office where he could ask some real questions without secretaries and executives and a quartet of what were clearly his new security guys, with their blue suits and square jaws, hovering around. They were the matching set to a pair each on the front and back doors of the building outside. But it didn't look like a private meeting was going to happen.

"So, what can I do for you?" Kolodnik wondered. "Like I said, I'm in the weeds. The Senate seat and all." The man was unbelievably easy and affable, as if he lived in a capsule of prosperity and lubricating charm. It was something Behr had noticed the first time he'd driven Kolodnik. The shooting had momentarily punctured the capsule, but now it was clearly resealed and Kolodnik was insulated once again.

"Right, congratulations on that," Behr said. The charm bubble made Behr somehow reluctant to roil the waters—any waters—and disrupt the serene good feeling that surrounded Kolodnik. Behr imagined the man would do well in Washington.

"Thank you. Quite an honor." A momentary quiet fell and Kolodnik looked at him expectantly. "So I imagine you've got a reason for the visit?"

Behr dropped his voice. "Well, yeah, as a matter of fact. I want to find out why someone was shooting at you, because then I'll know why someone was shooting at me."

Kolodnik nodded mildly. "Of course," he said, "it was very troubling. Very troubling," but didn't continue further, which forced Behr to.

"I was wondering if you'd heard anything about the police investigation. If anything came up on the security tapes."

Kolodnik shook his head.

"I've followed up, but they're not sharing much with me," Behr continued.

"I have people overseeing that. They'll brief me at such time as there's significant progress. Obviously this is something of great concern, and I'm taking it very seriously. But right now I can't afford to shut down the works and dwell on it. I always look ahead, no matter the trauma of the past. Even the recent past. I credit a good portion of my success to that."

Behr felt ungrateful and unseemly for bothering the man, for continuing to ask the blunt, unattractive questions, and for so ignominiously being stuck in an earlier time. But he went ahead just the same. "It's just the timing of it—do you have political enemies already?"

Kolodnik laughed lightly, without mockery but with genuine amusement. "Those would be the fastest enemies a politician ever gained, wouldn't they?"

"So no idea who could have done it?" Behr asked. When interviewing victims of anonymous violence, Behr didn't ask "Who do you think did it?" That was a limiting question, one that forced the victim to confront his attacker directly in his mind. The "could've" made it almost a game. Behr liked to sit them down and make a list of *could'ves* and assign possible motives to each person on the list, as if it were a creative exercise, and eventually the actual "who" and "did it" would often end up staring him in the face. But that took time and cooperation, and it didn't look like Behr was going to get much of either.

There had been an arrival in the offices while they talked.

Three men and two women. There were roller briefcases, computers, and an audiovisual projector.

Behr felt his little window of opportunity closing.

"Disgruntled employees? Ex-employees?" Behr had the unfortunate sensation he was peppering the man. "Business? Personal? I wonder if it would be possible to interview your staff?" Behr was hoping for a developed source, some third party that a staffer might mention, whom he could question when he or she was unprepared, in the hopes of jarring loose some information.

"Old business saying goes, 'It's not a deal unless both parties are sore about it.' I've always gone about it the exact opposite way. It's stood me well," Kolodnik said. "And I'll tell you something else, and it's how I've avoided all this recent *unpleasantness* in the economy. I never bought into the idea of overleveraging, and I've tried to avoid people who do. What I'm saying is: my business life is very . . . balanced."

A secretary ushered the group toward Kolodnik's office, then leaned over to Kolodnik and said, "The Trachtenberg group, sir." Behr couldn't tell if they were political lobbyists, real estate developers, or from a law firm.

"Be right in," Kolodnik said, and then turned apologetically back to Behr.

"You said you had people on this. I wonder if I could confer with them?" Behr asked.

"I asked an old senator I count as a friend for some advice when the appointment came in. You know—how to manage the demands on my time, weigh the equities, all that. And you want to know what he told me?" Kolodnik paused for emphasis. " 'Learn to hold it, because you're not going to have a chance to take a squirt for the next six years . . .' Well, four in my case, but you get the idea." Kolodnik was using his folksy gentleman's idiom to give Behr a message: he was too busy to deal with the matter further.

Just then an exceptionally well-tanned man in his mid-forties with blond hair going to gray, and a suit jacket sporting shoulder pads that were a shade too big, strode up.

"You ready to get in there?" he asked Kolodnik with great familiarity in his tone.

"Yep, right in, Shugie," Kolodnik answered, then made the introduction. "Frank, this is Shugie Saunders, my political consultant. Shugie, this is Frank Behr, the reason you still have a client."

"No, no, no," Shugie corrected with a porcelain-veneered smile that creased the suntan, "the reason I still have a *friend*."

Saunders shot out a manicure-soft hand, which Behr shook, as Kolodnik wrapped things up.

"You should come by the house, Frank. Not now. I'm about ready to decamp to D.C.—"

"We're going to get the seat. We're going to be confirmed right away," Saunders informed.

"But at the end of the summer, Labor Day, I'll be back for a bit," Kolodnik continued.

"So the attempt," Behr tried a last time.

"That's been downgraded as a priority at the moment," Saunders said with finality. "We appreciate all your efforts."

What could Behr say? Especially in the face of that powerful "we" that smacked of handlers and aides and institution, of government itself. Everyone he was dealing with was plural, from his client to his company and even Kolodnik. He thought about his own "we" for a moment. All it meant—all it would ever mean— was him, Susan, and his coming son.

"Like I said, Frank, bring the wife over to the house for some tennis when I'm back in town. Do you have a wife? Do you play tennis?" Kolodnik smiled.

"Not exactly," Behr said, and after a cordial pat on the back, Kolodnik was on the move. Saunders gave a parting nod and followed his man through the double doors into the office. The doors closed behind them and Behr was left in the waiting area empty-handed and as inanimate as the Johnson statues lining the streets of the town.

17

The shite holes that accepted cash were the same the world over. It was a truth Waddy Dwyer had learned long ago, after the military when he was in intelligence, and then in his life as a private military contractor and all 'round useful bloke: they were thin, through and through. Thin sheets, thin blankets, thin pillows on the beds. Wafer-thin slivers of soap and paper-thin towels in the bathroom. Cracker-thin walls with worn-thin industrial carpet on the floor. The places often liked to include the word "quality" in their names, as did the one he was at currently, though there was rarely much of it in evidence. But after what seemed like a lifetime of shite, it didn't bother Dwyer much. He'd always been stoic, ever since he was a rude boy on the streets, and the hardships he endured while plying his trade had made him a regular mean fucker. Though, it occurred to him, there were few things meaner than a pissed off Welshman in the first place.

He had left off his things—his labelless clothing and generic toiletries—at the Shite-Quality Inn, kept the hardware with him, and had driven north out of the city. He'd entered a different world, he realized, as he reached Kolodnik's office. The city was glass and steel shooting up out of a plain, but everything was marble and money out in this bloody suburb.

Dwyer grimaced as he slowed at Kolodnik's office building but did not stop the car. Anyone with a quarter of his field experience would've clocked the pair of yobs at the door for what they were: security for hire. He kept right on going, around the back, spotting two more, when another, a fifth man, big as a dray horse, came lumbering out the door. But this one didn't stay with his fellows. Instead, he moved on toward his car.

"Bollocks," Dwyer said, and tooled on out toward Kolodnik's home address.

"Well, aren't you the big-time Charlie Potato?" Waddy Dwyer said to himself as he crouched in the woods a good distance away from Kolodnik's home. Hidden in a stand of old growth oak, he glassed the lavish dwelling with Swarovski 10X42 binoculars. The house was a heavy-beamed Tudor, with decorative leaded glass windows along the ground floor, a peaked slate roof, and landscaped grounds, including pool and tennis court, surrounded by a tall, wrought iron fence. The place was more English manor than regular house.

He had parked several streets away, and had gone through the woods for a good stretch to get a look. With the binoculars, along with having seen the security at the office, it was fairly easy for him to deduce that Kolodnik wasn't at home. But the home security team certainly was. Another four men, at least, Dwyer determined, based on the two outside and the movement inside. He saw the telltale lumps under their jackets beneath the left shoulders. Probably Uzis or MP5s on slings, like the bleeding Secret Service carried.

He considered his options. A high-powered rifle from a quarter mile away while the man was at the kitchen sink. It was doable. He recalled a similar operation on a diplomat in South Africa more than a decade back. There were two on security there, who were put down after the shot, with the door kicked in and the target finished up close. But that was quasi-military, with plenty of support. There had been choppers for extraction. Here, a deer rifle with a telescopic sight was easily gettable, but night vision optics was not. It'd also be a cold bore shot, the barrel not warmed up. Then there was that leaded window glass to consider. It could cause a deflection, which might in turn cause a wound, not a kill—or, worse yet, a miss, with no chance of follow-up.

There was more poor news along with all this, Dwyer saw. Besides a pair of black Range Rovers outside in the driveway, and a Mercedes convertible in the open garage, there was a heavy-looking blacked-out Chevrolet Suburban that appeared modified with armor to his eye. There was also a moving truck being loaded with boxes and luggage. A team of darkie moving men was doing the hauling, and the security wasn't even helping, which was another sign of their professionalism. So it seemed Kolodnik was soon to be on the move, and there wasn't going to be much time for proper setup. There could be even more men inside, Dwyer realized, his mood blackening further. Four, six, eight, ten, or a hundred, it didn't matter. Kolodnik was covered tighter than a pair of balls in shrunken wool shorts. This thing was a walkaway. The operation was rogered. Right up the arse.

Back in his car, sucking on a Coca-Cola and a hamburger from some barf-hole drive-through window, Dwyer considered where he was at, and it wasn't a pretty place. He'd spent his life applying force for profit. He'd worked his plums off for three decades to create a skill set and a name, a name only whispered in certain circles, but one that was nonetheless *the* gold standard in the field. He'd built a business, starting at the end of the '80s, when the Berlin Wall came down and six million other soldiers were downsized and looking to go private. In the face of this competi-tion he'd dealt with all stripe of unsavory bastard, demanding to be paid up front, cash on the nail, and making his fortune. So a failure was one thing, and it was bad, but having things unwind and lead to arrests would be a disaster for his reputation and his business, and he hadn't hit his walk-away number yet. To come this far, to get this close, only to have it come apart during stop-page time was unacceptable.

Another five hundred thousand pounds would get him there, to the amount that would ensure security for the rest of his days. Living in Wales, unbothered. Diving in the Maldives twice a year. Two, two and a half years' work to get that last five hundred thousand quid, he projected. But it might as well be five hundred million he was looking for. The reason people hired private was to get their jobs done faster and better than doing it themselves and to transfer the risk of harm or arrest to someone else. So there was no room for error. Reputation was everything in his field. It was binary. Zero-sum. One either got it done every time, or one was to be avoided like botulism. Waddy Dwyer could either be the hero or the asshole. So here it was, decision time, and one last chance to get paid. Things had shifted from a finish to a cleanup. With the original objective now unreachable, that left Waddy Dwyer a single choice: containment. But first he was going to talk to that cunt Gantcher, because he goddamn sure wasn't heading home without his money.

18

Behr was driving back toward the city when he remembered the favor he owed, and dialed the number Susan had given him. After two rings, a cigarette-roughed voice answered.

"Decker," it said.

"Hey, this is Frank Behr. Your wife is friends with my girl," Behr said, trying to keep the tone of the condemned man out of his voice. "I was supposed to call you to meet up."

"Yeah, hey. And when you did, I was supposed to go," Decker said without enthusiasm but also without pause.

"So when do you want to do it?"

"When do you?"

There was no sense in dragging it out, Behr figured. "You on shift tonight?"

"Nope."

This didn't surprise Behr, knowing what he did about Decker's forced vacation.

"So how about in a little while?"

"All right. Where?"

Behr cast about for a place to meet and said the first one that popped into his head. "The Wild Beaver."

"Wild Beaver . . . ?" Decker couldn't keep the laugh out of his voice.

"I'm not far from it. Six o'clock?"

"All right then. Six o'clock."

Behr still had time to make it back to the office for a few ceremonial hours, but missing the marketing meeting as he had could result in a reprimand he wasn't much interested in. And there was another thing he was much more interested in at the moment—Bernie Cool.

Behr stopped at the library on Meridian and used his laptop and their Wi-Fi to do a background on Kolodnik. What he found was a pretty picture. As a matter of fact, it was a Rembrandt. Bernie grew up in Gary, ran track in high school, attended the University of Chicago, did two years at a large commercial real estate outfit, and then went on to Harvard B School. He married his college sweetheart, came back with his MBA, and began buying and refurbishing apartment buildings. By age twenty-eight he was breaking ground on his own developments. His operation had grown and grown since then. Industrial space, office parks, and towers throughout the Midwest. There were reams of information about Kolodnik's company and the deals it had struck and the construction projects he had put up. He'd had kids along the way, and there were civic distinctions and philanthropy. There were sub-three-hour marathon times, wins as a quarter horse owner, Boone and Crockett whitetails, and a club championship in golf out at Crooked Stick, where Bernie had even served as president a few years back.

Kolodnik was a Lion, and a Kiwanis and Rotary member, and the head of the state real estate association the governor had commissioned several years prior that advised on the statewide affordable housing panel.

Is that where he met the governor? Behr wondered.

It could have been, though it could have also been on countless other occasions at myriad venues and events. Indiana wasn't the largest pond in the world, and the big fish got to know each other pretty quickly. The most recent wave of press had to do with the Senate appointment, of course, and the one before that had spanned the previous three years and dealt with a venture that was something of a departure for him business-wise.

Kolodnik had partnered with a few other players on a large job: the Indy Flats horse racing track and casino—what was known around the region as a racino. It was a major development about twenty miles southeast of the city. There was a brand-new track and infield with a top-of-the-line grandstand connected to several hundred thousand square feet of casino floor packed with slot machines, video poker, and blackjack tables, along with restaurants, nightclubs, and even a few shops. Ground had been broken and a large, high-end resort hotel was under way; and a concert venue was planned. The project had been heralded as the financial salvation of the central Indiana economy. Everyone involved was expecting a windfall, and as such there had been a deal struck where the racino was supposed to pay the state a 250-million-dollar license fee, in the form of a roughly 75-million-dollar annual tax, to operate over the course of the next few years. From the tenor of the articles when the place had opened two years ago, this should have been a drop in the bucket. In fact, there were plenty of attendant op-ed pieces bemoaning the sweetheart deal and how the state was getting ripped off. But a year after opening, the economic crisis washed over the country and the world, and it didn't spare the Indiana gambling business. Apparently money had been lost by the consortium—lots of money, as in tens of millions—and now the venture was pushing the state for a rebate and renegotiation of the license fee. "Otherwise," Lowell Gantcher, the president of the company, said in the article, "the racino faces bankruptcy, and the area will suffer the attendant loss of hundreds of jobs." Behr wrote the name down in his notebook.

Predictably, there was another wave of op-ed pieces claiming the corporation had willingly entered into the licensing deal with the state, and now they had to live up to it.

Behr noticed that mention of Kolodnik in the articles had dwindled and ceased as the project moved from the development to the opening phase, and he wasn't sure how deeply Kolodnik was invested in the future of the racino, but from what he'd seen, and from the paucity of comments from him, Bernie Cool sure wasn't sweating it too much. Behr wondered what it was like, winning or losing tens of millions in the horse racing game. He'd sure as hell never played that much on the ponies.

19

Where in the bloody hell was Banco Alfaro?

That was Waddy Dwyer's question at the moment. The mobile number he had for his shooter was dead, as it had been for the past three days. There was no outgoing voice mail, no recording, nothing.

And why in the fuck did they call him "Banco," which was short for "money in the bank," when his real name was Juan, and he was such a bloody piece of shit?

That was probably a better question, Dwyer thought, but it wasn't going to help him much now. He needed to find Banco, to hear how he'd bollixed the operation, and if he and the backup shooter—and driver he was sure to have used—had been further compromised. There was an account number in the Caymans, where Dwyer had wired the first half of the money, but good fucking luck reverse engineering that into anything useful. Dwyer did have an address on a small apartment where Banco had been staying during prep. Of course the tie-dyed bloke wasn't going to just be sitting there, waiting for him or anyone else who might come knocking after the botched op. He would've gone into his hidey-hole for certain. But the address, 157 Keller Street, was all Dwyer had, which was why he was currently sitting outside the cheaply built, low-slung, tobacco brown apartment house.

He'd been squatting on the place for four hours and had yet to see a tenant come or go. He had his eye on the lower left-hand unit, marked MGR. on the building placard. Dwyer had knocked, gotten no answer, and had resigned himself to waiting it out. But here came a little man, walking with a shambling gait, a couple of grocery sacks banging against his knees. His skin was nut brown, including his mostly bald pate, and he wore a plaid utility shirt, twill trousers, and battered work shoes. He made his way to the manager's unit and barely had his key in the door before Dwyer was on him.

"Hey there, buddy," Dwyer said, adopting what the Americans called a Southern drawl. If he had to raise a ruckus to get what he needed, Dwyer preferred the cops to think they were looking for an American rather than a Welshman, and he found the Southern drawl the easiest jump for his tongue to make.

"Yes?" The manager turned.

"What's your name, bud?"

"I am Elihu," the man said with a Spanish accent.

"How you doing, Eli-yute? I'm looking for a good buddy of mine who was staying here for a while."

"Yes, sir, who?"

"Aw heck, he's hiding out from his ex-wife most of the time. His name's Juan, but he might've been going by something else."

"Yes, there is no Juan here. I'm sorry. He is *hispánico*?"

"Yep. Salvadoran fella," Dwyer said.

"Oh . . ."

"He would've probably just moved out. He has sort of spotted skin . . ." Dwyer didn't know what the condition was called, but Banco had some white discoloration on the skin on the side of his face.

"Yes, there was a guy, José Campos. He was here for six months only. Nice guy, very strong. Black hair, maybe this tall." Elihu held his hand up at head level. "He left last week."

"Hell, Eli-yute, that sounds like him. He happen to mention where he was moving?" Dwyer asked. There was nothing but a pause out of the manager. "Don't worry, I won't tell his ex-wife," he continued, adding the winks and eyebrow bumps the Southern fellows seemed so fond of.

"He did not say. He used to eat all the time at La Pasión. He loved *comida criolla*. He would bring me back *platanos*. Maybe they know." Elihu smiled blandly and finished opening his door.

Dwyer contemplated pushing him inside, closing the door, and hurting the man until he was good and sure he'd told everything he knew. Instead, Dwyer put a bland smile on his face, too.

"Thanks, bud," Dwyer said. He'd save that hurting for somebody else.

20

The Wild Beaver—with its ubiquitous smell of warm beer and the low ocean roar of happy hour—was nighttime dark, thanks to its lack of windows, when Behr walked in. He wondered exactly what the hell he was doing here and what had possessed him to choose the spot over the quietude of his usual haunt, Donahue's. His eyes cut around the bar for Decker, who wasn't easy to miss.

Sitting alone at a two-top table, back against the wall, was a man with a military haircut, worn desert-issue combat boots resting on the opposite chair, and a pissed-off look in his eye. His jeans were well ventilated, thanks to holes at the knees; and a tight black T-shirt stretched over his frame, which was that of a small linebacker. Small for the NFL, that is. Beefy biceps, marked with some high-quality ink, hung from traps built of humping a heavy ruck and rifle over exceedingly long distances. As Behr walked up to the table he saw that Decker wore earbuds connected to a battered iPod that was encircled by corroded duct tape still crusted with what looked like desert sand.

"Hey," Decker said, too loud, thanks to the headphones, which he pulled out as he stood and offered a hand. Behr shook what felt like a sandpaper mitt wrapped around a rock, and they both sat.

"What're you listening to?" Behr asked.

"Pantera, Coheed and Cambria, Charred Walls of the Damned."

"I don't know what you just said."

"Just a metal playlist." Decker offered the headphones. Behr put a bud to his ear and heard guitar-driven music, guttural singing, and driving drums. "Can't take this shit." Decker gestured into the air at the music playing in the bar. If pressed, Behr would've guessed it was Prince.

"Yeah, I don't really come here," Behr said.

"Whatever. Two-for-one happy hour works for me." Decker raised a pint glass of dark swill. The smell of licorice wafted to Behr across the small table.

"What are you drinking?"

"Deerslayer," he said, taking a big gulp and waving at a waitress.

"And that is?" Behr wondered.

"Jägermeister, Wild Turkey, and Coke, chilled and strained. Technically it's a black deerslayer. They usually make 'em with Sprite."

A chubby strawberry blonde with a bright smile and a pink T-shirt that was two sizes too small arrived at Behr's shoulder. "Hiya, what can I get you?" she said.

"Holly, get us another round of these," Decker said, then turned toward Behr. "Unless you have a regular drink."

"Sure, I'll try that," Behr said, and Holly went off toward the bar.

"Holly?" Behr said.

"What can I say, I'm a friendly guy." Decker shrugged, and nudged a pint glass, the second of his two-for-one, toward Behr.

"Thanks." Behr took a slug. "I've had better tasting gasoline," he said through the fumes.

"We drank these when we came off detail," Decker said, finishing the last few ounces in his glass. "When the object was to get as fucked up as possible as quickly as possible. It became a habit. You don't notice the taste after a while."

Behr appraised what sat across from him. Decker sported several-days-off stubble and though he couldn't have been much past twenty-six, there was an aged quality about him. But it was what was in Decker's eyes that spooked him, and Behr wasn't someone who spooked: nothing. There was just a depthless black that conveyed great familiarity with pain, violence, and death.

"So the girls are friends," Behr said, leaning back.

"Yep. Gina loves Susan like hell." Decker nodded.

"Seemed like they were having a good time when I saw 'em together," Behr said. "How long you been back?"

"Less than a year."

"Army?"

"Marines. Third Recon," Decker said. Behr recognized it as an elite unit.

"Regular infantry?"

"Scout sniper." Decker tapped on the rim of his empty glass for a moment before Holly arrived with the next round.

"Reload," she said in a singsong voice.

"Thank you, darling," Decker said as she left, and took a big swig of his drink.

"And now the IPD," Behr said.

"Only the dinosaurs still call it that."

"Guilty," Behr said and raised his glass.

"Brass hates that shit. Department-wide mandate to call it IMPD only. You were on the job for a while, I hear," Decker said.

"I was, and that was a long while ago."

"What happened?" Decker asked.

"Didn't work out," Behr said.

"I can see how that could happen." Decker drank again. For a moment Behr felt they were near the topic he'd been sent to discuss, but Decker moved them away quickly with a question. "And now?"

"Working at a place called Caro," Behr said.

"Oh ho"—Decker nodded—"explains the suit. Thought maybe you'd gone to law school or something. That's a plushy kind of high-dollar job, isn't it?"

"It can be. I've only been there for a little while," Behr said.

"So were you an officer? Ever consider making a full career of it?"

"Gunnery sergeant," Decker said, waving it away. "It's all in the DD–two fourteen."

They sat there for a moment, sipping. "Had enough of the Marines, then?"

"It was fun while it lasted," Decker said, then continued with effort, "but you get to a point when your contract's up, and you realize it's in or out for life."

Behr caught Decker rubbing a small tattoo on the inner surface of his drinking arm. It was a skull with a rictus grin against a bloodred background. The words *celer, silens, mortalis* forming a triangle around the graphic. Behr wasn't a Latin scholar but he knew the phrase: swift, silent, deadly.

"So you left?" Behr pressed on. After all, he was here for a purpose.

Decker sighed, shifted in his seat. "Like I said, it's all in my DD—two fourteen, I'll send it over if you feel like doing some light reading."

There had been a labored quality to the conversation from the start, and now this. Usually Behr could blame himself for the awkward pauses, but in this case he had plenty of help. "Look, man, you just tell me what you want me to know and we'll leave it at that. I don't need to check your military record."

"Fair enough," Decker said, the closest thing to a smile yet briefly creasing his lips.

"How'd you end up here?"

"India-no-place?"

"Yeah. I came out after college because the department was hiring," Behr told him. "You live in Indy before you joined up?"

"I was born in Missouri. Spent some time near Springfield growing up. Then Parris Island, Camp Lejeune, a few other fun places and points east."

"The folks still down in Springfield?" Behr wondered.

"No," Decker said as more black seemed to flood into those eyes of his and more light squeezed out, if that was even possible, before he continued, "grandparents. They raised me."

Five words over two sentences, an impressive average, even by Behr's standards.

Well, that's that, he thought.

The favor was to come, but he didn't guarantee results.

"Okay," Behr said, casting his eyes around the room, disengaging from the Decker project. As he watched pockets of office girls getting chatted up by snappily dressed guys, he spotted an attractive brunette by the bar, and noticed a worried, rather than sociable, expression on her face. He followed her gaze and saw a familiar looking young man next to her. Behr recognized the silver-framed aviators with smoked gray lenses, and, more than that, the attitude required to wear sunglasses indoors. It was Susan's little pecker-head friend Chad. And his back was currently pressed up against the bar, the forearm of a large man wedged against his throat. The geometry of the situation was pretty clear, even from a distance.

Behr zeroed in and watched it for a moment over the rim of his glass. The large man's face was purple with anger. Behr couldn't deny having pictured himself taking similar action in the past, but he'd never really considered it because of Susan. Chad was doing his best to stand firm, but white fear was leaking out from behind his spray-on tan. Things got worse when another solid-looking dude leaned into the fray at Chad's shoulder, clearly backing the first big guy. Behr turned toward Decker, put his drink down, and stood.

" 'Scuse me one sec," he said, and crossed the bar.

"Back door," Behr heard the second-to-arrive side of beef suggest to his friend, grabbing one of Chad's arms with a wrenching grip. The first florid-faced fellow caught hold of Chad's other arm and they practically frog-marched him along the length of the bar toward the rear. Chad's feet only occasionally touched the ground as he stumbled along, struggling in a growing panic that wasn't doing any good. A pair of girl bartenders in leather pants were head down and pouring drinks, oblivious to the situation. There were no bouncers in sight.

Behr moved around a pool table and interrupted the group's progress.

"Hold up," he said, putting enough bark in his voice to stop the procession.

The first man turned, let go of Chad, and fronted Behr.

"Move," he said.

"No," Behr said back.

"What's that?" red face asked, his words a wave of incipient violence and beer breath.

"What are you doing?" Behr demanded.

"None of your business—" the helper chimed in.

"Shut up," Behr said low and mean into the helper's face. It had the nearly physical effect of knocking him back a step, and it disengaged his hands from Chad's arm. Loose, Chad moved a few feet down the bar in a desperate attempt to escape further notice.

"Why don't you go back to your drinking," Behr suggested.

"Because this smart-ass motherfucker"—a thumb went in Chad's general direction—"fucked my girl"—the thumb now waved in the worried brunette's vicinity—"or tried to fuck my girl—"

"I'm not *your girl*, Bill," the brunette chimed in, "anymore."

Pain and rage flared in Bill's eyes. "Some shit went down. And I'm gonna push in his pretty boy face."

"If something gets pushed in, it's not gonna be that," Behr told him. Now Bill squared toward him, and Behr took in his thick neck, pimpled with razor burn and ingrown hairs.

"No? How come? *You* want to fuck him?" the man said.

Behr heard laughter around him and felt black anger in his gut. "Go file some tax returns or whatever the fuck it is you do and get out of my face, old guy," Bill spat, getting close and grabbing a handful of Behr's tie.

Lots of men in security work and law enforcement wore clip-on ties in contemplation of this very situation—for instead of a choking handle, which is what a regularly knotted necktie amounted to, the otherwise unfashionable clip-on will come off in an attacker's hand. Behr was one of these men. And it was what happened to Bill. The tie disengaged. Bill glanced at the length of faux silk in his hand, momentarily confused. But contact had been made and Behr didn't waste the opening.

He clapped a hand behind Bill's neck and drove a knee into his groin. The air went out of him with a gasp, and Behr felt him sag forward. He stepped back and let Bill crumple to the ground, but then he felt the thick arms of Bill's helper wrap around him from behind. Glancing down, Behr saw the canvas Converse All Stars that were considered so stylish by the kids these days.

Wrong footwear for the occasion, Behr thought and drove the rock-solid heel of his size thirteen Florsheim down onto the top of the helper's foot.

Behr felt the myriad small bones of said foot turn to pulp under his stomp, and the man's grip broke as he howled and shuffled in pain onto his remaining good foot. Behr spun him, and it took very little force for an ankle sweep to the man's weighted leg to deposit him on his ass with a thud next to his friend, who was curled up and drooling. Silence had fallen, besides the music, which Behr recognized as the old Pearl Jam song "Even Flow." All activity in the bar had ceased, as attention was directed toward the altercation.

"Are we done here?" Behr asked the pair on the ground.

Then there was a crashing noise behind him, and Behr whipped his head around to see a third big guy rolling around on the ground holding his throat, a pool cue loose on the floor behind him. Decker was just stepping back from the man, melting into the crowd of onlookers. Behr straightened. It was clear enough what had happened: Behr was about to get cold blasted, and then he didn't. A moment ago, on his way into the fray, he'd seen what looked like the remainder of the offensive line at a standee table, but stupidly hadn't clocked them as friends of the pair that was giving Chad the bum's rush. A pool cue shot to the back of his head could've really ruined his evening. Behr looked to Decker, who just shrugged.

Behr turned to Chad, who was wide-eyed and shrinking back against the bar. "Maybe you should call it a night."

Chad just nodded.

They stood in the dark, in the cool evening air, and were about ready to head for their cars. Decker had badged the lone happy hour bouncer, who had finally trundled up to the fracas, and the guy was plenty happy to let the three of them leave. Chad had at last gone on his way after an uncomfortable profusion of thanks. His mien—equal parts rattled, humiliated, and beholden—was almost more off-putting than his usual self-satisfied buoyancy.

"Well, that was interesting," Behr said, feeling like a high schooler on a date, when he and Decker were finally standing there alone.

"At least the music picked up there at the end," Decker added. Only the sound of passing cars filled the silence.

"Look, I don't know if I accomplished what I was supposed to here, so if you're up for it, and want to do it again . . ."

"Yeah, sure," Decker said, "you're lots of fun."

They went their separate ways, and Behr returned home to find Susan on the living room floor, organizing little blankets and clothing and other baby gear.

"How was it?" she asked.

"Fine. That Decker's a real handy guy," Behr said.

"Thanks for doing it, Frank. I know it was a big favor."

"Favors are my business," he said, heading off to take a shower.

21

Behr walked into the Caro offices at 8:25 to find a problem waiting for him, and it was one he recognized from the Payroll Place Web site. Karl Potempa was in the coffee area, pouring for a tall, gray-haired man Behr knew was John Lutz, the company president and client he was supposed to have met. Cups filled, they turned and saw him crossing to his desk.

"Mr. Behr," Potempa called out, warm yet stentorian, using a thumb to invite him toward a conference room. The "Mr." was something that was attached when clients were around, to impress them with the professional and civilized nature of the Caro Group. Behr grabbed his laptop and headed for the impromptu meeting, wishing he had more work product to show.

"Uh-huh, I see, uh-huh, hmm," Lutz said, his eyes raking back and forth over the lines of printed text that held the personal and financial information of his employees.

"We look for obvious flags—large deposits or purchases. Tax trouble or debt that could drive someone to cross the line. But as of yet, we don't see any of that here."

Behr had managed to get through most of the conference without looking like a complete fraud to the client. Lutz was merely a conscientious business owner eager to stop the thefts affecting his company, and it wasn't a problem for Behr to pepper him with preliminary factoids and generalized scenarios of worker malfeasance. To any casual observer it would seem that Behr had done much more on the case than he actually had. Potempa had sat in for the first ten minutes and his eyes, flat and knowing, made it clear *he* wasn't buying. What Behr saw there wasn't anger over a failure, however. It more closely resembled annoyance at the fact that Behr hadn't coddled the customer well enough on his own, he supposed, and that the complaint had climbed the ladder to the boss.

Then Potempa left and it got easier. Behr spent another forty minutes creating a blizzard of bullshit to distract Lutz. The nature of it brought a slightly sick feeling to his gut. There was no time over the past ten years when Behr would have bothered with a meeting like this, and if he lost business, so be it. But over the past months he'd led or at least been a part of several similar sits. File them under "client relations." In his past, as a solo operator, he'd probably spent 10 percent of his time on it, versus 90 percent on the work. Moving into the corporate world, he figured it would shift to a 25 to 75 percent ratio. He was wrong. Big-time wrong. Shortly after his arrival, he quickly deduced he'd be better off flipping things altogether, and making it 90 percent client relations, 10 percent work. He hadn't been able to make the final leap yet, to a complete goldbricking bill padder, but he'd probably get there soon enough. Finally, Lutz was satisfied and Behr got him out the door.

Behr went to his desk, where the smart move would've been to bust ass on the case in order to be prepared for when Potempa would have him in to rip him a new one. Instead he dove into the state business permit and licensing database. That's where he saw that, indeed, Kolodnik's company had pulled the construction permits on the Indy Flats racetrack project but was not listed on the state gaming license. That important piece was held by an LLC called L.G. Entertainment, the president of that entity being Lowell Gantcher. Behr remembered Gantcher from various articles that came up in his background check of Kolodnik, and it sent him on a new search into the man's personal history.

Lowell Gantcher had gone to college at the Kelley School at the University of Indiana, where he claimed a bachelor's of business administration. He worked for a large property management company and eventually did two developments: a stand-alone supermarket and a small eight-unit condo building. For some reason he hadn't been able to continue on that track, and began buying distressed loans. Then Gantcher and Kolodnik met at some point, because about three and a half years back they had partnered on Indy Flats.

In the more recent past, there were some interesting filings to the tax board, a petition to reduce estimated taxes based on a projected loss. That jibed with the news coverage on the racinos that he'd read of late, where video slot and poker machines that had been projected to take $350 per day during flush times were lately taking under $250. Some quick math told Behr that with between eighteen hundred and twenty-two hundred machines in play, that would account for around a $200,000 loss. Per day. Over the course of a year, the numbers would be staggering. And, finally, ten months back, the petition was denied, as was the request for a special assembly to convene on the matter. Behr made a note to swing by and pay a visit to Indy Flats to see for himself what was going on there.

It was close to 5:00, and an orange ball of afternoon sun was shooting through the office windows when Potempa's secretary showed up at his desk.

"He'd like to see you," Ms. Swanton said. Behr nodded, stood, picked up his paperwork, and followed her.

"Behr, sit," Potempa said. The client was long gone and so was the "Mr." right along with him. Behr took a seat across the desk from his boss. He saw that Potempa had a few fingers of amber liquor in a cut crystal glass near his elbow. Potempa saw him notice. "You want one?"

Behr shrugged, more out of surprise at the offer than a desire for the drink, and Potempa spun in his chair and poured a lean one from a decanter. He slid the glass across to Behr, who nodded his thanks and took a sip. It was a silk rocket of single malt that had to be eighteen years old.

"I get it," Potempa said. "You don't like the Payroll Place case. It's a hump job, a grinder. I'll put you on something else . . ."

Now Behr's surprise grew. "No, no," he began.

"Didn't expect it out of you is all," Potempa said. "You're not like most of those leather asses out there looking to do the minimum."

"Well, I'm not," Behr said.

"What is it, then?"

Behr took a moment, and then decided to speak to it.

"It's not about a different case, Karl, it's about the night in the garage."

"Still that . . ." Potempa started, suddenly looking weary. "I heard you called Breslau and that you visited Kolodnik," he said.

"Yes," Behr answered. If Potempa wanted more by way of explanation, he was going to remain unsatisfied.

"All right, look, there's shit about this you don't know," the older man finally said.

"Care to enlighten me?"

"Shit you don't need to know. Can't."

"Still, I'd like to," Behr said, forcing himself not to lean forward in his seat.

Potempa paused and scratched his chin. "Well, one bit I can tell you is: we weren't hired for security. It was just meant to be risk assessment, and an . . . advisory role."

"The political thing."

"That's right. We're not just steaming envelopes and running drivers' licenses here."

"I know that," Behr said.

"That exec protection bullshit was just something we threw in for . . . it was loss leader for—" Potempa stopped himself.

Behr suddenly understood. "For when he goes to Washington. So he'd be happy with you when he became *important*."

"And he is. He's happy. Thanks to you." Potempa smiled and put his hands out in a you-see gesture.

"Uh-huh," Behr breathed. "But he went with another company as soon as he announced."

"Well, it's unfortunate, but I've seen it before. They're looking for a little distance. We're hoping it's temporary. Look, Frank, this is a complicated situation. Caro is a sophisticated organization. Protecting people, property, that's just the surface. There's another layer—risk assessment, assets, digital proprietary—we're like . . . Do you play the piano?"

"The piano? No."

"Me neither. Well, I play a little. Not well. My daughter, now she . . ." There was a slight hitch in Potempa's voice, then he gathered himself and continued. "She was a hell of a little player. I could've had a ski condo in Vail for what I paid in lessons for her."

Potempa looked to Behr for the sympathetic laugh between well-to-do fathers. There was nothing there for him. "I picked up a few things coming in and out during her lessons, her practice." Behr's eyes went to the photos behind Potempa, to the pretty, dark-haired girl in them, who became a woman in the shots, and then went absent.

"Anyway, this place"—Potempa waved his hands toward the outer office and beyond—"is a grand piano. It runs on a complex set of levers and wires, various offices and pieces, all interconnected. And the personnel, we're all the keys. We each have our role, our note to play. Without any one of us, things aren't complete. But the A sharp doesn't necessarily know what the D flat is doing, when it's going to sound. And it doesn't need to. The keys all just need to be ready when they're called on to do their part. Like you were the other night. You performed, no question. And Kolodnik was goddamned lucky it was you there. But now it's time to stop the inquiries and go back to position until you're pressed into service again. The rest will work itself out. You know what I'm saying?"

Behr let the aria settle. "Maybe," he finally said, standing.

"Maybe," Potempa said, laughing to himself and pointing at Behr, who headed for the door and paused before leaving.

"What does she do with it now?" he asked.

"What's that?" Potempa wondered.

"Your daughter. The piano. Does she still play?"

"No," Potempa said, a new gravity joining the worn aspect. "She doesn't do that anymore."

Potempa turned his chair, picking his glass off the desk as he went, and faced the window. The room descended into a stony silence. Behr lingered for another moment and then left.

22

Spiker's Tavern was a taproom near the American football stadium. It had sawdust on the floor; a worn wooden bar; and was in a roughish—or at least an industrial-looking—part of town, so Dwyer knew it would make Gantcher nervous. He was sitting on a corner barstool, thanking bloody Jehovah that the marketing department at Guinness had finally penetrated America as he was hunkered over a decently poured pint of the stuff when a man entered who could only be Gantcher. Dressed in khaki trousers, tasseled loafers, and a melon-colored polo shirt, the tosser was a half step away from a country club and bleeding madras. It also looked as if he hadn't picked up a barbell in his life, and spent his time shielded from the sun in a sweet shop, pale and pudgy as he was. Dwyer watched him glance around the half-dark pub, struggling and nervous, and take a step in the wrong direction toward a punter in a Carhartt jacket before he rethought it and stopped. Finally he found Dwyer at the bar and Dwyer nodded, jumped off his barstool, and signaled to a secluded table, where they sat.

"If you want something you're gonna have to get it from the barman. No waiters here," Dwyer advised.

"No. I don't really drink much. I mean, wine, but I doubt they have much of a list," Gantcher said.

Dwyer said nothing.

"Never been here before, maybe I'll come back later and

become a regular," Gantcher chattered uncomfortably to fill the silence.

"I'm sure you'll be real popular in your poofter shirt," Dwyer said, causing Gantcher to pull back as if he'd been slapped. It was clear he wasn't used to chopsing like that.

Good, Dwyer thought, *at least he's listening now.*

"We've had complications, obviously," Dwyer said, using the silence. "This needs to be sanitized. Now. And I need more money."

"More money?"

"Correct. For operational expenses and fee," Dwyer said.

"How much?"

If word was going to get out and this was going to be the last job, then he needed the whole amount. "A million American."

"A million!" Gantcher lunged forward. "The whole job didn't cost that."

"But it isn't a job anymore. It's an emergency override, like at a leaky nuclear plant. And the money's necessary to buy safety," Dwyer said, knowing the effect the threat of his words carried.

"I know it is," Gantcher said, sounding forlorn, "but I don't have it."

Dwyer expected resistance. Rich blokes never *wanted* to pay. But when they were short of cash, they acted like they didn't like the idea, rather than admitting they didn't have the money. So the fact that Gantcher was sitting there actually volunteering he didn't have the cash was problematic. "The bloody 'ell do you mean you don't have it?" he demanded.

"I just . . . don't."

A beat. "How much do you have, then?"

"Nothing."

"Fuck off, nothing."

"Really. I'm tapped. I've broken T-bills. Drained retirement accounts, kids' college funds. I'm drawing down lines of credit now to keep my office open, and I'm almost empty."

"Look, man, you may think you're having problems now, but if this thing goes unmanaged and becomes the dog's dinner, you're going to know sorrow you never imagined," Dwyer said, causing Gantcher to go green.

"I've gotta go get to work, but we're going to meet again," Dwyer said, slamming his fist on the table, which lifted his pint glass with a rattle. Gantcher's eyes bulged with fear. "In the meantime, find some fucking dosh," Dwyer snarled, and with that he left Gantcher sitting alone in the bar.

23

It was a lot to think about, that soliloquy Behr had gotten from Potempa. And Behr was giving it plenty of thought as he sat in his car outside the office, waiting for Potempa's blue Cadillac to leave the lot. He'd told the client, Lutz, about the red flags an investigator looked for, and now he'd glimpsed a few himself. Potempa had been accommodating instead of pissed off. That was one. He'd been drinking. He'd even given Behr a drink. Maybe his boss had been in a sharing mood. Maybe. But Behr had been told to back off. Sure, it had been in gilded, metaphoric language, but the message was still clear enough. The words seemed to lock into place with the things that had been bothering Behr, and he knew that he wasn't going to back off. Quite the goddamned contrary. The Caddie pulled out, humping down in the swale between garage and street, then came up and turned right onto Maryland.

Behr was already in gear, and left plenty of slack between the vehicles, more than he usually would. It didn't really matter if Behr lost Potempa, since he could always pick him up again tomorrow, and whatever it was that had Karl Potempa so distracted, he was still former FBI, and getting burned on a tail of his boss was not the road to job security.

It was a fairly easy follow, with afternoon traffic flowing in between his and Potempa's car, as they crossed into the downtown area. Potempa turned onto Illinois and went halfway down the block before reaching the Canterbury, a boutique hotel, where he pulled over. A parked minivan started up and signaled in front of Behr, and he allowed it to pull out, then took the metered space, which had a good view of the front of the hotel.

As soon as Potempa got out of his car, a couple stepped toward him from under the awning. The man was midtwenties, with slicked-back black hair and a chin beard. He was just under six feet, thin but athletic, and wore a waist-length leather jacket and tight jeans. The woman, a girl really, was younger than the man, attractive, and had long blond hair that hadn't been washed in a long time. She wore a miniskirt with pale, pipe-thin legs shooting out from under it.

Potempa saw them, and the trio came together a few feet away from the hotel's front door. There was no handshake between the men. Potempa moved clumsily to greet the woman, but she hung back a step behind the young guy. The two men started talking, and while it didn't seem heated, it was a long way from friendly. Behr wanted to hear what they were saying, and slid down his window, but the traffic noise and distance made it impossible.

Behr considered what he was witnessing. The young woman was Potempa's girlfriend and the man was her brother? Or husband? The girl was a hooker Potempa had become infatuated with and the guy her pimp? That's when the young man reached to his waistband and pulled out a manila envelope, which he waved around a bit. This caused Potempa to lunge for it. But the younger man was light on his feet and slipped back a few steps out of range. Potempa squared with the pair and even from this distance Behr could see anger in the older man's hiked-up shoulders and clenched fists. There was some more conversation, then a halfhearted reach for the girl by Potempa, which she shrugged off. Then the group parted ways. The young pair backed up a few feet, still facing Potempa, before turning and walking briskly around the corner. For his part, Potempa stood rooted to his spot for a moment, before his shoulders descended and he moved back toward his car.

So two choices, a fork in the road, presented for Behr: follow

Potempa, see where he went, or track the young pair and that envelope Potempa had lunged for. Behr stayed with the envelope.

Behr fed the wafer-thin slim jim between the window and frame, and used it to reach for the latch lock. Countless seasons of alternating hot and cold weather had swelled and contracted the wood and left him a nice gap with which to work. The house was a small and aging bungalow common to the area. This one had a somewhat ratty lawn and peeling paint, and was not the kind of place Behr had been spending his time lately. He had picked up the couple, around the corner from the hotel, walking toward a five-year-old Lexus SUV. He followed them out of the downtown area for a few miles to the near west side and the formerly pleasant bedroom community of Riverside that had fallen on hard times that the weed and seed program hadn't been able to rectify.

The pair had gone inside the house, the man carrying the manila envelope, and after forty-five minutes of sitting there, Behr watched them exit. The girl now wore a short black dress and silver high heels, and the man was empty-handed. Then they got back in their car and drove away. Behr was tempted to follow them, to see where they were going, but he figured that envelope was sitting inside and that now was his chance to see what was in it and why it had so agitated Potempa. So he'd gone around the back and banged hard on the window in case someone else was home. No one was. No one came to investigate the noise, at least.

The notch of the slim jim found the latch, and Behr pulled, feeling it yield. His heart picked up its pace to a brisk hum as he slid the window up and glanced around the patch of backyard for any witnesses. He realized he was finally pulling that B and E Caro had been looking for. He fed a leg inside, sat, swiveled, and brought the rest of his body along.

Behr found himself inside a living room that was sloppy with clothing and scattered magazines and redolent of burned hashish. The place was sparsely decorated, but what furniture was there looked expensive, including a Persian-style carpet, a large flat-screen television, and a buttery-looking leather couch. There was also a high-end digital video camera mounted on a tripod standing in a corner. A mission-style desk pressed against a wall was buried in newspapers and held a computer with a webcam mounted on top of the screen. Behr hurried toward it to see if it was a security measure that was activated, but it wasn't. The computer, hard drive, and camera all appeared dormant.

Taking a quick tour around the house, Behr found the two bedrooms, one bathroom, and kitchen were all vacant. The same was true of the unfinished basement, which featured a brand-new side-by-side washer and dryer. He returned upstairs and gave the kitchen a closer look, which is where he found the manila envelope, resting on top of a yellow pages on the counter. The envelope was closed by a clasp and wasn't sealed, and Behr opened it to find an unmarked DVD in a jewel case. He set it aside and gave the living room a quick going over. On a cluttered coffee table Behr found a saucer full of ashes and a blackened piece of hash impaled on the end of a large safety pin. Next to it was a glass pipe, heavy with resin. As much as he looked, Behr could not find the other things he was looking for: a deed, a mortgage paper, credit card statement, a phone bill, or checkbook with the resident's name on it. He heard cars passing outside, and froze, ready to leap out the window, each time one occasionally slowed.

Before long Behr started to feel that sticking around was going to present increasing risk and diminishing return, and that it was time to leave. He cast a last look around, grabbed the envelope with the DVD, and let himself out the window through which he had come.

Behr had seen videos like it many times before, in fact it seemed he could hardly help but see them, even if he was trying not to— the Internet was so full of this particular type of material. He sat in his car four blocks away from the house with his laptop out, watching the DVD. It was amateur porn, shot in the bedroom of the house he'd just left. It wasn't badly lit, as the new cameras were very light sensitive. A girl walked into frame, in short shorts and bra, Behr was sure he recognized her as the one he'd just seen on the street and entering and exiting the house. He also figured he knew what would happen next: Potempa would join her in a compromising situation. But Behr was wrong about that.

While he considered it, the girl's clothes came off, revealing a slender and supple young body, pubic hair trimmed almost completely, with a tiny Playboy bunny tattoo on her hip. She lay down and started caressing herself. There was some banal conversation between her and an off-camera male about how horny she was, and then the man joined her in shot. He was young also, slim and muscled, but his face was never in frame, probably by design, as the width was occasionally adjusted, by remote, Behr assumed.

It's the sleazy guy from the meeting. If Behr had to hazard one, that would be his guess. The faceless man, tattoos of Far Eastern characters covering his forearms, "T-Bone" stitched across his abdomen in gothic script, pulled out his genitals, also groomed, and the girl serviced him with her mouth. Then the couple had sex, first in missionary position, her legs up, moaning and groaning into the camera. Next, she turned around and opened herself to the lens and he continued from behind in a three-quarter profiling shot, everything above his shoulder still out of frame.

The scene went on and on, and though Behr was tempted to speed the frame rate, he didn't. He needed to scan the whole disk so he didn't miss anything, like specific names being mentioned or any other important piece of conversation, or other people joining in. Nothing like that occurred, but the thoroughness paid off at about the seven-minute mark. That's when Behr began to realize there were edits, cuts to different angles, close-ups from below the genitalia known euphemistically in the porn world as scuba shots. The camera came off the tripod and started to move. All of it told Behr that there had to be at least one other person in the room, if not more, which meant that unlike some victims of spy cam setups, the girl had to know she was being filmed.

The whole thing was nineteen minutes and twelve seconds long. It was a clip like tens of thousands, maybe hundreds of thousands or millions, all over DVDs in porn shops and on Internet sites. But Potempa had been reaching for *this* one. Finally the girl went to her knees and the man finished in her face in a close-up. That's when Behr was able to finally recognize her. It was why his boss had been so interested in the envelope. Though she had her hair dyed blond now, the girl was Potempa's daughter.

24

Dwyer sat quietly in the back corner of La Pasión, the Latin restaurant his lead shooter supposedly favored, spooning black beans and rice into his mouth and watching the place unfold in front of him. It was a small, local spot, undecorated save tables and chairs and a *cerveza* calendar next to the cash register, so it was a bit unusual for him to be there. He'd sat and ordered, and after a while they had forgotten about him more or less. He saw that most of their business was takeaway. There were a few mothers with children who chatted in Spanish with the counter girl, who was also the waitress. She was a pleasant eighteen-year-old who spoke good English and had gone a little plump from too much *comida criolla*. There was a wizened old cook, his whites food stained and sweat soaked, who appeared from time to time in the kitchen doorway in the back. Dwyer asked a young, wiry busboy for a refill of his water and noticed a jailhouse tattoo of three teardrops near the webbing of his thumb and a scar on his face. The tattoo was gang or prison code, either of membership or signifying he'd killed. Dwyer didn't know whether the three represented a first killing or a total number of victims. Of course the kid could've been some aspirant who'd done the inking himself.

The waitress had come by to see if he needed anything and he'd asked for hot sauce. When she brought it to him, he'd made a little show of how hot it was, saying *"caliente"* and waving a hand in front of his mouth. It amused her and bought him some goodwill and an extra half hour of sitting there watching. Even so, he was at the limit of how long he could reasonably stay and hadn't yet spotted his angle, besides possibly the bus-boy, when two stout men in their early forties entered. In tight T-shirts that stretched over their arms and hard, round bellies, they might have been brothers or cousins. The larger of the two moved behind the counter and hugged the waitress warmly. It was clear from the indulgent nature of the embrace that she was not his daughter. The other man sat on a stool at the counter and waited. The waitress made him a *café con leche,* while the larger bloke popped the till drawer, removed a stack of bills, counted and split it, and handed over half to the coffee drinker.

Dwyer saw them notice him in the corner, size him up, and disregard him. He sized them up as well, and while they didn't seem like they'd provide much of a problem, they probably wouldn't volunteer whether or not they knew a José Campos just because he'd asked. He didn't see much point in getting into it in the middle of their restaurant during business hours though, so Dwyer stood.

"*La cuenta, por favor,*" he said, amusing the counter girl once again with his poor Spanish. He was just a novel fucking fellow. He paid his check, mildly overtipped, and exited. He got back in his car and took up a position where he could watch the men and follow them when they left. It was almost fiesta time.

25

Behr didn't sleep much that night. He'd driven by Potempa's house, and seen him through a bay window in his kitchen having dinner with his wife. He'd watched him go back and forth to the freezer for ice and refill his drink many times. He'd considered walking up to the door and knocking and telling Potempa what he knew. But he didn't. He just sat there thinking, wondering what Potempa, and his daughter, were caught up in, rolling the permutations around in his mind like a Rubik's Cube.

In the end, he didn't approach. He sat there until the house went dark, and he imagined Potempa sleeping, or at least in bed, lying there sleepless despite the alcohol. Behr's mind wouldn't feed him any answers, so he drove himself home to find Susan already down for the night. He slid into bed, envying her slumber. It was the body—the tiny one she was growing inside her—that demanded the rest, because he knew that by day her mind was filled with the anxiety of the coming child. The responsibility of it weighed heavy on her, as it did on him. She worried with a new mother's determined optimism. He envied her that, too.

For his part, he put up a futile struggle not to hope for everything to turn out well, as if his daring to wish for it would cause the universe to deny him that simple relief. He knew too well the blind corners and murky alleyways that came along with being a father. It seemed to be his sole area of expertise. He spent the rest of the night on his back in bed, between the worlds of the dormant and the waking, pricked by the knowledge that whoever he was hoping to track down probably wasn't at rest. He would rise early and be out the door before Susan stirred.

26

Waddy Dwyer couldn't believe how easy it had been.

It was as if the Americans built with bloody kindling materials.

The night had already been a hell of a busy one, and sleep wasn't going to be a part of it for him. The first piece had gone well, he thought, sniffing the intoxicating odors of gasoline and lacquer thinner coming off his shirt and skin.

As a matter of fact it was a thing of roaring orange beauty.

He pulled over behind a small grocery store and slathered his hands and lower arms in hand sanitizer. Then he stripped off his shirt, put on a fresh one, and stuffed the rank one in a Dumpster. No one of consequence knew he was in town or fuckall about what he was doing, but that was no reason to let the attention to detail drop. He got in his car for the drive through dark farmlands back to the city.

The second part of the evening promised to be more of a challenge. After all, the caballeros he needed to talk to could be pros or ex-pros, or could generally turn out to be a handful, so he'd need to be creative to get what he wanted from them.

Ah, just be a bit friendly, he thought, putting the car in gear and nosing it onto the main road, *and generous of course.*

27

The morning rose up in a hazy mass of purple sky bellied by thick rain clouds and smoke. The call from the police had come in half an hour earlier for Gantcher to get his ass out of bed and redline it down to the job site. Or what was left of it.

Three hundred and forty-two units, the town house villas in varying stages of completion, were now reduced to pockets of licking flame, glowing cinders, and smoke puffs. The beginning of the hotel tower was still standing but was now charred to a blackened cement spire.

Like my life, Lowell Gantcher almost said aloud. But it was a good thing he didn't, considering he hadn't noticed that a police lieutenant and a fire captain had walked up and were standing next to him.

"Heard you're having some trouble with your contractors," the policeman said.

"What do you mean?" Gantcher said, turning toward him. "I'm fine with those guys."

"They say they haven't been paid in three weeks." Hot pockets hissed around them as a slow, insistent rain began to fall.

"Bookkeeping changeover, nothing more. Their checks are cut, probably went out yesterday before close of business," Gantcher said, hoping it was the truth.

"Okay," said the cop.

"Are you saying that a disgruntled worker set this off?" Gantcher said.

"We're not saying that," the fire captain said. "It's too soon to say anything. Could've been bad luck or a colossal fuckup just as easy."

"How do you mean?"

"Best we can tell for starters is the fire originated in those units," the fire captain said, pointing with a stubby finger. "They were in the process of being wired for electricity. Maybe they weren't grounded yet. A power surge could've taken out a panel. Then those units, which hadn't been fully framed and insulated and fireproofed, went next. Your workers thought it'd be a good place to store the welders' oxy fuel bottles in there. By the time the flames reached the more finished units with all the paint and lacquer cans—well, the only thing that was missing was Mrs. O'Leary's cow . . ."

"Goddammit," Gantcher said, "if these guys were negligent, I'll sue the frigging contractor down to his last hammer and nail." Gantcher hoped it sounded convincing, the young developer distraught over his project going up in flames. The cop and fireman had no reason to know that he hadn't had a prayer of coming up with the funds to complete the job in the first place.

"Take it easy, Mr. Gantcher," the fire captain said. "Just like we don't know if it was intentionally set, we don't know if it was negligence either. Yet. All in time."

"Besides," the policeman spoke up, "you were insured, right?"

Gantcher felt the man's eyes bore holes right through him. He turned back to the smoldering flames and rubbed his eyes as if it were the smoke that was causing his tears.

28

Behr wanted to be the first one into the Caro Group that morning, to have a conversation with Potempa, for whatever it would yield, but he had something else he needed to do first. It was why he'd driven out to the southeast side in a gray, dripping rain and nosed his car up the dirt entry road to South County Landfill. This was a place he found himself from time to time, when he needed an answer or at least a thread to pull. Whatever was going on in town, Terry Cottrell seemed to know something about how it happened or who was involved. If he couldn't point Behr in the right direction, Terry would break things down into a likely strategy at the very least. The only question was: Would he? There had been bad blood between them the last time they'd met, and it was Behr's fault. He had pushed too hard on something and crossed invisible boundaries of friendship and trust. Behr had broken the unspoken code between them and had kept his distance accordingly, in order to let the wrong of it subside. But now it was time to lay it down. Which was why Behr had a large, expensive coffee table book called *French New Wave* resting on his passenger seat. A glamorous blonde graced the cover of the book chronicling the existential foreign films of which Terry was such a fan. It was a peace offering, just a token, but enough, hopefully, to bring about a thaw.

Behr parked by the double-wide trailer that was both office and home to Cottrell. When the weather was clear, he'd often find Terry outside, overseeing the dumping and spreading of waste at the landfill, or shooting rats with an air gun, or listening to music in the morning sun. It was usually later in the day, when the sun was ready to go down, that the Old Grand-Dad with a splash of coffee or cola would come out.

Behr rapped on the trailer door, surprised not to hear the sounds of jazz or a film bleeding through. After a moment the door opened and revealed a large gentleman fifty pounds heavier and twenty years older than Cottrell.

"Scale's closed for a half hour yet," the man said.

"Not here to dump," Behr said. "I'm looking for Terry Cottrell."

"You a friend of his?" the new man asked. Behr nodded. "He's gone."

"Gone? Where?" Behr wondered. But the man just shrugged.

"After the county hired me, he ran me through the workings of the place six months back. Then he packed out and left. Haven't heard from him since."

"He leave a number or an address?" Behr wondered. He had a cell phone number for Cottrell, but it was only good for leaving voice mails as it was rarely answered.

"Sure didn't," the man said. There wasn't much left to say. "Well, we're here if you need to do any dumping."

Behr tucked the plastic-wrapped book under his arm and walked back to his car, feeling empty.

29

"Can I get some coffee here!" Shug Saunders said, hearing the bark in his voice but completely unable to check it.

The fried eggs and hash browns were swimming on the plate in front of him, and he was pretty sure it wasn't due to the drinking he'd done the night before, but rather what Lowell Gantcher, the mewling son of a bitch, was telling him. Either way he had a growing suspicion he was going to retch.

Heads turned toward him at his demand. The Skillet was a small place—eight or ten seats and a counter—and the regulars there weren't used to strangers showing up in the first place, much less snarling at their waitress.

"Thank you, dear," Shug said, trying to put some sweetness into his voice when she finally arrived with the pot, and attempting to make it loud enough for everyone to hear.

"Uh-huh," the waitress said, and heads turned back to newspapers and plates and Shug and Gantcher were able to resume their conversation.

"Can you talk to the guy in the middle? See if he can, I don't know, make Dwyer back off or stand down?" Gantcher asked in a hoarse whisper, his coffee cup hovering in the air between them.

"The *middle guy* is running shit scared right now from this whole thing, man. I don't think I can call him for anything or make any kind of contact right now."

"Come on. Now's not the time for him to go MIA on us—"

"And as for the Welshman, from what I hear, once he's turned on, he doesn't have an off switch," Shug said. "Which is why you hired him in the first place, isn't it?"

"Oh god," Gantcher said. When he noticed his cup starting to quake in his hand he put it down on the table. "What are we going to do?"

"What did he tell you he wants?" Shug said, trying to think clearly.

"Money."

"Money?"

"That's right. To sanitize it, I think is what it's called."

"How much?"

"He said a million. So I suppose he'd settle for seven fifty, eight hundred grand."

"What the fuck? That's complete extortion."

"I'm not in a position to point that out."

"Well, I don't suppose you have it to give to him? Because that would certainly be the cleanest—"

"I don't have a piss to pot in, Shug," Gantcher said, scrambling it up and not even noticing. "I was wondering if you could, you know, go to Kolodnik on my behalf—"

"Oh come on," Shug cut him off, "I can't bring up the bill again. He's already landed on that—he's not doing it."

"No, I was going to say: to see if he'd extend me a loan based on my ownership piece," Gantcher said, his voice small.

"Oh, get real—"

"Now that I'm facing these rebuilding delays—"

"Are you a complete fucking idiot?"

The irony of the request was bringing on a migraine and Shug pinched the bridge of his nose. Three and a half years ago, this deal seemed so clear and simple. Back then Bernie Kolodnik's political ambitions were only a distant dream, the hundred K per year advisory fee Shug collected practically free money. It was cocktail parties and introductions for Bernie, which couldn't have been easier to make since he was a man of great success and integrity that everyone wanted to meet in the first place, and for

Shug it meant access—incredible access. Hell, he was probably the second person in the world to know about the Indy Flats racino project when it was born.

"Crapsake, Lowell," Shug hissed, "how could you mismanage things *this* badly?"

Gantcher had the good sense not to answer.

"It was supposed to be a simple build. A simple win," Shug went on.

"I know it," Gantcher said, shaking his head.

"You know how many frigging developers I could have steered this to? McLanahan, Aegis, Cyril Land. Who could've fucked it up like you?"

Some remnant of Gantcher's competitive spirit flared. "Come on, Shug, no one saw this slump coming. Aegis is balls-deep in overdue construction loans as we speak."

It was true. No one in the field was exactly unscathed at the moment. And none of the companies he named would've been willing to secretly kick back a piece of their end of the development in exchange for the introduction to Bernie, like Gantcher had been—which is why Shug had brought it to him in the first place.

It was to have been a straightforward build, launch, and sell. Long before Kolodnik's political career had even started. And when the deal was done and the sale complete, tens and hundreds of millions for everyone else and a quick thirteen-million-dollar pop for Shug.

But then profits dipped. The partnership had been forced to hold and manage the damned place. Gantcher and his team weren't equipped for that. Even in a robust economy they wouldn't have been any good at it. Gantcher had asked Kolodnik to go to the state legislature to ask for a special assembly where they would petition for a rebate on the licensing fee, which would have seen them through the tough time to recovery, and Kolodnik had. The man had asked. But the legislature had denied the request. Then, well, then the rest had started in motion, when whispers about the sitting senator's cancer broke, Kolodnik's name began being mentioned, and Shug saw the sock fill with the changing winds . . .

"A *racino,* for god's sake," Shug muttered, "getting a damned Gutenberg press and printing it yourself is supposed to be the only easier way to make money."

"I know, man," Gantcher said, his head moving slowly from side to side like a steer looking to graze. "But the question now is, What can we do?"

Shug's throat locked up. At the moment he didn't have any answers.

30

Ah, you'll be better after a bit of a kip, Dwyer told himself, standing over the sink, scrubbing the soles of his shoes with enzyme cleanser and a toothbrush. Only right now he couldn't afford to take one. That was one of the downsides of working alone. He'd used teams for the past eighteen years. He'd started out solo when he left the service, of course, until he could afford to start hiring on.

The ice-cold water pouring out of the faucet froze his hands stiff, but when dealing with protein stains cold water was required. Hot or even warm cooked the material right onto the surface that was to be cleaned.

It had been a hell of a night. After the burn job, he'd come back to the city and sat on the small house for a few hours, watching as the two stout men he'd seen at La Pasión arrived, then moved about, drinking beers, eating something at a table in the front room, and generally whiling away the late hours of the night. He'd wanted to make sure they were the only ones in the house, and eventually he had come to believe they were. Then he wanted to make sure they were good and tired before he got to them. Finally, the lights started going out, and he believed the time was right.

That's when he crossed to their door and knocked loud and hard. He didn't want them waking up confused as to what they were hearing.

He saw a light flick on, the front door opened, and an angry face appeared behind the screen door.

"*Que haces*, motherfucker?" the man, the one who had sat and drank café con leche said, tired anger in his dark eyes.

"I'm sorry to wake you, buddy," Dwyer said in his broadest Southern twang. "I was hoping you could do me a favor, and I could do you one in return."

"*Que quieres? Hablas español?*" the man said.

"What?" Dwyer responded.

"What the fuck do you want?" the man said, raising an aluminum baseball bat for Dwyer to see.

"I want to buy a piece of info, brother," Dwyer said, and fanned a handful of hundred-dollar bills. The man lowered the bat, opened the door, and let him in.

He needed to find Juan Alfaro, Dwyer told them when the other fellow, who'd cleared the till, had joined them. He didn't bother with a story about being friends, as he had with the old building manager. The two burly men sitting on either side of him, boxing him in in their living room, wouldn't have believed it and wouldn't have cared anyway.

Instead he told them it was a question of work. "I need him for a job and I'm willing to pay to find him."

"How much?" the till man, who was the more thickset of the two, asked.

"Five thousand," Dwyer said, dropping the money on their coffee table. They were experienced enough not to reach for it right away.

"If you will pay five for the information, how much you pay for the job?" café con leche asked.

"The job?" Dwyer said. "Hell, the job pays a butt load more than that."

"Maybe we do the job for you," the till man said.

"Well, sure." Dwyer nodded. "Where'd you serve? For how long? What was your specialty? How much combat did you see? Is your passport good? Is it under an alias? These are the ques-

tions my boss is gonna ask. He's always looking to hire on quali-
fied dudes."

The men waved the idea away with a *tsk*ing noise, as if it were
all too much trouble, which told Dwyer there wasn't much training to speak of.

"Maybe it'd be easier if you just told me where he is and keep
the finders' fee . . ." Dwyer suggested.

The men looked at each other and spoke in Spanish. Dwyer
kept a dumb look on his face even though he understood what
they said. *Why don't we call Banco and ask if we can say where
he is?*

"You know Banco," the café con leche drinker said. "He's very
privado. We call him for you."

Dwyer had an idea what would happen if they reached Banco
and described him and what he wanted, but he also saw his
opportunity, so he just nodded slowly.

Till man went and got a mobile and punched through the
phone's address book until he found the number and pressed
Send. The room got quiet and Dwyer could hear the muted
sound of Banco's phone ringing. It went on for a long time, a
good dozen rings, with no voice mail picking up. It gave Dwyer
the idea that they were calling a landline, not a cellular. Finally,
the till man's eyes flared.

"*Hola, guanaco. Soy Benito . . .*" Dwyer listened as the till
man—Benito—laid out the situation for Banco. He watched as
the man listened to Banco's response. The man's face was placid,
betraying nothing. He looked like someone reading a magazine
in a doctor's office, waiting for his appointment, despite the fact
that Banco was probably saying, "Don't fucking tell him where
I am!" or "Kill him!" or "Run!" The lad across from him was
good, Dwyer had to concede.

Dwyer held out his hand, as if it were his turn to talk. "Lemme
say hi," he said. Instead the man clicked off the call.

"He said 'chill,' he'll be right over."

"Great!" Dwyer replied.

Benito, the till man, stood and spoke to his *compadre* in flat

Spanish. Dwyer didn't flinch or in any way reveal what he'd heard: *"I'm going to get this guy a cooler. We can't let him leave."*

"Cerveza?" Benito offered, heading for the kitchen.

"Sure," Dwyer said. As soon as he stepped away, Dwyer turned to café con leche. "You can have that. Count it, make sure it's five thousand even."

Café con leche picked up the money and was counting greedily by the time Dwyer had crossed to the kitchen. The Česká was raised at head level as the freezer door closed, revealing Benito's face. Dwyer fired and saw the "cooler," a chilled .38, fall from the man's hand. Dwyer was back in the living room just as café con leche was picking up the baseball bat. It wasn't a fair fight.

The third to last thing Dwyer did was scroll the mobile and get Banco's number from the contact list, memorizing it, then erasing it. The second to last thing he did was wipe down the phone and drop it on the couch and pick up his five thousand dollars. Then he noticed he was standing in blood, so the last thing he did was step out of his shoes and head for the door carrying them.

Now that he was back in his shite hole and all was cleaned up, including his shoes, he went on his computer to reverse directory Banco's number. Banco had a bit of a head start, but hopefully it was one that Dwyer could make up.

31

Behr still got to work on the early side, and he watched as the office came to life around him. He would have preferred to be sitting in Potempa's chair when his boss arrived for the day, surprising him into sharing some information. It was a technique Behr had learned from an old NYPD detective and had employed in the past when he had clients of his own who balked at paying their bills. They'd walk in the door of their office to find Behr had gained entry and was seated behind their desk, leafing through their bills.

"Telephone, office supplies, cable, electric," Behr would say. "Why is mine all the way at the bottom of the pile?" Most of the time the shaken customer would pay him what was owed on the spot just to get him out of there. Of course that was when he was an independent operator. Now, at Caro, there was a billing department and accountants, and collection agencies after that, to chase down unwilling clients who refused to pay what they owed.

Behr figured *he* was owed something on this one too—namely answers. He'd put himself in harm's way doing his job for the company, after all. But Potempa had a career in law enforcement behind him and wouldn't be rattled by a cheap parlor trick like an office bushwhack.

Potempa walked in a little before 9:00, his perfect steel-gray coif floating above the tops of the cubicle dividers. Behr checked an urge to rush him with questions. He managed to sit out most of the day, doing a little work—as well as some Internet searches of Terry Cottrell that turned up nothing—but shortly after lunch, while the office was nearly emptied out, Potempa arrived back, and Behr made a beeline for his door. He had a hand against it before it had closed all the way.

"Karl, can I have a word?" Behr said.

"Make some time with Ms. Swanton—" Potempa began, before seeing the manila envelope in Behr's hand.

"Now would be better," Behr said, shaking the envelope a bit.

"All right," Potempa said, a slight rigidity gripping his body.

Ms. Swanton looked on with muted curiosity as Behr went into Potempa's office.

Potempa slid into his leather desk chair, and to Behr he appeared to have aged five years since the day before.

"Are we scheduling daily chats now?" Potempa said, a wary veil over his black eyes.

"I saw your conversation on the street in front of the Canterbury last night," Behr said.

"Oh yeah?" Potempa said, the veil dropping lower.

"Yeah," Behr said. A lot of people debated whether or not to tell a friend when they find out his wife is cheating on him. Behr preferred to lead with the truth, even if it was bad news. But then this wasn't about a cheating wife, and he and Potempa weren't friends.

"How'd that happen—coincidence or are you surveilling me?" Behr looked over Potempa's shoulder at the photos of his daughter, pictured her as a dyed blonde, and was sure of what he'd discovered. By way of answer, Behr raised the envelope and flipped it onto Potempa's desk.

"Is that . . . ?" Potempa almost barked, leaning forward and reaching for the envelope. He tore into it like a battlefield medic ripping open a compression bandage over a wounded soldier. A gamut of emotions played over his face as he slid the jewel case free: horror, elation, relief. "I can't believe you got it. I can't believe you got it . . ." he said.

"Karl," Behr said. "Karl," he repeated. Potempa finally looked to him, his hands shaking slightly as he held the case. "We have to assume this isn't the original. That there are copies. Multiple copies."

Potempa's shoulders sagged and he rocked back in his chair as the reality landed on him. "Right . . . of course . . ." It was too early for a drink, but Behr caught the older man's eye glancing longingly at the decanter on the credenza.

"Did you look at it?" he asked.

"I did—"

"Ah, goddammit, Frank," Potempa erupted, before his head sank into his hands.

"I'm sorry, Karl, I had to know what I was dealing with."

"And do you now?" Potempa asked.

"It's pretty clearly a sex-video blackmail scheme," Behr said. "But I'd like to know the particulars."

"Would ya?" Potempa said. His eyes went to the Scotch once again, but he turned admirably away from it. "I suppose you deserve to know," Potempa said. "But first the video. Is it . . . bad?"

"I have the girl as your daughter," Behr said.

Potempa nodded forlornly.

Any puritanical thinking about sex aside, Behr knew what he was asking. "Yeah, it's bad."

"Should I watch it?"

"It's pretty rough. I wouldn't if I were you," Behr said, somehow feeling that Potempa *would* watch it at some point, perhaps late at night, alone in his house or this very office, driven past the point of good sense by a morbid need to know.

"Does he hurt her?" Potempa wondered.

"No. It's what I'd call . . . consensual," Behr said.

"How'd you get this? Did you hurt *him*, by chance, or buy it?" Potempa wanted to know.

"Uh-uh, I entered his house and took it when he wasn't there."

"I'll have to get that address from you, I've wanted it for some time. I've had other guys on this and they didn't get this far . . ."

Potempa said distantly. Behr couldn't help but admire the man's skills. Though he'd come in with the advantage, and his boss was clearly struggling, Potempa had been the one to ask about a half dozen questions in a row and had Behr providing information, not vice versa. But enough was enough.

"Who is he—the guy you were talking to, and the one I assume is in the video?" Behr asked.

"My daughter's boyfriend. Lenny Brennan Barnes. Little pimp motherfucker. I hated the cocksucker the first time I saw him, and it grew from there." Potempa didn't go in for blue language most of the time, so it marked the depth of his emotions on the topic. "He got his filthy hands on my Mary and just . . . ruined her."

"What's he threatening?" Behr asked.

"To release it," Potempa said, thumping a finger on the DVD case, "on the Internet. To IPD e-mail addresses, Bureau offices. Her old high school. Local colleges. All over the damned place. To make it ugly for me. For her future."

"Unless you pay?" Behr asked.

Potempa made an "of course" gesture with his hands, and Behr didn't think much of it because of what was on his mind.

"Hold on, you said 'boyfriend'?" Behr said, trying to assemble it. "And I saw them together. They look like they *live* together."

"I know, I know. My daughter, she just . . . turned against me. By and by, I guess, though it felt like all at once. We started fighting. Over her friends. Men. Her lifestyle. Drugs. Back and forth like a couple of badgers, until it seemed like she was willing to go down herself just to see me suffer." Potempa shook his head. Suffering he was.

"But if she's party to it, if she's okay with the clip getting out there," Behr ventured as delicately as he could, "why not step aside and let it? The burn rate on this shit is like thirty seconds in today's world. It'll be forgotten before it's done playing."

He hoped to remind Potempa of what he, as a professional, already knew: that removing the leverage caused any extortion plot to fall apart instantly.

"Behr," Potempa said, "*she* may be out of her mind, and willing to play at this, but *I'm* not. I can't have it. I can't have it. You read me? That's my little girl . . ."

Even if Behr had never heard the English language, he couldn't have missed the desperation and vulnerability in Potempa's tone. Only a child in peril could bring forth such a sound. Only being a parent could make one that weak and susceptible. Behr just nodded, suddenly feeling as weary as the older man looked.

32

"Final numbers aren't in yet, but second quarter operating expenses are running constant at roughly negative twenty-seven thousand per day. Projected per-player revenue is off target day by day at two sixteen, one forty-two, one eleven, two nineteen . . ."

The numbers washed over Lowell Gantcher. All bad news. He looked around him at the paneled walls of the L.G. Entertainment conference room. He glanced at the people sitting at the long table. Senior operations managers, project managers, sales managers, accountants, bean counters of every stripe, the ineffective marketing ass wipes, the pricks from promotions with their dinner giveaways and frequent player cards as the height of their uninspired ideas. All of them sat there at the trough, waiting for their next paycheck. But the truth was, they weren't going to get them the following Thursday. There was no money left. They were alien beings to him, these workers, from another planet where you went to work, did your job, got paid for what you did, and lived on what you earned. If they understood overleveraging at all, it wasn't something they did. It wasn't their religion.

He was the real alien, he supposed. He wondered what he looked like to them: whether all the Xanax he'd been taking made him appear like a broken robot whose faceplate was about to spring off, or if their faith in him convinced them he looked normal.

It was supposed to be easy to be a CEO. The hard part was

supposed to be getting there. Twenty years of building, working long hours, sucking up to bosses and bankers, hitting numbers, winning bids. But now look at him. He'd tripped at the finish line and gone facedown on the asphalt.

Gantcher raised his gaze to the glass that looked out into the main office in time to see a bulked-up, stocky figure moving quickly. *Dwyer.* A rush of adrenaline hit him in a sickening burst that almost had him throwing up and lunging out of his chair to run at the same time. The figure continued past the room. It was just Williams or Willoughby or whatever his name was, some fireplug he didn't know well who worked in site planning. Gantcher caught himself gripping the edge of the table.

Relax, for god's sake, he urged himself to no effect, when Janine Mohrer, a young woman from accounting who issued checks for most of her day, walked in.

"Mr. Gantcher . . ." She interrupted the meeting, her face chalky white with fear, causing his own alarm to deepen in a way he hadn't thought possible moments before. "There's a problem with the insurance policy on the town house job. It had lapsed."

33

Lenny Brennan Barnes. That was the guy putting the squeeze on his boss.

Little pimp motherfucker. That's what Potempa had called him.

Behr ran him and discovered the résumé of an undergraduate hood scratching his way toward a master's. There was a drunk and disorderly, a grand larceny for a car theft that he'd pled to, possessing stolen goods, possessing drug paraphernalia, and pandering. All it told him was that Barnes was a dirtbag, as advertised. Behr was tempted to go to his house and have a real personal conversation about all things Potempa, but he couldn't risk pushing and causing the guy to go public with the video of the girl. It wasn't his move to make.

Behr had gotten to the office early, and he left just as early, making his way out while the place was still humming with activity, the Payroll Place file on his plate hardly an afterthought, his concentration fragmented, and Potempa nearly in tears. The conversation had only gone on another minute or two. There was no point in asking whether he'd been to the police, but Behr had done so anyway. A defeated shake of the head was Potempa's answer, and there was nothing else to say.

Instead of sticking around, Behr went to Donohue's, where he hung on the bar through dead early afternoon quiet and into the fore-end of the minor happy hour wave. He got a hold of the bartender Arch Currey, the gatekeeper of Pal Murphy's time, and requested an audience.

Pal owned the place and sat like a cardinal in a back booth, holding court. Nearly every piece of business information, both legitimate and illegitimate, of any consequence in Indy flowed through that booth. Pal would certainly know if any high-profile hit had been ordered in town. Whether he would tell Behr anything about it was the only question. Pal wasn't in the taproom when he arrived, and most of the barstools around Behr were full by the time the familiar visage of white hair, chrome glasses with tinted lenses, white dress shirt and smooth leather blazer took the seat in the booth that had magically remained empty despite there not being a reserved sign resting on the table.

They'd always been on terms. Nothing Pal had ever helped Behr with had come back to hurt him. For his part, Behr had shared some things that had been useful to Pal over the years. Other than that, Behr was a good customer, a regular, at Donahue's. Which made it all the more strange that Behr got no traction whatsoever tonight. Three hours and three nursed beers didn't yield him an audience. Pal was there, five yards away, occasionally talking to his waitresses, shaking hands with other patrons, conferring head-to-head with some old-timers, and getting his coffee refilled by Arch Currey every once in a while. Behr tried to keep his cool, but at the two-hour mark he broke protocol.

"Arch," he said, when the bartender moved by, "he's aware that I'm—"

"He's aware," was all Arch said.

Behr was trying to gauge whether it was a case of Pal having an inkling of what he was there for—because he would certainly have heard it was Behr in that parking garage—and had no information to share, or if some more direct insult was being communicated. Things were pretty chilly when it came to acquaintances willing to help him. He wondered if it was coincidence or like forest animals going to their burrows before a storm. Maybe Pal knew something, but it was too big for him to get involved. That thought made Behr uncomfortable. Then he got a new idea.

He needed someone who knew things but didn't know any better. There was a different Murphy besides Pal—a *McMurphy* anyway—who might be able to help.

"Some other time," Behr said to Arch, and tossed a quick two-finger wave Pal's way as he headed for the door.

34

"Uh-oh, nightmare walking, psychopath stalking," Kid McMurphy said, his face falling, when he saw Behr.

Kid swallowed a gulp of his drink, which looked to be only water. Stepping off a riser after his sound check, Kid looked pale and much thinner than the last time Behr had seen him. "Kid McMurphy" was a stage name. The singer was Pal's nephew, and he shared the family talent, albeit unpolished, for information tracking. "What the hell are you doing here?"

"Here" happened to be the Vollrath Tavern, which had been in operation on Palmer since the day it opened as a speakeasy back during Prohibition. It still retained the old-time saloon feel, with its ornate wood-and-mirror bar and tile floor, as when John Dillinger used to frequent the place. Nowadays it was a live music venue, and tonight it happened to be hosting one Kid McMurphy and band.

"Hoping to ask you a few questions," Behr said.

"What makes you think I'd help *you*?"

"I just think you're a helpful guy," Behr said evenly.

"You know, that dude was plenty pissed off about that thing," Kid said a bit sulkily. Kid had introduced him to a source of information when they'd first met, and Behr had been none too gentle with the man.

"I'm guessing he got over it," Behr said. He hadn't come here to discuss past matters. "You don't need him as a friend anyway—you're better than that."

This seemed to brighten Kid's mood. "You think so?"

"Yeah. Come on, you've got talent and what does he got?" Behr had heard Kid on the radio, and the last few bars on the stage just now. He wasn't bad.

"You know anything about your uncle cooling me? I can't seem to get booth time with him," Behr asked.

"Could be. I don't know anything about it directly, but that's 'how he do,' as the bros say. Either way, the minute I saw you here, I figured you must be fresh out of friends."

The truth in the musician's words landed on Behr like a cold, wet blanket. He thought of his usual sources and how little they'd yielded—and those were the ones he could find. The news about Pal was more troubling. The old man was secure enough to say "I don't know" if it came to it, but he'd refused Behr an audience altogether. *Bad sign.*

"Maybe I could buy you a few of those whiskey and Cokes you love so much and we can have a talk?" Behr asked.

"I don't think so . . ." Kid said, causing Behr to think he was on the verge of another strikeout. "Caught a wicked case of pancreatitis a little while ago. If I drink now, I die."

"So you're sober?" Behr asked. Kid's pupils were the size of pinheads and he didn't look fully zeroed.

"I still take pills."

"Oh, good," Behr said.

"But they don't do shit without mixing 'em with booze."

"I'm sure you'll keep trying."

"You got that right."

They moved off to a corner of the bar, away from Kid's bandmates and the tavern staff, and Behr broke down what was happening from the night of the shooting, his visit with Kolodnik, the lack of security footage, and Breslau telling him to leave it alone. Kid appeared to half listen, his head turned away, bobbing to some inner sound track, until Behr got to the part about the sex DVD he'd recovered, then Kid slowly turned and faced Behr and suddenly became all ears. When Behr mentioned the name Lenny Brennan Barnes, Kid came to life.

"That's a name I've heard," he said.

"You know him?"

"Nah. Never met him. Been at places he's been at, but never met. Word is he's one scurvy motherfucker."

"He runs girls? What else?" Behr wondered. He noticed the Vollrath was filling up around them.

"Hmm," Kid said, scratching his stubbly chin, "I don't know about his business. But if I wanted to, I'd talk to this girl Sunshine Jane."

"That her real name?" Behr asked, writing it down.

"No, Ann Marie something. Who cares? She goes by Sunny. Everyone knows her by that."

"Okay. What's her deal?"

"She's this freaky-deaky massage girl. Smoking hot. Works on all the big business dudes and politicos in Indy."

"Hooker?" Behr asked. "Rub and tug?"

"Not even," Kid said. "She gives regular rubdowns, but *she* gets off. Grinds her snatch on the corner of the table while she works or something."

"Classy," Behr said.

"Whatever. She told me about it one night after a gig, but I was mad wasted, so my memory's not too crisp . . . Those days are sure over, though, I'll tell you," Kid lamented of his liquor-soaked past.

"Where can I find this Sunny?" Behr asked.

"She's got a Web presence. You could book an appointment. You look kind of tense." Kid broke into a sniggering laugh at this, which Behr rode out. "But this time of year, long as it's not raining, she'll be at the Palms, no doubt."

"You want to take me down for an intro?" Behr chanced. Kid winced like he'd stepped on a nail.

"No, dude, and in fact if I'm left completely out of this shit this time, it'd be much appreciated."

Behr just nodded and felt his BlackBerry buzzing, as a guy who seemed like the club manager walked up and tapped Kid.

"Two minutes," he said and moved on into what was building into a decent happy hour crowd.

"You gonna stay and take in the future of rock and roll?"

Behr shrugged. "Yeah, sure." Then his BlackBerry beeped, announcing an incoming text message. It was from Susan and read: *Where the heck R U? The Deckers have been here 4 half hour.*

If Susan had mentioned the dinner to him, he'd forgotten it completely.

"Gonna have to be when you play Conseco, Kid. I've gotta be somewhere," Behr said, sliding off his barstool.

"Your loss," Kid said. Behr took a step for the door. "Hey, man," Kid called out. "What was it like getting shot at?"

Behr looked at him for a moment. "You know how it is not drinking?" Kid nodded. "It's even worse than that."

Behr headed for the door.

35

The house smelled like rack of lamb with olive oil and rosemary, Susan's specialty, when Behr walked in the door and found them at the table.

"This is restaurant quality, Susan," Decker said, waving his fork over his plate.

"You're not drunk already, are you, Eddie?" Susan shot back.

"Maybe just a little," Decker said. He wore a weathered, olive drab polo shirt with sleeves that cut into his biceps, Gina a dress that was shorter than most pregnant women would've dared.

Then Susan saw Behr and turned her face up to him for a kiss. "Sorry, Frank, it was ready to go so we didn't wait."

"Rightly so," Behr said, sitting. "How are you all?"

"Jealously watching Eddie suck down all your liquor," Gina said. Behr saw a prim glass of white wine in front of the women, while Decker had a tumbler filled with what looked like Wild Turkey on the rocks.

"Where were you?" Susan asked. "I tried the office."

"I was out."

"I called your cell."

"You used the landline. It comes up 'blocked,' which is what happens when people from work call from their private lines, so I didn't answer."

"Ah, the artful dodger," Decker said.

"Gotta be. Second thing they teach you in detective school," Behr said.

"What's first?" Gina Decker asked.

"How to bill," Behr said, with Decker murmuring the line along with him. It was an old saw in law enforcement.

"By the way," Susan said, "I spoke to Chad and heard what happened the other night at that bar."

Behr and Decker looked at each other guiltily across the table.

"Like a couple of schoolboys, the both of 'em," Gina said, obviously having heard the story from Susan.

"Don't worry—you two get your merit badges," she said, "and thank you," and that was the end of it.

A pleasant meal passed, filled with lots of chatter, mostly on Susan and Gina's part, and some laughs. The men bussed the plates to the kitchen and the ladies took over from there. Behr and Decker retired to the living room for yet another drink while they waited for the blueberry cobbler to warm up. Decker had had a good three or four refills of his bourbon during the course of the dinner—not measured shots, but big, generous home pours—and Behr had stayed head-to-head with him, so neither was feeling any pain as they hit their seats.

"Extremities almost completely numb," Decker said, "almost where I want to be."

"So when are you back on active duty?"

"Staycation's over tomorrow," Decker said. "Modified for a week, and back to the gerbil wheel."

"Is that what the job feels like?" Behr wondered. It had been a long time since he'd been on, a long time wishing he was—he couldn't remember anymore.

Decker stared out over the rim of his glass. "The job's not so bad. It's me." Behr understood him well enough but was surprised to hear him go on. "When I was in—the time I spent training, going out with Cal—he was my spotter. We switched it up, but he was mostly the spotter. We'd set up in a position near the airport, in places I can't mention, and lay hell down on the Ali

Babas for forty-eight hours straight before they'd dope us out. Back here, I can't sit still for half an hour. Without a drink in my hand . . ." He laughed. "Over there things were just . . . clear. Take out this target. Set a pomzie surprise on a trail—"

"Antipersonnel mines?"

"Yeah. Or a mud cutter—they were sort of my specialty."

"Mud cutter?"

"It's when you bury a short-fuse grenade on a heavy-use trail and remove the pin but leave the handle in place. Step, step boom. Or throw a fifty-caliber party on this group of unregistered bad guys. We've got wounded and you need to use your snipecraft to allow the cas evacs in. I knew exactly what I was supposed to do and how to do it. Now, being back. Living like this. Sleeping with my boots off. In a bed. Married. With a pregnant wife. Trying not to crack dipshit motorists and to act like a normal clean-cut citizen . . . I don't know . . . It's great. I'm lucky . . . But now, I'm just powered down. Like I hit the mute button or something . . ." Decker raised a hand in front of him and rubbed his fingers together as if he were trying to grab a hold of something slippery. "Life now's like eating steak with a balloon on my tongue."

Behr just looked at him and took a big drink of his bourbon. He rattled the ice in his glass when he was done. Behr felt like another, and he could see that Decker just about needed one, but he couldn't move. Then Decker leaned in.

"Look, I don't want to get too personal, but I could use some intel on what's coming down the pike on the kid front."

He took the question in. Obviously Susan had mentioned to Gina that Behr had once had a son. He had to assume that they also knew the boy was no longer alive, though perhaps they didn't know the circumstances of his death. Either way, it wasn't what Decker was asking, and it didn't make Behr want to revisit the terrain.

"Well, I remember this: about six days before and six days after the birth, until when her milk comes in, your wife sure isn't the woman you married. Hormones. Try to remember that when you think you're living in *The Exorcist*."

Decker just nodded. Behr saw he wasn't looking for jokes and something resembling sobriety descended on him. The young cop's question deserved a real answer and he only hoped he was worthy of giving one.

"What do you want to know?" Behr asked, doing his best to keep the iron cauldron lid in his chest sealed up tight.

"Well, I'm pretty sure Gina's got a handle on the basics. But I want to do things right, and the way I came up, I don't have much of a . . . role model."

Behr turned and looked at Decker, who finished off his drink. For a minute he sccmcd young, actually resembling his twenty-something years. Behr wanted to help him, and cast about in his brain for a way to do it.

"That doesn't matter," Behr began. "When you become a father, the—" he looked for the right words "—the slights and grudges, whatever you want to call the shortcomings of your own childhood, they get pushed aside. They've got to, because they've got nothing to do with the kid that's coming. You don't want to be the same father you had, and you don't want to be a direct reaction to that either . . ."

That's when Behr saw it happen: Decker's eyes went a flat, distant black. A palpable darkness filled the air, and Behr got the feeling Decker wasn't really in the room with him anymore. A silence grew to an uncomfortable length, and Behr did something he didn't often do, which was reach for a social convention and continue in a more positive vein so the whole conversation, the whole night, didn't crumble to dust.

"It's a fresh start is all I'm saying. You're gonna feel that you need to find a way to be more or better than you are, for the sake of the kid . . . And you will. You'll do it. It'll be an inspiration like you've never had before. So try not to worry about it."

Everyone knows the best salesmen believe wholly in their product, and, as such, Behr realized he wasn't much of pitchman for the bright side.

They both looked at their glasses and grunted and made their way to the counter where the bottle was. That's where the ladies, bearing plates of cobbler, found them and added a sooth-ing social balm to the proceedings. Susan and Gina talked and laughed. They all finished their desserts, and it seemed Decker came back to himself.

"So, boys and girls, I'm fizzling out here," Susan said after a bit.

"Me too," Gina said, and they all stood.

"C'mon, Jeeves," Decker said to his wife, throwing an arm around Gina's neck, and then turned to Behr and Susan, "that's her chauffeur's name. I got me a designated driver."

Gina gave him a shot to the stomach. "You get a driver, and I get to carry a bowling ball around for nine months," she said.

Decker just laughed. "That's the price for twenty minutes of glory," he said, then stuck a hand out to Behr. "Sorry to leave you hanging, buddy. Nothing worse than an incomplete bender."

"Nah, it was good enough, and I'm up plenty early tomorrow, too," Behr said.

"Work?" Gina asked.

"After I push some pavement," he said, thinking ruefully of his morning run after countless drinks.

"What time?" Decker asked as they reached the door.

"Six o'clock, Saddle Hill," Behr said.

"See you there," Decker said with a cockeyed, drunken grin. He weaved off toward the car in a way that told Behr just how unlikely that was going to be.

The company was gone, the dishes washed, the lights off, and Susan was asleep, when Behr crossed a line he didn't ordinarily with someone he'd met socially. He went ahead and ran Deck-er's background, starting with his military record. What he saw there was impressive and vivid. Decker had been a Recon Marine, which was an elite branch, and his Military Occupational Spe-cialty was Scout-Sniper, as stated. Behr saw that Decker had entered the service when he was seventeen, and also had seventeen confirmed kills logged per his service record. It was a big number when one considered what it meant. And Behr knew that the CKs on the record only represented a percentage of kills, and that most snipers had many more unconfirmed. That meant that the big kid sitting in his living room trying to figure out his life had dropped the hammer on twenty, two-dozen, thirty, or maybe more human beings.

He'd been awarded two Bronze Stars, a Silver Star, and a Purple Heart for his work. He'd been to recon school and demolition school and jump school at Benning, home of the Army Rangers. Then Behr saw something that really caught his eye. Family: none. That got him off the Department of Defense site and out into the world of civilian information. He discovered that after his discharge, Decker had served a nine-month stint with a defense contractor called K-Bar USA, and then Behr continued into the regular news and municipal record bases for Franklin, Indiana, and then Missouri, where Decker said he'd grown up. Once he was searching Missouri, the story wasn't hard to find.

The Springfield *News-Leader* reported the basics:

> An area man snapped at his home outside Springfield yesterday, killing his wife, daughter and infant son with a deer rifle. The man, identified as William Lawrence Decker, also fired at his thirteen-year-old son, hitting the boy, who ran and escaped, before turning the gun on himself. Decker, a teacher, had been unemployed since moving to the area a few months earlier. Neighbors said the family kept to themselves, but seemed normal, and saw no signs of the outburst. The boy was admitted to Cox South Hospital in serious but stable condition and will survive the incident.

Behr sat there, his blood running cold, a headache pounding at his temples as the liquor left his system. He imagined Decker as a boy, as a young man, and even now, wrestling with why he had survived, why he had failed to save his family, and whether he would've been better off stopping and letting another bullet from his father's gun rip through him and take him to a place beyond doubt. A lone follow-up story mentioned that "the boy" had been sent to live with his dead mothers' parents once he'd recovered. After that kind of childhood, the military was probably about the only thing that made sense.

Behr shut the computer, sorry he had checked, sorry he knew, and even sorrier that it had happened in the first place. It seemed like a world of sorry out there that got deeper and darker the later the night grew. Not knowing what else to do, he peeled off his clothes and crawled into bed.

36

Dwyer had invested his entire day in his stakeout and was completely knackered after nearly thirty-six hours straight awake and on the job. He also found himself someplace he didn't often visit, which was at the limits of his patience. With the telephone number he'd gotten from the La Pasión boys, Dwyer had been able to use a reverse directory program on the laptop back in his room. It was a bit sloppy of Banco to have ended up trackable by landline, but he must've figured he needed comms in his hide, and he'd know that a mobile would have to be turned off and the battery removed to make sure he wasn't traceable by that. In the end, it had taken him a hell of a good deal of work to uncover the address, 1701 Wilmette Avenue, and find the building. This told him that Banco hadn't completely abandoned his fieldcraft. He was still being careful. The lime green stucco apartment house wasn't a half bad hidey-hole either, out of the way and nondescript as it was. Now though, sitting outside wasn't yielding any more answers for Dwyer, and he didn't expect he'd be lucky ducky enough to catch Banco leaving or coming. It was time to go in.

The building was poorly secured, and earlier in the day, he'd found a way inside. As far as he could tell, there were no security cameras on the doors, nor was there a video feed on the front door buzzer that might have been run through a backup recording system. The ground floor of the building had a long front-to-back hallway with a steel door in the rear that had been wedged open, probably to allow for a cross breeze, and the only thing stopping entry was a locked wire mesh gate. Dwyer had gripped the cheap knob and given it a good yank, and it had popped right open.

He'd gone upstairs to the second floor and looked at the door to 2G but couldn't figure a way through without blasting it off its hinges, and that wasn't going to be conducive to a conversation once he was inside. So he'd retired to the rented car to give it a think. After a few hours, once darkness had descended, Dwyer had finally picked up his mobile and dialed.

"*Sí?*" Banco answered, as if he'd been woken.

"I'm here. Outside," Dwyer said. "Let's talk."

"The door will be open," Banco said after a long pause, and rang off.

Dwyer didn't bother with getting buzzed in but instead popped the cheap gate once again, this time with a handkerchief in his hand, which he also used to turn the knob to Banco's door.

He entered the small, sparsely furnished apartment and saw Banco, sick and pale, propped in a bed with soiled coverings, backed up against the wall in a corner away from the windows; and one whiff told him Banco was suffering gunshot sepsis. The cheap curtains allowed enough streetlight in for Dwyer to see there was an assault rifle pointed at him. Banco's gaze seemed firm and his grip steady enough that it discouraged Dwyer from rushing him and grabbing the barrel and ripping the gun away.

"*Qué pasa, 'migo?*" Dwyer said.

"You found me," Banco said, shifting a bit, in apparent great pain.

"Sure."

"How are Benito and Boli?" Banco asked.

Dwyer understood he meant the men from La Pasión.

"Fine," he said.

"They told you where I was?" Banco asked. Dwyer didn't respond, just shrugged. "Because they didn't know . . ."

"The number was enough. I paid them for it," Dwyer said.

"I called them back a few times, couldn't reach them," Banco said.

"Probably out partyin'," Dwyer tossed. He moved closer and noticed piles of gauze bandages and white cotton undershirts and rags stained red and yellow with blood and pus on the floor at the foot of the bed.

"Let me see what you got?" Dwyer said, taking another step closer. Banco tipped the barrel of the gun up toward Dwyer's chest, stopping him, but flipped back the bedsheets and lifted away a wet, bloody bandage, revealing a hit in the meat of his flank just above his hip bone.

"Goddamn in and out. But still . . ." Banco said.

Dwyer went near the wall of the small kitchenette and flicked the light switch. A fluorescent kicked on in three stages and threw enough light for him to see the black entry point the width of a pencil. Banco leaned forward and Dwyer saw where it had come out, that hole the diameter of a two pence piece. Red splotches and streaks surrounded the wound, which oozed a thick and foul green.

"That's close enough," Banco said, leveling the assault rifle at Dwyer more directly. He recognized it now. It was an H&K 33, of German make, the rifle of the Salvadoran army, and Banco's old service weapon.

"What in fuck's name happened, Banco?" Dwyer asked.

Banco shrugged. "I got the call. I went to the location. Just like the plan. I set it up—the elevator, the lights, the car—and I waited. I opened up on 'em and was walking him down to finish. But the fucking car was armored . . . and he had this guy with him—"

"You knew he'd have a man with him," Dwyer said, doing his best to tamp down his anger.

"Well, this motherfucker wasn't the one I expected. And he was good. Or lucky," Banco said with disgust, gesturing at his wound.

"What type of guy?"

"Big. And tall. Dark hair, dark suit, mustache," Banco said and it made Dwyer wonder for a moment before he refocused.

"What about your backup shooter?" Dwyer asked.

Banco just shook his head.

"You didn't use a backup shooter?" Dwyer was shocked. A three-man team was minimum industry standard. "Are you fucking retarded or something, man? At least the bloody driver should have been a backup . . ." Dwyer tailed off when he caught the look in Banco's black eyes.

"Fucking 'ell, you went in solo?" Dwyer asked, equal parts incredulity and disgust. "Why?"

"I needed the money, man," Banco said simply.

"You were paid fifty K, with another fifty coming at the finish."

"There's no work. I couldn't afford a split. It's been two years since I've had any job worth shit. I needed all of it."

"And look at you fucking now," Dwyer said, his fury leaking out. "I thought you were a bloody professional."

Short money, the root of all botch-ups, he seethed to himself.

"Help me get well, and we'll go finish this thing together," Banco said.

"I don't know about the second part there, Braveheart." Dwyer shook his head. "The target's all buttoned up now . . ."

A look of fear came over Banco as he realized what his failure meant. The two men stared at each other. Dwyer had been on ops down in Salvador with Banco. They'd been on bivouac together, a thirty-day stint, in shit jungle doing nasty things. That kind of time created a bond. He'd directed Banco's fire, and Banco took orders and responded under pressure. That, and because he was familiar with the city, were why Dwyer thought to use him.

But now . . . but now . . .

"Just so you know, Waddy," he said, "I have some things in place if anything happens to me. Information you don't want getting out."

Dwyer stared at Banco. He didn't particularly believe him. The guy had been no-bullshit, ex-army when he'd met him a dozen years ago. But he couldn't be sure one way or the other whether Banco had put some insurance in place, so he played along.

"If anything happens to you? You've got one foot in the boat and it's ready to cross the river, man . . ." Dwyer said.

"You've got to help me," Banco said. The fear he'd been doing a good job keeping out of his voice made itself heard for the first time.

Dwyer acted like it affected him. "What do you think you need?"

"Sterile dressings. An IV drip of lactated Ringer's solution. Or at least saline. Plasma expander if you can get it. And antibiotics—cephalosporin or even penicillin. Dilaudid or Percocet for the pain."

"Fucking 'ell, anything else?"

"Find me a doctor who'll fix me without talking."

"That could take a while, being it's the first time I've been in this shite burg."

"I'll be here waiting."

Dwyer wasn't going to be able to get a thing for Banco at this hour, short of robbing a bloody hospital. He fetched Banco a cup of water from the kitchen—he thought it was a nice touch—and took a last glance back and left, closing the door behind him.

37

At ten minutes to six in the morning, the air still night crisp, Behr trotted down the street in warm-up mode, toward Saddle Hill. He was thinking about why he had drank so much last night and why Kolodnik had found himself in the casino-building business and why he seemed to have moved back out as quickly as he'd gotten in. That's when he saw Decker, dressed in shorts and a red T-shirt that read "USMC—American Spartans," in the middle of the street, doing squat thrusts.

Behr came to a stop. "Surprised to see you here," he shouted, since Decker's headphones were on.

"You said oh-six hundred," Decker said, pulling out an earbud.

"What's today's selection?" Behr asked.

"Alt rock playlist. Okkervil River, Black Keys, the Dead Weather. You know, the Jack White spin-off."

"Terrific," Behr said. It was too early to inquire further as to who and what any of the bands were.

"So what do we got?" Decker asked.

"Ten up, ten down. Full speed."

Decker glanced at the upward slope of Saddle Hill, humping away over a rise, a quarter mile into the distance.

"Big hill. I thought this town was flat."

"Mostly is," Behr said.

They started out, and things quickly turned from a hard

morning run to a full-bore pride competition—the kind Behr knew from his football days and supposed were common in the military, too. Behr led the way and set the pace; but by the fifth trip up, he found he couldn't stay with Decker, fit and fast as the young prick was. Behr put his head down and pushed and felt the alcohol from the night before sweating out of him. By the eighth go-round, he'd started to make up considerable ground and wondered if Decker might fade. On the tenth trip down the hill, Behr lengthened his stride and got within twenty feet of Decker, in time to see him turn his head and spew vomit. Behr figured he had him, but instead saw there was no fade in the guy. Decker didn't break stride. If anything, he accelerated and reached the bottom a good ten yards ahead of Behr.

They both grabbed their shorts and sucked air, and then Decker started laughing.

"Guess I shouldn't have had those nightcaps when I got home," he said.

"Didn't slow you down any," Behr said.

"Pounding ground till you puke's a way of life in the corps. Especially with a freight train running up my back," Decker gave Behr a whack on the shoulder. "Thanks, I've been going marshmallow since I got out."

Behr had Decker as a boots-on-the-ground, triggers-up type, but if this was soft, he wondered just how hard-ass the guy must've been when he was in. They walked the short distance to Decker's car, a steel-gray Camaro with meaty-looking black tires that were Armor All-ed to a high sheen.

"So, time to go pretend you're working?" Decker asked.

"Something like that."

"Gina heard from Susan that you took some rounds not too long ago," Decker said, as he opened the car door.

"Been trying to figure out who flung 'em," Behr said, "but I seem to be the only one around who cares." Whether or not Decker understood what this meant wasn't clear, but a version of that dark, distant gaze visited his eyes for a moment.

"Anything I can do to help, let me know," Decker finally said, then got in his car, which he started with a rumble.

He had begun to drive away, when Behr leaped behind the Camaro, pounding on the trunk. Decker stopped and poked his head out the open window.

"As a matter of fact . . ." Behr began.

38

Kid McMurphy was right: Sunshine Jane did have a Web presence and Behr didn't need her real name. Behr was at his desk, making a brief appearance in the office, which had a very half-assed attitude going at the moment since later in the day there was a company outing—a spring party out at Potempa's place. Making the most of the lax atmosphere he'd done a Google search for "Sunny, massage, Indianapolis," and she was the first hit. Hers was an elaborate Web site that featured tasteful photos of her—a fit, healthily suntanned, dark-eyed, dark-haired woman in her early twenties—shot in a semiprofessional massage-room setting. Her hair was pulled back into a prim ponytail, and she wore plastic-framed glasses and a white coat that gave her a slightly medical air. Her guidelines stated that she offered Swedish, deep tissue, and acupressure massage, that outcall was preferred, and rates were to be handled by e-mail. The small print on the site listed it as registered to Sister Golden Hands LLC.

Once Behr had printed a picture and felt he'd be able to spot her, he continued his digging and found her profiles on various social networking sites, where the photos got less professional and more telling—shots of her out at various bars with her girlfriends, who seemed like a pack of good fun or a hell of a lot of trouble, depending on how you looked at it. She was also shot in the clutches of an array of strapping young men, her hair down in a wild mane of ringlets. It was clear she liked the nightlife.

Why not? She's twenty-four years old . . . Behr figured. There were also several shots of her standing proudly next to an alpine-white BMW 650i convertible—one even showed the license plate SUN-EEE. This sent him to the muni tax database, where he saw business income listed for Sister Golden Hands LLC as a mere $28,000 for the past tax year. This told him something and he made a note of it.

Finished with her for the moment, he went ahead and completed three more background checks on his sorely neglected Payroll Place case. He was less than focused, and really just killing time before heading down to the Palms at Bella Vita, which wouldn't be open until lunchtime. The Palms was an outdoor bar right at the marina on Geist Reservoir in Fishers that offered a real island party feel for the postcollegiate set, including a deck area, an outdoor swimming pool, and even featured a sand volleyball pit. But the thing was, he'd actually gotten a ping on one of his background checks.

A young woman, Olga Miroslav, who worked in accounting with a perfectly good credit score and no bankruptcies, had taken out a restraining order on a once live-in boyfriend named Salvatore Rueben. He had counter-filed a restraining order against her as well, but both had filed to have the orders dropped after a few days. Simple case of break up and make up? *Maybe,* Behr thought. But it was enough for him to make a note to run this guy Reuben. Instead of actually doing it, though, he glanced around to see that Potempa and the case managers were tucked away in their offices, and hit the door.

The suit and tie was about the worst possible combo for someone trying to feel comfortable at the Palms. Surf shorts and bikinis were the uniform of the day, a smorgasbord of firm young flesh on parade. And the day was evolving into a cloudless and unseasonably warm one. Full-sized plastic palm trees painted in primary colors ringed the pool, full of splashing drinkers, and on the volleyball court a competitive two-on-two game was under way. Speedboats and WaveRunners trolled in and out of slips, making the most of the start of boating season. The party was on like an MTV spring break special.

Behr rolled up on the bar, ordered an ice tea, and felt the eyes of the staff and the nearby patrons on him. They probably had him as a narc or an Alcohol and Tobacco Bureau goon, but the awkward impression of authority was what he was trying to project, so he kept the jacket on. After twenty minutes and a lap around the place, he saw her, stunning as advertised, with the flowing ringlets of dark hair, smoky eyes, and full red lips that broke in a lazy sensual smile when he introduced himself.

"Hey, Sunny? Frank Behr." She took his extended hand, and he felt the bones of hers, defined and fragile beneath a glove of warm, tanned skin. She wore a white bikini top that barely contained her, a sarong-type thing knotted below her flat, pierced belly button, and Ugg boots on her feet. Regardless of her skill level with the bodywork, he imagined her company was in high demand.

She was standing with a burly dude, about twenty-five years old with a buzzed dome, dressed in digi-camo shorts, Timberlands, and a pair of Gargoyle Intimidators.

"Hey," she said. "Do I know you? You a client?"

"No. I want to ask you a few questions though."

"About what, bro?" the burly dude said, doing his best Terminator impression, sans accent. Behr ignored him.

"Oh, I'm partying though," Sunny said, the smile just flickering slightly.

"I want to talk about Lenny Barnes," Behr said, and felt a ripple of regret as he made that smile fall away for good.

"Dude, I don't want to talk to you," she said, crossing her arms, "and I *definitely* don't want to talk to you about *him*."

"If you're a cop, flash a badge. If you're not, it's time to catch the fuck-off express—" the burly dude said. Behr raised a palm in front of his dark shield glasses and spoke only to Sunny.

"Ken Jergens."

"Who?"

"Guy I know, works over at five seventy-five North Pennsylvania. You ever see that return address on correspondence?" Behr said. For a moment she was intrigued, and Behr went on. "I'll give you a hint: it's a government building. The kind that'd be interested in twenty-eight thou declared and a ninety-thousand-dollar car."

Dawning knowledge spread across her face. "It's the IRS."

"That's it. And this guy, Jergens, he's like a Gila monster—you gotta break his teeth out to get him off you once he clamps down."

"Screw you," she said. The smoky look departed her eyes and was replaced by a stony stare. Behr had been going on an instinct that she was in a largely cash business and there might be some jeopardy, and he saw he'd hit a soft target.

"*I'm* not the one who's gonna get screwed . . ."

"Sunny, you want me to—" the burly dude began.

"No," she cut him off and turned to Behr with a direct stare. "Let me just give you a treatment instead. A series of treatments even. I'm pretty unbelievable. Trust me, you'll feel great—"

"Sunny," the burly dude bleated.

"I don't want a rubdown," Behr said. Then turned to the guy. "Just go buy her another drink. It'll all be over soon," Behr said. Behr's jacket was unbuttoned, and he didn't mind if the handle of his Glock might have been visible to the guy. Sunny ground her teeth for a moment and then relaxed.

"Fine," she said. "It's fine, Nolan." Behr waved the burly dude away, then he and Sunny retreated into the shade of an umbrella.

"How'd you find me?" she wondered.

"Uh-uh," Behr said. "And no one knows where anything you tell me comes from either."

"Fine," she said again. "What do you want to know?"

"What's the deal with Barnes and Mary Potempa?"

"Potempa? Is that her last name? Mary's his girlfriend. Whatever that means with a guy like Lenny."

"What kind of guy is he?"

"He's . . . not a nice one," she said uncomfortably.

"And you know this how? Firsthand?"

"No. I don't do that. And I'm an independent."

"He runs girls?"

"Yeah."

"You know what he wants with Mary's father? You know who her father is?"

Sunny shook her head, her curls sliding across her smooth shoulders.

"What about Bernie Kolodnik?"

"Who's he?" The girl seemed open and innocent on this one. She really didn't know. Behr felt his frustration rise. Kid had advertised that she was wired in.

"Bernard Kolodnik. Big-time developer. Bernie Cool?"

"Oh, yeah, I've heard of Bernie Cool—"

"He's going into politics, being named senator . . ."

"Right, right, politics" she said, and then a shrewd look came to her eye. "Well, there's this political fixer guy, Shugie . . ."

"Saunders? White teeth, dark tan, a little older than me?" Behr asked.

She nodded.

"I know him."

"Everyone knows him, he knows everyone," she said. "That's his thing. I mean this guy is out in the bars, the clubs, events, everywhere, like he gets paid for it or something. Anyway, my friend Lori . . . sees him."

An errant volleyball bounced near them and rolled under a table. A chunky girl, spilling out of her bathing suit, top and bottom, ran over and collected it, laughing. Behr paused until she was gone.

"She dates him?"

"Not exactly. If I tell you, are you gonna go after her with this IRS jam too?"

"No."

"She's an escort."

"Last name?" Behr had his notebook out.

"That's up to her. And, dude, *please* put that book away. I don't want to look like an informant here."

Behr pocketed his notebook.

"Where do I find her?"

"Lorii Love at Indyblacktieclub.com. That's two 'i's on the Lori on the Web site. There's a personal e-mail for her."

"I'm not sending her an e-mail, I want her damn address," Behr said breezily.

"Fine," Sunny answered back but in a tone that said *you sicken me*. "I'll text you. Gimme your digits?"

Sunny took out her phone and Behr told her his number while she clicked away a message.

"Indyblacktieclub.com is Barnes's organization?"

"Yeah."

"Go on," Behr said, hearing his BlackBerry bing.

"Lenny hooked her up with Shug originally. Just a usual date, but it became a real regular thing. The guy's freaking in love with her. It's pretty sickening. He's like fifty and always talking about their *future*. I mean he's *fifty,* the future was yesterday, dude . . ." Behr waited her out. "Anyway, a while ago she tells me that Shug was talking, you know, *after* . . ." She got lost in her thoughts for a moment. "Gross. I don't know how she does it. She's such a cool girl . . ." But then she circled back on topic. "And he needed a special detective to get something done, and she mentioned it to Lenny, and Lenny knows the perfect guy."

"What's *something*?"

"I have no idea."

"Who's the perfect guy?" Behr demanded.

"I don't know."

"You know. And you're gonna tell me," Behr said, closing the distance between them a few inches.

"I don't. I really don't. I would tell you if I did. Shit, I'm telling you everything already. You've got me slung over a damn barrel."

"All right. What *kind* of detective—IPD?"

"No, private. A private investigator."

"So Shug needed something done. Lenny had a private investigator," Behr reiterated.

"That's it. Exactly," she said.

Behr felt like he'd reached maximum extraction from her. He asked her ten minutes of follow-up questions, but none went anywhere and it was time to shut it down. He nodded and started walking away.

"Hey," she called out, "you're not really gonna bone me on my taxes, are you?"

"No, I'm not, honey," Behr said, "but we all gotta pay eventually."

39

" 'ello, dear."

"Waddy!" Sandy's voice came through the mobile loud and clear, from a mountaintop in Wales all the way to America's god-forsaken flatland, and put a pang in his chest. He tried to call every day when he was away for work. It was tougher years back before mobiles and sat phones, but now he was fairly religious about it.

"How are ya?" he asked.

"We're all fine up here. Nobby's doing a little better with the kidney medication."

"Good news, that," Dwyer said. Nobby was their shepherd, named after the legendary footballer. The shep had a hell of a bark, and unlike the saying, his bite was worse. Dwyer worried about his Sandy when he was away, both because of the enemies he'd collected, and run-of-the-mill arseholes, though she was plenty handy with the iron. He'd made sure of that when they'd first gotten married twenty-four years ago, and he occasionally made her go out and practice. She could fire tight, three-shot bursts while walking with an MP5, but her real skill was with a handgun. She was a cracking good shot with a SIG 9mm.

"You putting the alarm on nights?" he asked.

"Of course, dear."

"Locking the gates?"

"Of course, dear."

"The cameras up?"

"They are. Just how you left 'em," Sandy said. "Any idea when you'll be home?"

"Not quite yet," he said. "Soon as I can though . . ."

Dwyer felt relaxed after he rang off, like he could go to sleep straightaway. Of course he couldn't and wasn't going to. Instead, he nosed the Lincoln into a spot in the big parking barn, slapped a cap on his head to look the part of an American punter, and headed inside.

40

The Indy Flats racino looked like the old Flamingo did in the pictures of early Vegas: an overbuilt facade, grand and flashy, standing lonely by a road in the middle of nowhere. Glowing red and gold and liquid neon purple even in daylight, it almost invited—implored—other structures to join it.

Behr had driven south from the Palms with a sick feeling in his gut over the connection he'd unearthed between Potempa and Barnes and Kolodnik's man Shug Saunders. He had no idea what, if anything, it meant, but he didn't like it. Potempa was a stand-up guy, by reputation and as far as Behr knew personally, but he was suffering over his daughter, and that could make someone vulnerable to all kinds of pressures.

He'd made his way around the city, got on 421 south, and began to pass square-box housing tracts that gave way to cornfields and eventually horse country. After a dozen more miles, he started seeing billboards and finally reached the exit for the racino. As he neared it, he passed a massive construction site that signage announced as the future Indy Flats Hotel and Villas. But something had gone wrong—most of the villas had been burned to their footings and an unfinished concrete tower was charred black. Cement trucks, backhoes, and other equipment, some of it fire stained, stood dormant.

He'd read about the massive fire. It was front-page news and the story featured comments by Lowell Gantcher, who vowed that the project would be rebuilt and opened on time for next Memorial Day as planned. Gantcher's name had caught his eye, since it had come up in his investigation of Kolodnik as a one-time partner. He'd gotten the idea that he'd like to talk to this Gantcher, or at least see his operation. It was why he'd come. He steered for the six-story-tall parking structure, where it was easy finding a spot among the pickup trucks and SUVs—too easy.

Inside, the place was a real carpet joint, as they said in the old days. And not just carpet, but marble and colored glass and mosaic tile and leather chairs filled the high-ceilinged space that spoked off the racetrack grandstand and was just as tall and cavernous as that structure. It was lavish, a show palace, built if not to rival the Las Vegas mausoleums, then at least to outstrip the riverboats and Indian casinos that dotted the region. Behr made his way around the casino, the gaming floor choked with machines that whirred and boinged—poker, blackjack, roulette, and craps—all automated. By law, no cards, dice, or dealers were allowed—just machines.

The gambling pit was ringed by theme bars and restaurants, including the Bassmaster Café; the Small Batch Bourbon Still; a Mine Shaft steakhouse; and Winners, a grill that featured sports betting and had flat-screen televisions broadcasting games and races from all over the country and the world. There was also a nightclub.

Behr grabbed a glossy five-color brochure off a display and learned that the burned-out second stage of hotel construction that he'd seen was to include a world-class eighteen-hole golf course. Starting at a few hundred grand, players would be able to get a time-share. But to his eye it seemed unlikely that Vegas: The Midwest Branch would be springing up at Indy Flats anytime soon, considering that the clientele didn't appear to be high rollers but mainly truckers and farmers dressed in fleece and Colts sweatshirts and Carhartt jackets, and retirees riding scooters, oxygen tanks in tow, sucking on cigarettes while camped out in front of nickel slots.

Since most patrons used player cards to track winnings, there

wasn't even much in the way of clinking coins or tokens. Nor
was there the crisp snap of cash as it was fanned on tables and
shoved into strongboxes, no shouts of "Changing five hundred!"
nor cheers as a dealer busted and the table won, and it rendered
the place oddly muted. Nothing was quite as depressing as a dead
casino, and it didn't bode well for the future.

Behr found a spot with some railbirds in the poker room, taking
a look at the high-stakes Hold'em tables. It was harder to follow
the action without stacks of clay checks in front of the players,
who had to rely on screens built into the table at each seat in
order to see their bankroll and their opponents'. But the game
took on a quiet rhythm of its own and moved along much more
quickly without a dealer handing out the cards and constantly
reshuffling. Before long, a slick young casino host named Brad
approached Behr.

"Can I find you a game, sir?" Brad said, shooting the cuffs of
his expensive Italian suit.

"Maybe in a bit." Behr nodded. "Just taking a look. I've only
played live deal."

"No problem. I can get you a players card. You'll catch on
quick."

"How're the crowds? If I came down on a Saturday night, how
long would I have to wait to sit?"

"Well, it wouldn't be longer than a few minutes," Brad said.
"We're a little busier than weekdays, but you know, there's never
any more than ten names on the wait-list."

"Guess they thought the place would be packed when they
dumped all the money into it, huh?"

"Something like that. I sure did. Took my master's a few years
back in hotel management and that's what I was looking for
when I signed on here. We get some play on weekends—young
professionals and college kids with dad's credit card. You know
how it is."

"Lots of action at the bars and clubs?"

"The bouncers stay busy. Seems like there's a dustup just about every night."

"Sounds like fun," Behr said.

"It's stupid, but it's all right. Just guys liquored up, failing to score, and looking to vent."

"The American way," Behr said. "What's gonna happen with the place? How are they gonna fill it?"

"Bosses say there's gonna be a law passed soon—live-deal, full-blown casino action. Either it passes or I'm heading out to look for a job in Vegas. That's what we hear, anyway. We get these company-wide e-mails."

"From who, Lowell Gantcher?"

"Not him. Vice presidents usually. But I've met Mr. Gantcher. He comes walking through, shaking hands."

"What kind of guy is he?"

"He's a decent boss, and that's all I'll say about that. Haven't seen him lately. Heard he's here today though . . ."

Behr tried to appear only mildly interested. "Really? Corporate offices are here?"

"Sure. Nice suites above the casino floor. I've been up there a few times. Once when I got hired and then when my check didn't come in the mail recently and I had to go ask for it . . ."

"The eye in the sky," Behr said, folksy.

"You got it," Brad said, eyeing a group of housewives who looked like they wanted some action. "Let me know if you want to sit."

Behr nodded his thanks and watched for another five minutes. There were some heated words exchanged between a husky, milk-fed farm boy who took a pot off a pair of wiry Asians, who in turn criticized his play. Apparently he'd done it all wrong, though he'd taken their money. But it settled down quickly and Behr wandered away in search of the corporate offices.

The main cashier's cage, brass bars shining, stood prominently down a carpeted path near the main entrance. Just beyond it was a small vestibule done in white Carrara marble that housed a set

of brushed gold double elevator doors. Standing sentry in front
of the area was a pair of broad-shouldered bookends who'd only
be able to board the elevator one at a time. The men wore blue
suits and had earpieces and seemed several clicks beyond regular
casino security. To Behr's eye they were high-line hires. Getting
a word with Gantcher wasn't going to be as simple as waltzing in
and chatting up the secretary. All the same, Behr started heading
toward them to give it his best shot.

I've seen that fucker before.

Dwyer was sitting at the bar, a Ford cap pulled low, sipping
some vile swill called Monster for energy, when the thought
flashed through his head. The blue suit, the mustache, the con-
fident walk—it was familiar. After a moment he called up the
location. It had been outside Kolodnik's office. First at Kolodnik's, now here. And he sounded a hell of a lot like who Banco
described from the night of the shoot. Dwyer had originally
made him for one of Kolodnik's hired crew. But if he was, there'd
be no reason for him to show up here, unless Gantcher had hired
the same company and the bloke was reporting for his shift here.
He was a pro in the field, that much was clear to Dwyer. It didn't
take long before one recognized his own in the game.

Dwyer had been planning on having a little chat with Gantcher,
but seeing his newly installed protection had made him pause.
Now he figured it could wait. Spotting this big laddie had just
taken priority. The way the hired security were standing made
it clear they didn't know the man he'd seen at Kolodnik's, and
they sure weren't going to be mates straightaway. The casino was
too massive for the whole place to be affected, but the energy
in the immediate area changed quickly and Dwyer knew what
was coming. Some words were exchanged and the posture of the
hired hands grew more rigid, and then the other man extended a
business card that got looked at and jammed back into his chest.

The pair initiated the scuffle. They wanted to take down the lone man, to throw him out, neutralize him or hold him in some capacity, but it didn't go that way. The man from Kolodnik's snapped his arm free from the grasp of one of the others and grabbed the attacker by the wrist, yanking him forward and off balance into a Russian arm tie. Then, with a very intelligent piece of footwork, the lone man spun his opponent and jammed him into his own associate, effectively cutting off his opportunity to join in. As the pair grappled for a piece of the loner, trying to get him around the waist and legs, he stuffed their takedown attempts by dropping his weight on the one he held and winging an elbow at the face of the other to keep him back. If the pair would've committed to an all-out attack, they might have been able to quickly take down their man, but perhaps they were concerned about causing a ruckus in the casino, or they lacked the skill. It was either that or the suits. Dwyer had seen men otherwise rough-and-ready rendered oddly subdued when dressed up on a job, as if the elegant attire seeped into their manner and stripped away their animal nature. If that was the case, it certainly didn't happen to the other fellow. His grunts and expletives echoed around the marbled elevator bank.

Finally, with a great push, the lone man shoved away the one he'd caught and stepped back several yards, opening a chasm it would be hard for the pair to cross without going for something of a rugby tackle. Backing away, eyes on them, the lone man from Kolodnik's headed for the door and was gone. Dwyer caught a glimpse of the pair smoothing out their ruffled lapels, collars, and ties and pulling out mobile phones. That was all he saw of them, though, since he followed the loner out the door.

Dwyer caught up to the man in the enclosed breezeway that joined the casino and parking structures. There were only three or four other people in the space, playing slot machines, which normally wouldn't have been enough to obscure Dwyer's presence had the lone man been paying attention—a solo foot surveillance was a lot more difficult to pull off than the telly made it out to be—but Dwyer neared him in time to hear the man's mobile ring. He took it out and answered as he walked, not slowing, wanting to get away from the casino quickly, Dwyer imagined, and began a conversation, which gave Dwyer the chance to fall back a decent distance as they entered the parking garage.

It was tricky to stay with the man finding his car while Dwyer found his. Dwyer went up the interior staircase, heading for a higher level than the big pro, but was able to see the tall man's legs for a while as he walked toward his car, then the man went out of sight. Contact broken, Dwyer sprinted for his Lincoln, jumped in, rammed the stalk into reverse and barked the tires backing out in front of an old couple in a pickup truck driving so slowly it was going to take them fifteen minutes to leave the structure. The old coot farmer raised a fist in frustration as Dwyer pulled away and wheeled around the corner. But Dwyer quickly found he had no reason to hurry. The big pro was sitting in his car, an aging but well-kept Oldsmobile, talking on the cellular. Dwyer continued on down the row to an empty parking space by the exit, and settled in to wait for the big pro to leave.

41

"Behr, it's Decker," the voice came through his cell phone gruff and friendly. "What the hell's up?"

"Not a thing," Behr said, his breathing still returning to normal, as he walked out of the casino.

"What are those bells?"

"Just someplace I'm leaving," Behr said, the double doors to the casino sliding shut behind him.

"Sounds like a bachelor party."

"Long way from a party," Behr said, nearing his car.

That pair of rabid attack-dog son of a bitches had almost truly uglified his day.

"Heading up to Lowell Gantcher's office," Behr had declared when he'd walked up to them and was challenged.

"You have an appointment?" the first one had asked, a hard layer of unwelcome in his tone.

"Want to go up and make one," Behr said.

"Go somewhere else and call to do that," the other said.

Behr pulled out his Caro business card. "Look, buddy, I'm in the trade. I'm not gonna go up there and do anything but request a time. How about a little professional courtesy?"

It was a reasonable ask. Behr figured they probably wouldn't go for it, but the least it should have garnered was a respectful "No can do" and maybe a hint about how to get an appointment.

Instead, upon seeing the card, one meat shield looked to the other, and it got physical. Whether they'd wanted to give him the bum's rush or a full beat down, he had no idea, but he was surprised his announcement was what set them off. And behind the aggression Behr had seen something else he hadn't expected in the men—fear.

What did they, or their client, have to fear from a pro in the field?

Behr was flipping this around in his mind, glad to be leaving Indy Flats under his own steam, when Decker called.

"So that thing you asked for," Decker said, "I did some file diving for you . . ."

It was a big favor that Behr had asked, and when it came to favors, he vastly preferred doing them to claiming them, especially the first one. But after their run, Decker had offered and the piece of information was fairly impossible for him to get any other way, so he'd been unable to resist. Now Behr was impressed not only at the speed with which Decker had come through but that he'd bothered at all. That was a rarity these days. He closed the car door behind him and took out a pen.

"Go."

"Very little traffic left that garage around the time of the incident," Decker said. "I got an Indiana license plate for you: IXN three sixty-two."

Behr wrote it down.

"Car is an aqua blue metallic 2008 Impala. Entered at seven thirty."

"Stolen?"

"Doesn't seem so."

"Plate reported stolen?"

"Nope. Registered to a Campos, José."

"That's gotta be bogus," Behr said.

"Probably."

"Here, write it down," Decker said, and gave Behr a street address on Keller, in an untrendy, predominantly Latin part of town.

"Did you get this from the security footage?" Behr wondered. "Any image of the driver?"

"Nah, didn't get a look at that. If footage exists, it's under lock and key," Decker said. "This was off a log."

"So someone logged information from a security tape?" Behr pressed.

"Don't know. The entry gate that dispenses tickets records the plates of the cars going in. Then there was a note in the file that said: 'matches car leaving at time of incident.' Pretty sure it's your guy though," Decker said, "unless he left on foot, which seems unlikely."

"Yeah. Probably dumped or sold the car by now."

"Yep, someone got himself a great deal on an aqua metallic Impala . . ." Decker said. "Anyway, I figured that Keller Street addy was a bogey too, so I did a utilities check." Behr had a momentary surge of envy for the access the police had and how much more difficult it was for him to track down the same information. "There was a secondary account established—one of those triple-play deals of phone, cable, and Internet—and it had the Keller Street billing address on it too, but a service call was listed a month back to seventeen oh one Wilmette Ave. I'm guessing that if either of 'em even are, that's gotta be the live one."

"You're damn good," Behr said, writing it down. "Can I feed you the rest of my casework?"

"Hey, it serves 'em right for bringing me back on desk duty and not plunking me right back on the street. You should see the shit I'm working—cleaning up paperwork on DWIs and stolen Girl Scout cookies."

"Try not to have too much fun."

"Well, if there's not anything else, I should probably get back to pretending I work for the city," Decker said.

"Look, there's one more thing," Behr began, awash in gratitude and guilt all at once. "Something I did, I'd feel better if I just told you . . . I Googled you. And I'm sorry."

There was silence on the line before Decker answered.

"I ran you too. So I'm also sorry," he said.

Behr knew it meant Decker had learned about his time on the force, the arrests he'd made, the way he was sent off, and how his son had died by accidental gunshot.

"I might've done a little more than just Google," Behr added.

"Yeah," Decker said, "so did I."

And that was the end of it.

42

This cunt's becoming bloody difficult.

Dwyer had his hand around the CZ, thumb on the safety. He had followed the big pro back north on 421 toward Indianapolis until the road turned into the main interstate. It was an easy tail in medium traffic and, not knowing the city, Dwyer couldn't be sure exactly where they were headed when the big pro exited the interstate and rolled into the run-down part of town, until all of a sudden—bang—he did know, and a sense of disbelief, concern, and disgust exploded inside him. The big pro slowed and parked in front of 1701 Wilmette. Banco's building.

Dwyer stuck to his training, rolling slowly by and turning three consecutive rights in order to reach the head of the block on Wilmette again, behind the big pro, where he could observe him and the building but not be seen.

How the bloody hell had the man come to be here?

Dwyer racked his brain but couldn't, for the love of god, put it together to any satisfactory degree.

The big pro crossed to the front door, traced a finger down the tenant list, and pressed a buzzer. He waited a long time, but there seemed to be no answer. Dwyer had been willing to leave Banco alive, for the time being, to find out more about what had happened, who else might know anything, and to make sure his little insurance policy was only fictional. If the man recovered, miraculously, Dwyer could use him to help with the cleanup job he was doing. He was at the very least content to let the man die on his own. But that was yesterday. Now one thing was for certain: if the big pro was buzzed in, the Saiga shotgun was coming out of the trunk and Dwyer would enter and erase both of them right-bloody-now.

The big pro stood there, ringing the buzzer repeatedly to no avail. Either Banco wasn't there or was smart enough not to answer. Dwyer imagined the big pro would find his way around the back door before long, and wondered whether he should take him there, before things went any further. But then the big pro took out his mobile and put it to his ear—he was answering a call, as he hadn't dialed one. He checked his watch and hurried to his car at a pace that was just short of a run.

Dwyer was tempted to go in and cauterize the bleeding vessel that was Banco, but he'd have to go in shooting to do that, and he preferred to be elsewhere when Banco expired, not standing over him with a hot gun. He was also more than a little curious as to who the big pro was and where he was headed next, so he put his car in gear and followed.

43

"I want to thank you for this bonding opportunity with everyone from your company *but* you," Susan said quietly the minute he was within earshot, "and for getting to feel like a total dork. The fact that it's about a million degrees and I can't even drink is just a bonus." She looked beautiful in a sundress despite the fact she was sweltering in the unseasonable spring humidity.

Behr had been buzzing the front door of the address Decker had given him, getting no answer and planning to come back with a bump key to make entry, when Susan had called. He was already forty minutes late for the company picnic, with a twenty-minute drive to get there. By the time he arrived, cars choked both sides of the street.

"Sorry," he said, glancing around Potempa's backyard at his coworkers, who were dressed in short-sleeve dress shirts and sunglasses, and eating cold shrimp and drinking beer in the afternoon sun. He saw Potempa, in a Panama hat, standing nearby next to a cooler. He drilled into Potempa with his eyes, but they were under the hat's brim and behind sunglasses too, and they told him nothing.

"This whole thing is awesome. Really awesome," Susan went on. "I have every bit of detail I need to re-create Betsy Malick's salmon recipe."

"Okay—"

"And Cheryl over there"—she pointed to a tall, gawky woman

about her age—"she's hoping to be Mrs. Reidy one of these days. They've been dating for three years but she's pretty sure they're 'getting close.' "

"I get that you're not pleased," Behr said.

"I'm just a little low on humor. And patience," she said.

"Never cross a pregnant woman," Behr said. "Noted."

"Glad you dressed for the occasion . . ." Potempa said, swinging to a stop next to them. Behr had had the good sense to shuck his jacket and tie in the car, but he had to acknowledge he wasn't doing much of a job of fitting into the Caro corporate culture. Potempa jammed a frosty Michelob Ultra into his hand. "Drink that and grab another, you're behind." It was the kind of comment usually made in jest, but there wasn't much mirth to the way Potempa said it.

"Thanks," Behr said. "Have you met Susan? Suze, this is Karl Potempa—he runs the whole shooting match."

"I said hi to Mr. Potempa earlier." Susan smiled.

"And I told her to call me Karl then," Potempa said smoothly, showing Behr how good he must be at the client-relations game when he had less on his mind.

"Listen," he said to Behr quietly, but not quietly enough that Susan didn't hear, "some clients may be stopping by, and John Lutz is one of 'em. If you see him, make yourself as scarce as your work product on his case."

Behr could only nod, and Potempa moved on.

"You're pretty popular around here."

"Oh yeah, the fair-haired boy."

"What's going on?"

"Nothing. Just office bullshit. Can I get you a plate?" Susan shrugged and Behr headed for the buffet.

He was standing over a massive platter of barbarically rare roast beef when Pat Teague's laugh boomed across the backyard. Behr felt his head whip around at the sound. He hadn't seen nor thought much of Teague since the night he'd asked Behr to fill in on the Kolodnik job, and the morning after. Teague stood next to a raw bar with Reidy and Malick, chortling into the rim of his beer bottle, and a chill spread over Behr despite the warm air.

Particularly dark notions can grow slowly. The mind turns away from the worst. It was human nature. Behr had trained himself to stare nasty thoughts down, but he wasn't immune to the instinct to block out, to avoid; and it could take something random, seemingly unconnected, to break through and spark an idea. Another peal of laughter shot across the lawn, and he looked at Teague. It was just laughter, but it sounded malevolent to Behr. He was staring it in the face now.

It took Behr five minutes chatting around the party to learn that Teague had twin sons and two daughters. Another two minutes on his BlackBerry to get Teague's address out in Thorntown. For the rest, the schools they attended, and which teams they played on, and whether those teams had games on the night in question, he'd need a computer, and had a feeling where he could find one. He dropped back to Susan's spot with a fresh bottle of water for her and she said, "I could use a ladies' room."

"I'll walk you inside," Behr said.

The air-conditioning was kicking and the house felt like a crypt. No one was inside, not even Potempa's wife, who was out back, playing the hostess. Behr helped Susan find the powder room, and after trying two more doors found himself in Potempa's study.

Behr could hear the chatter of the party outside through the window mere feet away from where he stood, but his boss's computer woke the second he touched the mouse. Unlike an office terminal that might've needed a log-in password, this one was already up and online. Looking around the study, Behr saw framed photos of Derek Schmidt and Ken Bigby, two Caro boys who had been killed on the job the year before. There was also an array of family photos similar to those in Potempa's office, including one of his daughter, taken about five years back in her high school cap and gown. She was a lot more innocent then, or at least she looked it on her graduation day. Behr recognized the opportunity at his fingertips, and fought down the temptation to search Potempa's computer and browsing history. Instead he went right to checking the school zone, and then, when he found that Teague's children attended Western Boone Junior and Senior High, he went to those Web sites, specifically the athletics' departments. Behr's eyes kept traveling back to the door, expecting it to fly open with a red-faced Potempa wondering what the hell he was doing.

He heard a door open and close outside.

"Frank . . . Frank?" came Susan's voice. If she kept calling out, it could attract attention to his whereabouts, but he found himself unable to abandon what he was doing and go to her. She gave up after a moment, going outside to look for him, he supposed. His luck held, and he got what he needed before deleting his searches and putting the computer back to sleep.

He dialed the school and found a woman still in the office despite it being so late in the afternoon, and he asked her about the outcome of the girls' lacrosse game on the date in question.

"No game that night," came the response. "Season just ended the week before."

Cold knowing hit Behr in the belly as he gripped his Black-Berry. He asked a few more questions, just making sure there was no boys' JV baseball game, and no girls' varsity swim or track meet either. But he knew there wouldn't be.

"Nope. No, and no, sports fan," came the woman's response.

Behr staggered back onto the patio, heading for Susan. He saw that Teague had shifted positions away from the raw bar to some chairs, where he sat with Potempa and Curt Lundquist, Caro's house counsel, who wore a guayabera shirt that looked all wrong on his stalklike frame. Behr considered the information. There were countless other reasons why Teague could have needed the night and had begged out. He'd been moonlighting—pulling a security shift at a bar or club, driving for someone else off-the-books, or working some case independently. Maybe he'd been fighting with his wife and wanted to take her out to make it right. Or he was cheating on his wife and had plans with another woman. It was also likely Teague just didn't feel like working—he didn't strike Behr as the hardest charger in the office—and had wanted to stay home, watch *The Simpsons,* and fart into his La-Z-Boy. But nothing Behr could come up with could quell what he was thinking—that he was working in some kind of bullshit factory—or what he was really feeling about the shooting that night: *Teague had known it was coming.*

"Where were you?" Susan said as he reached her.

"I had to make a call," Behr said vaguely.

"Would it be okay for me to go? I'm French fried."

Behr nodded and saw a new arrival across the backyard. It was John Lutz. Behr put a hand on Susan's arm.

"I'll leave with you."

"Should we say thanks or good-bye?"

"Nah, come on. Let's blow this pop stand."

44

Behr kept his eyes focused on the rear of Susan's Jeep Liberty—
she'd gotten it recently when the size of her belly and the coming need for a rear-facing child's seat made continuing to drive
her beloved Miata fairly difficult and pointless—but things were
getting slippy in his head. He was taking in both too much information and not enough by a long shot at the same time, and
he was having trouble processing where it all stood. He'd heard
about professional golfers blowing up on the last hole of a major,
turning a three-stroke lead into a two-stroke loss as they found
the water, the trees, the gallery, and a bunker in succession after
avoiding them successfully for the prior seventy-one holes. When
they came off the course, they all commented how "things happened so fast." Golf and fast didn't go together—these guys took
a good five minutes between shots—but still, Behr understood
the sensation.

They were almost back home, where Behr was going to peel
off and continue on his way, when he caught a flash of a silver
Lincoln Town Car in his side view mirror and felt like he'd seen it
before that day. It was way back there and not the most exotic car
on the street but he *noticed* it, and that was almost never nothing. The thought was only half formed and went out of his head
as the car dropped away out of sight, and before he could call
Susan and tell her to drive somewhere else with a dead end where
he'd *know* if it was a tail, they were turning onto their street and

pulling up to their place. Susan had turned into the driveway and was already on the steps, and he had parked on the street since he was going out again but hadn't moved from behind the wheel when the Lincoln came driving up the street. He froze behind the wheel as the car drove past without slowing, the driver's eyes forward on the road. He waited a beat as it continued on, then swung his door open and leaned over, dropping his head below the edge to license plate level. He caught the first three letters, D-U-F, but couldn't grab any numbers. He also saw that the car bore an Illinois plate. He straightened in his seat.

Halfway up the steps, Susan paused and looked to him. He gave her a wave, put his car in gear, and drove away. The Lincoln was long gone, but he had other places to go.

45

Waddy Dwyer was hungry and tired. He missed his wife and was, until five minutes ago, in great need of a piss. He knew one thing for certain, though: he was going to take it out on all of them. He had a gallon of petrol and a sleeve of Styrofoam cups, which he was tearing into strips and stirring into said petrol. He didn't have the time or the wherewithal in his hotel room to make proper napalm by melting soap into the gasoline, but this would do quite nicely. The mixture, which was nearing the consistency of jelly, smelled comfortingly chemical and took him back to the defoliated jungles of his past. A two-liter soda bottle, a funnel, and a prepaid mobile phone—all the ingredients for a quality firebomb—most citizens had no idea these were sold at every gas station that had a well-stocked convenience mart. Whether they had need for a firebomb might've been another question altogether, but he unfortunately did.

Sitting around waiting for Banco to recover, or to fall weak enough for Dwyer to take his rifle away and finish him was one thing, but now that Banco was getting his doorbell rung by the big pro, the ultimate precaution needed to be exercised.

He'd followed the big pro and a pregnant blonde, his wife or girlfriend it seemed based on the solicitous hand placed on the small of her back, to an address that struck him as their home. He wasn't sure but thought he might've been burned on the tail right there at the end. It disgusted him. With even one backup operative and an alternate vehicle it would've never happened. No matter. He'd take care of the car soon enough, and he'd be sterile once again. He ran the address but didn't come up with anything by way of a name. The big pro was a pro after all and knew how to scrub personal information. There was another way to get the man's identity, and it was somewhere he was going already. He still had lots to do. He kept on stirring.

46

Behr stood in the parking lot next to the gold Chevrolet Traverse that Teague drove, feeling conspicuous and hoping he wouldn't have to wait long. He'd already been inside the office. More specifically the equipment room, where among the heavy-sided black plastic cases that housed sensitive and expensive surveillance equipment—bugs, voice stress analyzers, cell phone taps, GPS trackers, and the like, as well as the company's large gun safe—he grabbed a simple low-tech set of gear: a ring of bump keys and hammer. One specially crafted bump key would open *any* pin tumbler lock of the same make, so he had 90 percent of the standard domestically produced locks covered with what he currently had jingling in his pocket. It was the simplest form of lock beating this side of a battering ram, and a lot more subtle.

Behr waved lamely at two departing coworkers who had caught a ride from the barbecue and come back to claim their cars. It told him the party was over, and he guessed Teague would be along soon. He considered slim-jimming his way into the Traverse or, better yet, smashing the window with the barrel of his Glock, and reviewing the contents of the car. There was nothing in it, Behr realized. Teague would know better. After another four or five long minutes in the day's last light, a Buick Enclave rolled up, its windows open, Reidy behind the wheel and Malick in the passenger seat. Teague piled out of the back and walked toward him with that rolling gait of his, and didn't break stride when he spotted Behr.

"What's up, buddy?" Teague asked, hale and hearty, and inscrutable behind a pair of dark sunglasses as he neared the car.

"You tell me," Behr said, squaring to him and stopping his progress toward the driver's door.

"What's that, big guy?" Teague said, his keys out.

"I want to know what's going on," Behr said.

"Nothing's 'going on,' " Teague said, all hint of jocularity now gone from his voice. "Unless you keep standing there, in which case we're gonna have an issue."

"Do we already have one, Pat?" Behr asked. Teague didn't move, but his mouth fell open, and Behr was about to follow up with more pointed questions when Reidy honked his horn.

"You ready to go, Patty?" Malick called out. "Six dollar pitchers of Leinenkugel's at Taps and Dolls. You coming, Behr?"

"No, he's not coming," Teague said, putting a shoulder into Behr's chest, moving him back a step, unlocking his car, and getting in.

"See ya tomorrow, then," Malick said, and drove off.

Teague's Traverse revved and shot gravel at Behr and left him in a billowing cloud of exhaust. He stalked off toward his car, thinking about his next move with Teague and wishing he had something in front of him to punch.

47

Behr walked along the filthy, ground-down carpet runner of the second story hallway of 1701 Wilmette. He'd returned to the building, which was a low-slung cracker box, typical in this part of town, cheaply built and aging badly. It was a wonder that someone had bothered to install carpet in the first place. The front door's Kwikset had proved to be of little challenge for the bump key. He wasn't well practiced, but after he flat-hand buzzed every apartment except the one he was going to, announcing "Pizza delivery!" to the few answers he received, he was surprised that no one rang him in. So he slid the bump key into the lock, flexed the hammer back, and let it go with a *thwap*. He turned the key and heard the tumbler click open, and he was in. It was so easy and smooth his heart didn't even get to racing.

But it sure was now, as he neared the door in question. This time the bump had to be slick and precise and he only hoped he got lucky again, because he didn't know what was waiting for him on the other side. Behr slowed his pace and walked quietly up to the side of the door, keeping his back to the wall and his body to the side of the frame so he wouldn't disturb the hall light sliding under the door into the apartment.

There was no one in the corridor, and Behr bent and saw he was dealing with a Weslock. It wasn't an expensive brand. They sold by the boatload at Home Depot. A sixteen-pound sledge-hammer would do the job for certain, but that wouldn't allow for much conversation once he was inside. He fingered through the keys on his ring and found the Weslock equivalent. He removed it from the ring to prevent any telltale clinking noise. He grabbed a deep breath, crouched, and slid the key into the lock. One last quick look up and down the hall. He flexed the bump hammer. And bang.

He turned the key—which rotated—and stood. Twisting the knob, he put a shoulder into the door and found himself inside a dimly lit, foul-smelling little apartment. A man around thirty years old with black hair and long sideburns, and sporting faded ink, rested on a filthy bed. He jolted in surprise at Behr's entry and began reaching for something, though he was hardly able to move. In the grainy half-light Behr made out the silhouette of a weapon, a rifle, leaning against the wall on the far side of the bed. With a lunging stride, Behr crossed the room, rolled along the foot of the bed, and knocked the weapon away from the man. They wrestled for a moment, but the man was weak. He groaned and gave up nearly instantly, shrinking back against the edge of the bed. Behr got control of the weapon, raised it at the man, and gestured him up with the barrel. As the man climbed to his feet with much effort, Behr's thumb found the safety and he discovered the weapon was ready to fire.

Behr took a step back to give himself room and noticed the man's skin was mottled, as if he'd been doused with acid, but before long Behr recognized it as a skin condition, probably vitiligo. He also noted, with little satisfaction, that the assault rifle he held was fitted with a flash suppressor and brass catcher and was military grade. It was the same one that could've killed him, the one Breslau had suggested was home-modified. He was staring at the shooter.

"Who are you and where are you from?" Behr demanded.

The man didn't answer, but it wasn't due to defiance. He was doubled over clutching a wound on his side. There was an IV bag of saline hanging from a nail in the wall. The tube had ripped loose from the man's arm during their struggle.

"I'm not going to hurt you. You understand English?" Behr said.

The man nodded.

"You know who I am? You recognize me?" Behr said.

The shooter nodded again. Behr noticed food and drink on a countertop in a kitchenette.

"Someone's been here, bringing you supplies?"

The man nodded a third time.

Behr took a step forward. He kept one hand on the pistol grip of the assault rifle and used his other to move the shooter's hands back. He saw that a round had entered low on the man's left hip and ripped away the flesh at his flank. What remained was a viscous dark green that was going black.

"Did I do this to you?" Behr asked.

The man nodded.

"Who trained you? Who hired you? You were hired, weren't you?"

"Yes," the man croaked, revealing a Hispanic accent.

"Why were you shooting at—" but it was all Behr was able to say. He heard a single digital beep, then a hiss, and an instinct beyond any training he'd ever had caused him to throw himself on the floor behind the bed as the apartment exploded into a ball of orange fire.

Gasoline fumes and flames ripped through the air of the apartment as Behr reached and yanked the shooter down. But it was too late. The guy had caught a big stripe of a viscous, flaming substance that stuck to his back like a paintbrush slap. The man screamed as Behr tried to roll him on the floor and squelch the flames with his hands. While the flames didn't spread, they just kept burning, down deeper into the man's back, searing through his clothing and then his flesh. Behr found a blanket and tried to smother the flames, and finally had some success right around the time he realized he needed to get out of the apartment because it was burning around him. The heat was overwhelming—and worse than that, he was suffocating as every bit of oxygen in the place was consumed by the blaze.

The door was cut off by fire, so Behr grabbed the rifle, tore away a melted window shade, and smashed out the glass.

"One way out," Behr gasped.

He grabbed the man's charred and limp body and fed it out the window feetfirst and hoped for the best. Gravity sucked the man out of his grasp and Behr heard a thud before he grabbed the window sash, sprang through the opening, dangled, and dropped. He hit the ground with a painful roll and sucked in cool, fresh air and saw he'd ended up right next to the shooter, who was still and emitting a whimper as plaintive as any sound Behr had ever heard. He looked for some unburned flesh near the shooter's wrists and forearms—there was little—and hoisted the man up and over his shoulder and headed for the front . . .

48

Enough was bleeding enough.

Dwyer had to admit it to himself. The solo play was over. Dwyer had been inside. He'd brought Banco some Gatorade, a sandwich, fresh bandages. He'd left some simple saline intravenous fluid and tubing. He'd explained he couldn't get the more therapeutic stuff without a license, and that he was working on it. He'd left him something else too, a last surprise. It was just under the lip of the kitchenette counter. The mobile phone's internal clock was timed for fifteen minutes. Dwyer planned on being across town, under the shower nozzle in his shite hole by the time everything was finished. He was just leaving, taking his time, sitting in his car for a bit, making sure he'd thought everything through, when the big pro showed up.

Bugger me, Dwyer thought, another few moments and they would've been face-to-face. He watched the big pro go to the door, try something with the buzzer, wait a bit, and then set about letting himself in.

"He's bumping it," Dwyer said aloud. It was clear enough to him, even from down the street, what the big pro was doing. He'd seen better, but the bloke wasn't half bad at it. The man was dogged. He was a hunter.

Dwyer's anticipation grew as the big pro disappeared inside. *Two for the price of one,* Dwyer thought. His eye went from building to dashboard clock and back as he waited. And then he heard the muffled *crump*. There was the sound of breaking glass. Smoke appeared from the far side of the building. Then he couldn't believe his eyes at what he saw next: the big pro giving a fireman's carry to Banco's limp body. Dwyer opened the car door and set a foot on the pavement, ready to run straight at him and put two in his dome before he knew what had happened, but then a series of residents made their way, coughing and frightened, out the front door of the building. It was show enough for Dwyer. He put the car into Drive and took off before the police and emergency services arrived to set up a perimeter.

Now, pacing around his room, Dwyer took out his mobile. Going it alone was one thing, but he'd have to be a frigging idiot to go any further so. He dialed a number from memory and waited while it rang, and then he heard the familiar voice come through.

"'Ey?" It was his boy, Rickie Powell, a hard Sandhurst chappie and regular hooligan who'd earned his nickname 'Ruthless' many times over.

"Oi, Rickie. Dwyer. Where are ya?"

"Waddy, ya fuckin' Cambrian! On Ibiza."

"Work?"

"Nah, 'oliday."

"*Bewt*. Which side?"

"Which side? You think I'm in Ibiza Town with all them rich quiffs? I'm in fucking Sant Antoni, getting smeared on cider and porking fat German chicks."

"Sorry to interrupt your vital mission, but I'm on a damage-limitation job and could use you to rally up."

"Fucking 'ell. Can do."

"Tidy."

"You're doing me a big favor. These Bavarian twats can drink their weight in beer, I'm goin' broke . . ."

It went on like that for another five minutes before Dwyer snapped to and asked, "Can you come in on a blank, then?"

"Not without flying back to Leeds first. Me blanks are in the safety deposit box at the bloody bank—just have my legitimate passport with me," Rickie told him.

"Come on straightaway, then, no matter," Dwyer said. "Go and get yourself packed, we've got work to do . . ."

49

Behr sat with his back against an ambulance on the dusty lawn in front of the building, coughing out smoke. He'd given his name and brief description of what had transpired, first to the 911 operator when he called in the fire, then again to the first patrolman on the scene. He watched while paramedics and the police and fire departments arrived simultaneously and put out the building fire, which they'd managed to contain to a few neighboring apartments, made sure the residents were safe, and EMS tried to stabilize the shooter. A paramedic gave Behr water and oxygen and cleaned and bandaged the burns on his hands, which were only first and second degree.

He'd been lucky. The shooter had been far from it. They had him on a stretcher, on his side since his back was so badly burned. One paramedic hung an IV and placed an oxygen mask over his nose and mouth, while the other worked the radio.

"We've got a male—Hispanic, I believe—in his thirties, late or early unknown . . . Abnormal respiration . . . We have black nasal and oral discharge . . . Burns greater than sixty percent of his body . . . Deep burn pattern . . . Chemical accelerants . . ."

The care-giving paramedic spread gauze along the burned man's back and looked up at his partner. "Christ, I think this guy's been shot—lower left quadrant. Not too recent either . . . He's septic."

"Probable GSWs, lower left quadrant," the one on the radio said into the handset.

"Repeat. Did you say GSWs or burns?" a voice came through the radio.

"Yeah, GSWs. Burns also."

"Shit, he's shocking," the one on the ground said. "Pulse two ten, and spiking."

"Let's move him, stat," the radio op said.

"Trying to stabilize him first."

"Nothing *to* move if we wait, partner."

"Roger that, let's roll."

"He's hypovolemic, we're on the move," the radio man said into the handset.

They used straps to secure him to the gurney and carried it toward the ambulance. Behr got a chance to see the shooter's face as he went by—his lips grossly swollen, one eye glassy and blank, the other burned shut, the hair on the back of his head gone. Whatever information the man had may as well have been locked away in a Swiss vault. Behr didn't have much experience with serious burns, but he didn't see the guy making it.

Behr stood as the ambulance was closed up and did his best to order his scrambled thoughts. He'd tracked down the shooter. The man was for hire, some kind of pro—ex-military, a mercenary—something he didn't see every day. Someone—his support or handler—had brought in supplies. And someone had firebombed him. Or Behr. Or both of them. He didn't get much further than that, because as the ambulance sped out, sirens wailing, a dark Crown Vic rolled onto the scene and a familiar, unwelcome figure climbed out. It was Lt. Breslau, chesty and overheated in his suit, his jaw in major pump mode over a lump of gum.

"You okay?"

"Yeah."

"You need further medical treatment?"

"No."

"Good. What kind of Caro business brings you out into this mess?" Breslau wanted to know.

Behr could only stare him in the face. "Unofficial," finally came out of his mouth.

"Who's the well-done slab of meat they just carted away?" Breslau asked.

"José Campos. It's an alias," Behr said.

"Great, a spic John Doe to unravel."

"When that fire's out, you're going to find an assault rifle in that apartment. Military. Not jerry-rigged," Behr said, wondering exactly what the hell he was trying to prove.

"This is about the garage shoot, then?"

"Yeah."

"Of course."

"What's that mean?"

"Christ. You protected the principal. That's great, man, well done. Congrat-a-fucking-lations, you did your job. But that's not enough for you. No, you need to go and find the shooter. Are you on some kind of glory run here?"

"Glory run? What the fuck are you talking about?" Behr said, his blood fizzing with instant anger.

"Can't let it go. Can't get off the rush from all the kudos. Gotta prove it out to everyone . . ."

Behr felt his knuckles straining in tight fists. He wanted to use them.

Breslau gave a half laugh. "You think I'm a douche bag, don't you? You do—I can see it on your face . . ."

Though dying to answer, Behr managed to hold off.

"Just know this: *I'm* not the douche bag caught on camera entering a security office in that parking garage."

Behr thought with disgust of the rent-a-cop who'd obviously reported him. But the disgust went deeper, because wasn't *he* just a rent-a-cop too? For slightly better wages.

"How the hell'd you even end up here?" Breslau suddenly wondered.

"It's called investigation," Behr said, and saw the muscles of Breslau's jaw freeze. Now the cop was just as angry as him.

"You're being small-picture here, Behr," Breslau said, fully squaring on him.

"I am?"

"Yeah. Look, the police, a place like Caro—whatever—they're all gears in a bigger machine. And you, Behr, you're sand in the gears. Sand in the fucking gears."

Behr said nothing. He just stared and choked on the burned gasoline taste in his throat.

"Don't you think we've been looking for the shooter?" Breslau asked.

"I don't know what you've been doing."

"We've been looking for the shooter. We have been. And we were going to find him—"

"Before or after he was barbecued?" Behr shot back, causing Breslau's volume to triple.

"We were going to find him and lock this thing down! But I'll tell you this, and I really hope you read me on it. We are *not* in the business of taking a straight-up random shoot, or even an attempted murder beef, and turning it into some unsolvable high-profile conspiracy case. You got me?"

Behr didn't nod. He didn't move.

"And believe me, when I say 'we,' I mean 'we.' As in 'to the top.' So mind you don't head from 'sand in the gears' status toward 'shit on my shoe.' Because if you end up there, I will scrape you the fuck off."

Breslau spat on the ground and stalked away toward his car while Behr turned his gaze back to the smoldering apartment building.

50

Waddy Dwyer was inside the master bedroom, sitting in a plush Ultrasuede chair and admiring the custom-milled woodwork when the shower cut off in the bathroom. He'd had a moment, after coming in through the window, when the water was running, that he could just sit quietly and appreciate the house. Where he was from, where space was at a premium, size and scale said wealth and power. If that perception were the reality here, though, this wanker would be Superman. But it was a lie. That much was clear. Because his initial look over the house told Dwyer that this guy must be auctioning off the furniture for spare cash.

One of the double doors to the bathroom swung open and Gantcher emerged in a puff of steam, wearing only a monogrammed towel around his baggy waist.

"All scrubby-dubby, are we?" Dwyer said, causing Gantcher to freeze, and a wave of gooseflesh to pucker across his skin.

"How'd you get in here?" he said, his mouth flapping. "There are—"

"Two poofs guarding the front, occasionally walking the perimeter," Dwyer said. "I saw 'em. They didn't see me."

Gantcher's eyes traveled toward the bedroom's double doors and then back to Dwyer.

"Who tried to get to you today?" Dwyer asked.

"You saw that?"

"Your security stopped him. Who was he?"

"They . . . they told me his card said Frank Behr. From the Caro Group," Gantcher said. "They thought he might've been . . . someone else."

"I know who they thought he was," Dwyer said, his voice hard. Now he had a name for the big pro.

"What do you want?" Gantcher said too loudly. Dwyer saw what he was trying to do.

"Drop the volume," he said. "You know what I want." Dwyer took in Gantcher's hairless, pink, flabby body. "Look at you there, with your man babbles," Dwyer said with disgust. "How much steak and lobster, clarified butter, and sweets have you shoveled down your gob, you soft bastard?"

Gantcher didn't respond, just stood there looking wounded.

"You ought to have some insurance money coming your way about now, righto?"

"The fire," Gantcher said, confirmation playing on his face. "Holy shit, I had a feeling that was you."

Dwyer said nothing.

"They're going to be coming to me now, asking," Gantcher whined. "*Investigating*. They've already called . . ."

"Well, you've got nothing to worry about, ain't you? Your bloody hands are clean. Now what about it? My money."

"The thing is, you see," Gantcher started, "the insurance policies on the development—they were lapsed."

"The fuck do you mean 'lapsed'?"

"There was a bookkeeping error. A shortfall. Damn it, I'll tell you, it's the same thing I told you before. I'm tapped. My company is tapped. You know how expensive fire, loss, and liability insurance is on a job of that scale? I couldn't pay the premium, and now . . ." Actual anger flared in the man and replaced his fear for a moment. "You really dicked me over here, Dwyer. You burned my damn job! How am I supposed to finish—"

"Huck up!" Dwyer said, jumping out of the chair and putting the fear right back into Gantcher. "How the fuck were you gonna finish the job in the first place, if you couldn't even pay the insurance?"

"All right, all right," Gantcher said, backing up, "fair enough." A moment passed. "So where do we go from here?"

Dwyer took a slip of paper from his pocket and thrust it into Gantcher's hand. "Wiring instructions. A blind account in the Isle of Man. My name's not on it. If you don't want to see me again, have the money in there within forty-eight hours. And hear me on this, you damned jeefe: you *don't* want to see me again."

Gantcher nodded, his eyes on the slip of paper. Dwyer headed straight for the bedroom's grand double doors, pulled a sleeve over the hand that gripped the knob, and headed out and down the stairs. He descended a wide staircase and let his heels ring brazenly against the marble of the vaulted foyer.

Dwyer exited through the front door, like a boulevardier out for a stroll, where he rabbit punched the closer of the two guards in the back of the head. They were the same two lummoxes he'd seen at the casino. On shift for too long—which was something only an amateur would do—they were rendered too tired to be sharp. The man went out and down, straightaway, landing on his face with a crunch that meant new dental work. Dwyer caught the second one, just turning in surprise, around the body and rocked him into a wicked *harai goshi*—a sweeping hip throw— that had him flying through the air briefly before being viciously deposited on the stone steps headfirst. The man's face and chin took the brunt of the fall. Dwyer was already down the driveway to the street and in his car before they even started to move.

51

You're sand in the gears.

Behr recalled hearing varying versions of this complaint his whole career, and while he understood it conceptually, seemed powerless to change when he needed to. He made his way on a tender ankle from the car through the near-midnight dark to his place.

"Are you okay? What the hell happened to you?" Susan asked the minute he walked in the door, bringing him out of his thoughts. Between the stink of smoke on him, the soot on his face, and the bandaged hands, there was no chance he was getting off without an explanation.

"Nothing to worry about, I'm fine," he said. "There was a fire."

"I see there was a fire. Where? What kind of fire?" she demanded.

"I was . . . looking to do an interview . . . and a device went off."

"A *device*?"

"I believe they call them improvised explosive devices."

"Jesus, Frank! What's going on here?"

Her question was straightforward enough, but he knew where his answer would lead the conversation.

"What do you mean?"

They stood there, eyes locked, for a moment—and then she plunged ahead. "I know you're working the shooting," she said. "Okay? I know." The look on his face asked "how?" and she continued. "The other day when you were in the shower I opened your notebook." Even though it was beside the point, the admission caused him to see red.

"Why are you opening my notebook?" he asked with some heat.

"Why are you pursuing this thing when they told you not to?"

"Because I want to know," he said, his decibel level rising. "And because no one tells me what to do."

"That's great, Frank. And what about us—me and the baby? You have responsibilities now—"

"I was shot at, Susan—"

"I know you were. And it makes me sick that I could have lost you. Which is why I was hoping you'd walk away from it and just leave it alone."

"Well, I can't," he said.

A thought occurred to her and she looked into his face. "You're doing this because you're bored."

"*Bored?*"

"That's right. With the grind of the Caro job. With the suit and the BlackBerry and the bosses and the supervision. Maybe with me. Our life . . ."

"You've got to be kidding, Suze," he said.

"Then tell me it's not true," she said.

"Not the part about you."

"And the rest of it?"

He couldn't answer. Not in a way that wouldn't blow things up between them like the firebomb he'd just survived. So he bit down and didn't say another word for a good minute or two.

"I'm sorry," he said, his voice at its quietest register, "but I can't break off now. I'm close to finding some things out, and then I can hand it off to the police and it'll be done. Then it'll be nose to the grindstone. I promise you that."

It was between them now, like a boulder, but she chose to relent.

"How are your hands? Do they hurt?" she asked, touching him softly on his arm.

"No, they just itch right now," he said.

"Can I do anything for you?" she offered. He shook his head. "All right then, I'm going to bed."

"Fine," he said, "I'll be in with you in a few minutes."

The smart move would've been to go off to bed with Susan right then, to reassure her that he was as reasonable and responsible a choice in a partner as she could possibly want. But he hadn't had time to run the partial plate on that Lincoln he'd seen earlier, so he sat down and started in on the Illinois Department of Motor Vehicles database. It was an uphill climb with only half the digits he needed, but he kept trying. He also ached to head out and brace Lenny Barnes, to interview Lori the escort, to learn more. But he held himself back from pushing that course, because if he pumped Lenny Barnes it would invariably track back to Caro and likely cause the video of Potempa's daughter to go viral, destroying the man. Behr just couldn't do it to the guy.

At the ninety-minute mark, he had made some minor progress and realized he wasn't going to get much further. His best guess was that the Illinois-plated Lincoln was registered to the largest rental car company in the world. He could farm out cracking the company's database to a hacker, but in the end, the car would likely come up rented to an alias. That was if his guess was even right, and it wasn't one of the dozens of private Illinois citizens who owned the same vehicle.

Behr shut down his computer. His hands had progressed from itching to stinging, and were now throbbing, along with his head. He picked up the phone and called over to the hospital where they'd taken the shooter.

"I'm not supposed to release this, so please don't share it with anyone," the duty nurse said after he'd explained who he was, "but since you tried to save the guy, I'm sorry to tell you our burned John Doe expired of shock and burn trauma."

Behr thanked her and hung up the phone. His night was over.

52

The isolated telephone interface, better known as a tap, was a nifty piece of equipment; just a little box that clipped into the telephone line where it entered the house and allowed him to listen to conversations via his laptop. It was true, no one used landlines much these days, but Dwyer had the frequency sweeper and signal intercept pieces to monitor mobile phone calls as well. The only tricky part was placing the box. In days past it would have been a broad daylight operation with a team that could have posed as utility workers with dummy uniforms and trucks and the like. Now he was solo, and all props kept to a minimum, so he was left with the dead of night. He'd stolen out of a copse of scrappy trees and across a dirt-patch rear lawn in dark clothing and balaclava, the Česká tucked in his belt, and went to work, hoping that Teague wasn't on his game and that he didn't end up with a hot round behind his ear.

Dwyer doubted he would. It had been three years since they'd met at the hotel bar in Dublin during the World Wide Detective Association's annual convention. Dwyer wasn't a member of the WWDA, but he often ducked into the city where it held its yearly event. It was as close to marketing as he could get in his profession. Certain members of the organization knew of him and referred him to their fellows who were in need of some off-the-books assistance. Carrolton, a longtime friend from the service, would then get the call and broker the meeting.

Besides, Teague didn't even know it was Dwyer he'd met. The man had been under the impression he *was* Carrolton, Dwyer's representative. There was a Carrolton, of course, but Dwyer had wanted to meet Teague himself while preserving his anonymity. What he'd learned in the sit-down was that the old Fed was big as a half beef, and he liked his whiskey. He'd drained a good four or five Tullamore Dews during the meeting, which had just been a general introductory chat with no specific job discussed. Dwyer's experience was that that type of drinking, if it didn't stay the same, generally only went in one direction over time, and that was *more,* so he imagined the old boy would be pretty hard to wake in the middle of the night. All the same, he had treaded lightly. He'd known too many lawmen's wives who slept like sparrows and were plenty handy with the family shotgun.

Before long Dwyer had the line tap placed and was back in the car, which he drove around the corner to a place where he could receive the signal. He'd waited while the sun took its time getting up, as did the ex-Fed and his family. The program on his laptop chimed to life, but it was only to hear Mrs. Teague ring a friend for afternoon plans. Two of the four kids made calls, one about meeting a friend before school, the other about something that happened on a television program the night before.

Four bloody kids, Dwyer thought, *no wonder the ex-Fed needed a few extra bob . . .*

He'd been hoping to pick up a transmission that would mention Kolodnik's location, a vulnerability, either right then or at some point later on, but he got no such break. It was with irritation that Dwyer watched the ex-Fed and his whole damned family set off for their day.

"Fuckin' 'ell," he said aloud, and realized that even a few years ago working all night and coming up with nothing would've rolled right off his back. He was getting old, he supposed, and still in need of that kip, too. But it would still have to wait. He needed to head out for the airport, which he'd do after a quick shower at the shite hole. He put the car in gear.

53

"Ms. Miroslav," Frank Behr said, as a woman carrying a purse and a briefcase arrived at her office.

Olga Miroslav was pretty and dark haired and quite surprised to see Behr sitting in her cubicle at the main branch of Payroll Place. John Lutz had been surprised too that morning when he got the crack-of-dawn call from Behr asking for the interview. He was as happy to arrange for Behr's admittance to the offices as Ms. Miroslav seemed miserable when she learned why Behr was there.

"How would you describe your duties?" Behr asked once she'd put down her things and settled.

"I chart the pickups at our clients' businesses and design the routes for the armored cars," she said with a bit of a Slavic accent. "And schedule drop-offs and bank deposits also."

"You do all this by hand, using maps?" Behr asked, though he already knew the answer.

"No, the computer does it. There's a mapping program. I just input it," she told him.

"And then if you need to make any changes . . . ?" Behr wondered.

"I tweak it after the computer makes the route," she said.

"Why's that?"

"Road construction. Businesses closed for holidays. Things the computer don't know about."

"I understand you have visitors to the office sometimes," Behr said, changing course with some information he'd picked up yakking around with her coworkers before her arrival, seeing if it threw her. "That you have lunch down in the cafeteria with a Salvatore Rueben."

"Sally is my boyfriend," she said, nodding, looking uncomfortable with the topic. She wore fairly heavy base makeup, but her color was mottling beneath it.

"I see," Behr said, making a note. He was writing for effect, to let her see him documenting the conversation. "And what does Sally do?"

"For a living?" she asked.

"Yes. Does he have an employer?" Behr inquired.

"He's . . . self-employed."

"I see. What's his business?"

"He's in . . . distribution."

Behr didn't have to ask what he distributed. He'd run Sally Rueben after discovering the restraining orders and the guy had drug arrests. To complete the investigation properly, Behr would have to finish the backgrounds, interview a dozen other potentials, to rule many things out. And maybe he would when he had time, but for now he noticed Ms. Miroslav's hands were shaking.

54

A whore in the morning was rarely a pretty sight, and this one was no exception. In fact, she proved the rule. Behr had felt he should get in to the office and show his face, but leaving Payroll Place down in the wholesale district he realized the address Sunny had texted him for her friend Lori was close by. Unlike speaking directly to Barnes, he believed he could explore the connection of this "certain investigator" and Kolodnik's camp without mentioning Potempa, or his daughter, and then make a retreat. Or maybe he was just telling himself that so he could go get what he needed. Either way, he reached McCrea Street and the old industrial building that had been converted to high-dollar loft apartments. He made his way inside as a food delivery kid exited, took the elevator to the fourth floor, and set to banging on the large steel door for a while before he heard a muffled female voice from inside.

"Keep it in your pants . . . Just a sec . . ." she said.

A deadbolt lock bar clanged open and the door rolled to the side, revealing a woman who wouldn't look young for long. She'd slept in her makeup, and there'd been a lot of it. Her eyes were caked in black smudge, her lips smeared red, and concealer rubbed off in patches revealed purple blotches and acne pits. Whatever mask she'd applied the night before was long gone. She was rank with cigarette smoke, dead cherry perfume, and body sweat. It was a wonder people paid for this. But her body was shapely and her flesh looked firm, and she hadn't hit thirty, which was a kind of magic elixir to some men.

"Hey. Can I help you with something?" she asked.

"Invite me in," Behr said.

"Why?"

"Because I need to talk to you."

"Oh shit, cop?" she wondered.

"Nope."

"If you're not a cop, you are some kind of law guy, no?" she said.

Behr nodded. "I could use your insights on something," he said.

"Am I in trouble?"

"You're not," Behr said, "yet." Then he went to a leverage point that worked on every prostitute he'd ever met. "But my partner is over at Lenny Barnes's place with his foot on the scumbag's head, and if you don't help, my partner's gonna squash him like a grape."

She swallowed and stepped aside, letting him enter.

"Look, just be cool with Lenny. I'll help you as much as I can," she said. The pimp victimized his women—emotionally, financially, often physically—but the psychological bond was deep, and the women stood up for these parasites, even when it cost them everything. Sometimes even their lives. The door rolled and clanged shut behind him.

Her loft was cavernous, with high ceilings and casement windows, and was stylishly decorated in a modernist yet comfortable design. The furniture wasn't custom—she wasn't rich—but it came from a higher-end chain store. The place was clean. He imagined she did outcall, and doubted she entertained clients much at home due to the personal-sanctuary feel here.

"What's it about?" she asked.

It was clear Sunny hadn't warned her about him. *Good girl,* he thought.

"Well, it's about a certain client of yours," Behr said.

"I figured. Do you want some juice?" she offered, crossing around a divider into her kitchen.

"No thanks," Behr said, following, and keeping a close eye on her. She poured herself a glass.

"You know we don't talk about our clients," she said. "It's an unwritten rule."

"Yeah, like doctors."

"Or priests," she said, flashing a smile.

"I'm not asking you to identify him. I already know this guy sees you. And I'm not looking for bedroom dirt."

"So it's like anyone I'd know, an acquaintance as much as a client . . ." she said, getting comfortable with it. "All right."

"Shugie Saunders. When did you meet him?" Behr asked.

"Oh, Shugie," she said cryptically. "When did I meet him . . . let's see . . . a little less than two years ago."

"Where?"

"Over at the lobby bar at the Conrad. I was drinking with some friends. He came out of a dinner at Capital Grille and swung through for a 'capper. He saw me and beelined it right over."

"How'd it start—regular attempt at courtship?"

"Nah. He's not stupid. He'd set it up with Lenny. After a minute, he asked quietly if I was the escort. I said yeah."

"You hook up that night?"

"Uh-huh. We had a few rounds with my friends. He got loaded up. Acting all swag, putting an arm around me, calling me his 'little cocksucking blonde.'"

Behr eyed her to gauge whether that was a problem for her. But she just laughed.

"He's a pretty big deal in this town, you know? His political connections . . . But that bravado shit sure didn't last long," she said.

"How's that?"

"We got a room and went upstairs and I rocked his world," she said, with more than a little pride. "After that"—she snapped her fingers—"he was a regular. A *regular* regular. He pretty much paid for this place," she said, and laughed again.

"Okay," Behr said, hoping to steer toward the topics that mattered to him, "so about six months after that, you're all regular together, did you ever hear about his dealings with Bernie Kolodnik?"

"Sure."

"On anything outside of politics? A big construction project. A casino."

"Come on, man, Bernie Cool and Indy Flats? I heard about it *real time*. Shug talked about it like it was his kid practically. It was his big plan for our future. What'd he call it? His *thirteen-million-dollar play,* something like that. Pop. His thirteen-million-dollar pop."

"So he had some kind of profit participation. Did Kolodnik give him a piece?"

"I doubt it. I'm guessing it was under the table, because Shug was always telling me: *you* don't talk about this."

"How'd it sound to you?" Behr wondered.

"Pretty damn good, if he was gonna get *that* rich . . ." she started, but then just shook her head. "You hear a lot of apple-pie promises in my field. You learn to wait until they come true . . . Anyway, yeah, if he wasn't telling me about the deal, he was talking about it on his cell."

"All right," Behr said. "Jump ahead to more recently. He had need for a detective or an investigator at some point, and you—"

"That's right. And my manager—well I guess you know who I'm talking about, Lenny—knew someone, so I made the connect."

Behr felt his pulse race the way it did when he was hitting pay dirt. "*You* made the connect."

"Yeah. I told Shug I could help him out. We all met here—Shug, Lenny, and Pat."

"Pat," Behr, said, the word barely getting out of his mouth.

"Yeah, Pat the detective. He and Shug went out to Fogo de whatever—that Brazilian meat place. Lenny split. He didn't go.

He and Pat weren't friendly. Pat was up his ass about something, so Len was throwing him the introduction as a favor."

"This Pat the detective," Behr said, tapping his pen on his notebook like it was just an afterthought hardly worth asking about, "he that burly fella, last name Teague?"

"Yeah, yeah. I guess. I think so. Something Irishy sounding."

Behr heard a ringing in his ears, and was distracted by the sun glare coming through the windows. He didn't know if he was even speaking English for the rest of the interview. He just wanted to get out of there, and go face-to-face with Teague. He needed to hear how Shug would get rich off his piece with Kolodnik out of the way. And that was just for starters.

"You gonna call the dogs off on Lenny?" the girl asked. "I did good for you, didn't I?"

"Yeah, I'll call 'em off," Behr said, heading for the door. "You did good."

55

Ah, here he comes now . . .

Waddy Dwyer saw the broad shoulders and buzz-cut head of Rickie Powell bouncing out of the Continental Airlines doorway of Indianapolis International Airport. He wore dark, gold-framed Elvis sunglasses, and an Affliction T-shirt that resembled a full torso tattoo, as he was an MMA freak, though he'd been banned from some UK feeder league after three straight disqualifications. The boy did love those head butts.

Dwyer had switched cars to a smokestone metallic Mercury Grand Marquis. That Lincoln was a notch too flash for his liking. He'd reserved a full-size when he'd first arrived, but they'd upgraded him unasked to the luxury class ride. He hadn't wanted to take the time and cause the notice that switching would have. But now the Lincoln may have been spotted, and besides, it stunk like petrol and ass sweat, takeaway food, and concentration—like all work vehicles did eventually. He flicked the lights and tapped the horn, and Rickie changed course toward him and then tossed his duffel bag in the backseat and slid into the front.

"'Ello, fruit," Dwyer said by way of greeting.

"Waddy, you big queer, good to see ya."

"You steal them glasses from Kanye West?"

"His little sister, actually," Rickie said.

"What I figured," Dwyer said, pulling away from the curb.

As Dwyer drove back to the city, he briefed Rickie on the particulars of the situation, from his original hire to the blown attempt, all the way through the fun and games of last night. He poured in every detail including all the private security involved. Rickie mostly looked out the window as he listened, but nodded like a metronome, clocking each fact, locking it all down in his mind.

"On the bright side," Dwyer said, "Banco's dead. I called as a concerned citizen looking to donate blood in case 'my poor neighbor who was hurt in the fire needed a transfusion,' and some nice lady in the administrator's office told me there'd be no need."

"You've always been clever with the incendiaries," Rickie said.

Dwyer finished with a rundown on Frank Behr, booted cop, private investigator, and general pain in the bollocks, whom he'd done a background on that morning, and the very man who'd pulled Banco from the fire.

"This knob's a regular National Peace Scout, ain't he," Rickie said. "You want to spike his computer with kiddie porn, fit him up?"

"His reputation's been buggered for years, don't think it would slow him down much, and he might have enough sway with the cops to avoid any real hassles," Dwyer said, pulling over. "No, I'm going to sink a deep choke on 'im and keep it locked for about three fucking minutes." It was an amount of time that caused death.

"You sure that's a good idea, Waddy? You know what happens when pros lock up: everyone gets hurt. And he sounds like a strapping fucker," Rickie said, laughing.

"*They* go down harder than anyone when they're shot on and their legs is yanked out from under 'em," Dwyer said through gritted teeth.

"Just taking the piss, man," Rickie said. "Where's your sense of humor?"

"Shit stirrer," Dwyer said, turning off the car.

"What are we doing here?" Rickie asked of the massive military surplus store they'd parked in front of.

"Need to do a little shopping," Dwyer said. "You got a cap you can wear? They've got cameras all over these places, and with them glasses they'll probably think you're some celebrity."

56

Behr jerked the front door of the Caro Group open and strode across the office, hoping to see Pat Teague. There was no sign of him and Behr quickly discovered it was *not* business as usual that day at Caro. For him, anyway. His personal effects, which weren't many—a mug, a pencil cup, a few framed photos, a phone charger, a flash drive, a jar of Tums, and a pack of Big Red—were in a cardboard box on his desk. The company computer had been removed and an envelope left in its place. He knew what was inside before he even opened it.

Glancing over the tops of dividers Behr saw the heads of his colleagues ducked down toward their computers and papers. He'd never witnessed such hard work. Nothing like some spilled blood to refocus the troops. He opened the envelope, which contained two checks in the same amount. One was his pay for the last two weeks. The other had the word "severance" on the memo line. There was a Post-it note on that check that read: "Speak to Curt Lundquist."

Behr put the box of effects under his arm and marched across the office past Lundquist's secretary to his closed door. He knocked too hard and didn't wait to be invited in. Lundquist was seated behind his desk on the telephone when Behr entered.

"Let me call you back. There's something I need to deal with right now," Lundquist said, rising. He hung up and gestured at his guest chair.

"Have a seat, Behr," he offered.

"Why?" Behr said, "How long is this going to take?"

"Not long," Lundquist said. "I'm going to need your company-issue sidearm and BlackBerry."

Behr unclipped the holster from his waist and put the Glock on Lundquist's desk, along with his BlackBerry.

"Good riddance," Behr said.

"Yeah, I know what you mean," Lundquist said, then he slid a piece of paper across the desk. "Gonna ask you to sign that. It's a nondisclosure of case information, protocols, everything to do with working here."

"Signed one when I started," Behr said, taking a fancy pen out of Lundquist's holder and scrawling his name.

"We like to reinforce it," Lundquist said, and advanced another piece of paper. "This one says you accept the terms of your dismissal and waive your right to future suit."

Behr took this piece of paper and crumpled it into a ball. He wouldn't have talked to anyone about sensitive information in the first place, but he was fine signing the NDA. He wasn't going to sue either, but he sure wasn't in the mood to give them comfort over that fact. He tossed the wadded paper in the general direction of Lundquist's recycling bin.

"Why am I fired?" Behr asked.

"Officially? Neglect of duties."

"And unofficially?"

"You've repeatedly engaged in unsanctioned inquiries. And you've irritated the shit out of IPD," Lundquist said. It wasn't a shock to Behr—the moment he had seen the envelope on his desk he'd known Breslau had dimed him.

"So, in my capacity as house counsel for the Indy office of the Caro Group, Worldwide, I'd like to—"

Behr slammed the door behind him as he exited, cutting off Lundquist's words. He headed for Potempa's office. He understood the man was in a world of shit at the moment, but Behr had done plenty in the line for him and exercised copious discretion on his behalf. For that Behr was owed better. It was a simple matter of contract. He reached Ms. Swanton outside Potempa's closed office door.

"I need a minute with him," Behr said.

"He was unexpectedly called out of town, Mr. Behr," she told him.

"Is he in there? If he is, I need him," Behr said.

"He's not in the office. Really," she responded.

Behr ground his teeth in frustration, but the truth was: whatever he got face-to-face from Potempa was bound to be no less frustrating.

"That's fine," Behr said. "Look, I know this isn't your deal, but tell him the following: I recommend surveillance, visual and telephone, on Olga Miroslav at Payroll Place. And put someone on her scumbag boyfriend, Salvatore Rueben. File's not complete, but I'm thinking that might help close it."

She nodded as she scrawled the names on a steno pad, then she looked up. "I'm sorry, Mr. Behr," she said.

"May as well call me Frank," he said, and walked away.

He cut for the front door, feeling the eyes of his ex-coworkers on him, all except for that one set.

He paused at the reception desk in front of the new girl. "Where's Pat Teague?"

"He called in."

"Sick or personal day?"

"Didn't say on the voice mail, just that he wouldn't be in."

"Thanks," Behr said. "You need my key?"

"They changed the outer lock first thing this morning."

"Okay then." Behr nodded. "See ya." And he left.

57

Behr's knuckles gripped the steering wheel as if to tear it off the stalk as he drove out to Thorntown. He parked in front of Teague's ranch style and watched it for half an hour. There were no signs of movement inside, no cars in the driveway. He played out versions of the conversation he was going to have with Teague and couldn't picture them going any way other than the man laughing in his face or at least blanking him completely. The thought filled Behr with rage. Finally he couldn't sit still any longer, got out of his car, and passed the garage. Though it was closed, Behr looked in through one of its small square windows and was disappointed to see it empty of vehicles.

He returned to his own car and sat there again, his fingers drumming on the wheel, and his insides tightening like a diver's cylinder being filled with pressurized air. That's when he saw Teague's Traverse roll up and park in the driveway. Teague got out, dressed in suit pants, dress shirt, and sunglasses, and headed for his door carrying a paper bag and a newspaper.

Behr was out of his car and at the door before Teague was inside his house.

"Hey. Teague!" Behr called out.

"What do you want?" he said, turning and pushing in.

"You hiding from me?" Behr said. "That's not gonna work."

"Fuck off," Teague said, dropping the bag and newspaper as he made to close the door in Behr's face. But Behr stepped forward and blasted it with both hands like he was hitting a blocking dummy. The door flew open and Behr followed it, stepping inside.

"I want to know, Pat, and I'm not leaving until I do," Behr said.

"Get out of here or you're a dead man," Teague answered.

"This is gonna happen," Behr stated.

Teague shook his head.

"Lose the Maui Jims," Behr yelled, and slapped the sunglasses from Teague's face. What flashed in Teague's eyes was not fear, it was anger, and Behr knew it wasn't going to be easy.

Teague threw a stiff-arm palm that caught Behr's face, driving him back a few feet. He was softening a bit around the middle, but Teague was still a big, thick ex-Fed, and he came at Behr, snapping out a steel telescoping spring baton that he pulled from his pocket. Behr heard it and felt it whistle past his head as he leaped out of its path.

He squared with Teague, who feinted high, then changed levels and swung the weapon again, this time low at Behr's thigh. Behr tried to check it as he would a leg kick, by raising his shin and turning it toward the blow, but took the shot across the outside of his kneecap. A white-hot bolt of pain lit through him, but he managed to deliver a looping overhand right that caught Teague high on the side of the head. Teague stumbled back, and Behr closed the distance, collared him behind the head in a sort of Muay Thai clinch and gained an over hook that took the baton out of play, before it eventually got knocked to the floor.

Tied up as they were, they did the dance, and Behr felt in Teague the balance of an ex-lineman. They staggered into a piece of furniture that was coat and hat rack and mirror. Baseball caps scattered and the glass cracked. A potted plant was knocked on its side and dirt spilled across the foyer floor. After a minute, Behr found he couldn't take the man down, and neither could Teague him, so the dirty boxing commenced. Fists, elbows, and shoulders flew across the tight span between the men. At that range more landed than missed. It became a question of chins and will.

Behr heard Teague's breathing begin to go ragged and labored.

He knew the older man hadn't put in the gym time and road-work he had, and he pressed the advantage, upping the speed and the output. Behr's blows began landing more cleanly, thumping Teague's head back. Teague threw a knee to the body, his desperation growing. But Behr leaned into it and stuffed it, and his abs held like a retaining wall, and then he felt Teague sag.

Wrapping an arm behind Teague's neck, Behr doubled him over, landing a standing guillotine choke that he closed but didn't finish. Instead, Behr dropped his weight over the man, cranking Teague's neck, and dished out a set of three knees to the body, the last of which found the liver and deposited Teague on his broad ass.

He gasped and keeled for a moment before Behr grabbed him by his matted, curly hair and turned up his bile- and puke-streaked face.

"What did you know?"

"Nothing," Teague began. Behr drew his fist back and blasted Teague in the ear, which burst red with blood.

"What did you know?"

"Nothing," Teague said again, but when he saw Behr rear his fist back once more, quickly continued, "nothing clear. Nothing for sure."

Teague sucked in a breath and went on. "Most of this shit's way above my pay grade, man, but suffice it to say not everyone loves Bernie Cool."

Behr drilled a punch into Teague's mouth. "Start getting specific or I'm gonna start getting ugly."

Teague gave a sickly smile. Blood ran over his teeth and he spit it on the floor. "What do you call this?"

"The warm-up lap," Behr said, and kicked Teague in the floating rib with the point of his shoe. He put some leg into it, enough for a thirty-yard field goal. Teague groaned and doubled over into the dirt from the fallen plant. When he finally caught some air, he pushed himself up, leaning on one hand.

"Okay. Okay. Shit, your stand-up game is tight . . . SB-5373X."

"SB, what's that?"

"Senate bill. Proposing a tax break on the racinos."

Behr had read about it when he was researching Indy Flats. It was the massive relief bill that would allow the Indiana racinos to survive and compete with those in Ohio, Michigan, and Illinois.

"What does it have to do with Kolodnik?" Behr asked. "He's out of his piece of the casino interest, and that's a state senate vote anyway," he said.

"Everyone knows the senators out of Washington tell the state legislature which hand to wipe with," Teague said, rubbing his side.

"Kolodnik wasn't going to be senator until five minutes ago," Behr said.

"Well, best as I can tell it's a story of eighteen months. That's when Kolodnik's ex-partner—"

"Gantcher," Behr said.

"Yeah, Gantcher. That's when he broke ground on the hotel. Then the business went into the dumper. They're losing six figures a day, man. It's a bloodbath."

"What's it connect to?" Behr was writing now, his swollen knuckles clenched around his pen.

"About a year back Gantcher and some others in the state gambling business request a special assembly so they can propose SB-5373X."

"I read about it. The legislature told them kiss off," Behr said.

"That's right. But with that kind of money on the line, they're not just going to walk away. So about seven months ago Gantcher goes to Kolodnik, even though he's out of it, to get him to use his juice to get a special assembly, you know, to safeguard the economic engine that is the racino business. Bernie Cool's a stand-up guy, so he asks. But they reject the request."

Teague pulled himself heavily into a more upright seated position. He wasn't going anywhere, though. He was talking now.

"This worries Gantcher, big-time. Same with his competitors—the other racino and casino owners in the state—who are now quickly becoming his asshole buddies. They all get together and have a meeting with Kolodnik where they fucking tell him to go to the governor and *demand* an assembly. They figured he and the gov are so tight he can do it."

"What happened?" Behr asked. He fought to keep writing and to resist the urge to just let the information wash over him.

"I don't know. I suppose the meeting didn't go well. Kolodnik didn't go along. He's not the kind of guy to be pushed, and I guess that's when he decided he needed security."

"This is what, six months ago, when he hired Caro?"

Teague nodded.

"How'd he decide on Caro?"

"How'd he *decide*?" Teague laughed. "*He* didn't. It was decided *for* him. See, there was this thing I was working for Potempa on the quiet—"

"The daughter," Behr said.

"Yeah, that fucking wild-child daughter of his—"

"I know about her. I've seen the video," Behr said.

"Fuck me! You've seen the video? I never got that far on it. Man, I wouldn't mind getting a look—"

"Shut up," Behr said. "Where'd it lead?"

What couldn't I get out of Potempa? Behr wondered.

"So he asked me to sort this thing for him, since we go back the furthest, and I'm on it, talking to this jackwad Barnes trying to work it out—"

"Lenny Barnes, daughter's boyfriend," Behr said.

"Yeah. He and the daughter want to leave town. They want to move to Hawaii or something and open a business. The guy's looking for fifty grand from Potempa . . ."

An agonized look crossed Teague's face, probably from a cracked rib. That pain comes on slow and builds.

"Look, I've known Karl Potempa a long fucking time. I can read when a man's in the shit. And that's where he was. He don't have leaks—like gambling or liquor—but on this, I saw he was weak . . . he was wide-open. So I'm in there, working out leverage on how I'm going to squeeze Barnes, make him walk away or take him down on pandering—I'm just trying to keep the video squelched, you know, for Karl—"

"Yeah, yeah. Father to father," Behr said.

"Right. And I get called to this apartment to meet, and Barnes has got this girl he runs there with him, and this douche bag of a john is there too, drooling all over her, with an idea on how we can all make a lot of money."

"The john was Shugie Saunders," Behr stated.

"Yeah. Damn, you've gotten a lot." Teague's hand found his bleeding ear, as if just discovering it wasn't working right, but he went on. "And Saunders says he has a prominent client for us, a guy he advises that needs some special services, yada yada—"

"What the fuck is 'yada yada'?" Behr said.

"Nothing. 'Special services.' That's all he said then. We go out and have dinner and talk about the services and coverage we provide. He calls Potempa the next day and hires Caro. I'm an experienced E.P. guy, so it isn't long before I catch a Kolodnik detail, and after the first one, they start requesting me."

Behr took it in.

"Round this time people start talking about Kolodnik getting the Senate seat. Thinking was: business as usual, the casino owners grease through their tax measure, no problem. But now it looks like Bernie Cool's ready to be the law-and-order senator. Instead of helping, he's gonna stick it in their eye to make a point, so they needed to make sure he never got there."

Behr understood what happened from there. Still, he wanted to hear it.

"Gantcher and the other casino owners paid you to kill Kolodnik," Behr said.

"Not to kill him. They did pay me. Paid the note on this place clean," Teague said, glancing around his house. "But they just asked for a tip on where he would be at a given time. There was going to be a team of shooters. Said it would come when I was on shift. I knew it would be bad press for the company, for me, but I figured Caro could survive it . . ."

"Why didn't it go down that way?"

Teague straightened and gathered himself a bit.

"The thing was, after riding with Bernie Cool a few times, I just couldn't . . . be there for it. You know what I mean? I just couldn't. The man is a *prince*."

Behr did know what he meant. In a charm derby Kolodnik had most everyone beat.

"So you started subbing me in," Behr said, "and it was 'fuck the new guy.'"

"Not exactly . . ."

"No?"

"The body man—me—was never supposed to be hit. It was supposed to be a clean deal, I swear to you on that—"

"Whatever it was, *you* didn't want to be there that night."

There was a period of silence. "No."

"Who were the shooters?"

"No idea."

"Who did the hiring?"

"Again, I don't have a clue. Not a damn clue."

Behr eyed Teague. "So you went ahead and served me up."

"I hardly knew you. We weren't in the Bureau together—"

"Sure."

"I didn't know what else to do. Shit, looking back, of course it was a setup and the bodyguard was going down too. I just didn't see it at the time. You did damn good though. Better than I would have. Behr, it wasn't personal."

"To me it was."

Another period of silence elapsed, this one prolonged.

"That's it, then? All you did was give the location?"

Teague shrugged pathetically.

"Are they going to try again?" Behr demanded.

"Kolodnik's in D.C. Confirmation is any day. He's made now. I'm pretty sure that ship has sailed."

"And how much does Potempa know?"

"He doesn't know shit about this, just that we had a fat new client and after my first time out with him, I was requested. Anything he thinks, it's meaningless. The man's a fucking puddle since watching that video." As Behr had suspected, Potempa couldn't stop himself from looking at the thing.

"Potempa's just screwed up—he's not dirty," Teague said with a near laugh.

"Unlike you. You're screwed up *and* dirty, aren't you?" Behr said, extinguishing the humor.

Behr looked down at Teague, the man's head sagging forward. He didn't know if he'd gotten 10 percent of the details or 90, and had no idea how much of it was the truth. He also didn't know what to do with him now. Taking him to the cops would stop his own investigation cold, and Teague would be out on bail in three hours. A trial would happen two years down the road, and everyone else responsible would be long gone. On the other hand, Behr couldn't torture him. He couldn't sit on him. He couldn't kill him. He had no other way to shut him up besides the old-fashioned. Behr used his foot again, this time planting it in Teague's chest, and knocking him onto his back. Then he put the edge of it across Teague's throat, stepping down with some weight on the trachea.

"You're not going to show up for work. For a while. And you're not going to be reachable either," Behr said, "except by me when I need bits and pieces filled in."

Teague nodded, his eyes bugging from fear and the pressure and lack of air. Fragments of mirror glass ground into the floor and Teague's shoulder with a grating sound.

"You're not going to say anything about this to Potempa or anyone else at Caro." Even as he spoke, Behr knew he was wasting his breath. Teague was going to tell whomever he was going to tell and do whatever he wanted to do. Teague's gurgle had heightened to a high-pitched wheeze. Behr took his foot off Teague's windpipe and walked out the door.

58

Behr sat at his kitchen table in jeans and trail shoes, having finally retired the suit. He had a couple of gel packs from the freezer and had started in icing his left eye, where Teague had clipped him with a right, then moved on to his leg, and was concentrating on his right knuckles and wrist, which had incurred some damage as he was dishing it out, when he heard the front door open.

"Frank, are you home?" he heard Susan ask.

"In the kitchen," he called out.

"What's going on?" she asked, still out in the living room.

"Nothing much," he said. He heard the rustle of plastic shopping bags.

"I just got a call from the manager over at Glen Arbor. Why is your jacket and tie on the floor? We need to make our move on that unit if we're going to—" She appeared in the doorway and stopped talking as she took in his condition.

"You've been fighting."

"Yep."

"What happened?"

"Bit of a story."

"Start anywhere."

"We'd better pass on that apartment," he said.

"Why?"

"I got fired today." Silence fell between them, along with a palpable patina of worry.

"Oh my god, oh my god . . . oh my god," she said, sitting down heavily across from him.

"It'll be okay."

"Oh my god." She actually grew pale.

"Breathe," he instructed.

"I don't want to be this person, Frank . . . but I'm not working and the baby's almost here."

"It'll be okay," he said again.

"How?" she asked.

"The shingle goes back out." He shrugged. "I've always gotten by."

"Starting from scratch clientwise this time, though."

"Yep. Something will come along . . ."

"*Something will come along.*" He saw her face set in anger. "I can't believe this. We've got to let the apartment go . . ."

"Like I said, it's not a good time to—"

"You were hedging before you lost your job."

"Maybe I was," he allowed.

"And you're out careening around on this thing—"

"I was minding my damn business and got shot at—"

"You wear a gun to work," she said. "Are you really minding your business?"

There it was, a topic they'd never broached before. She hadn't mentioned a problem with what he did until now. Had she been holding back, or had things changed? It didn't matter. Here they were.

"You know what I've realized, maybe since the baby started getting close?" she asked. "That I spend my nights alone. Whether you're out working, or even when you're home. You're not focused on this baby, and you're just . . . unreachable."

It lay there, half lament, half accusation, all true. Behr cast about for a response.

"Look, it's been a tough time. That's my fault. But I'm trying . . . to focus on the baby. And I do love you, Suze. Isn't that enough?" he offered.

"Not if you won't let me do the same back to you," she said, and then searched for words. "People think unrequited love is the worst fate imaginable, but the truth is: being without either half of the equation is awful. Because it just makes you feel empty."

He felt like a child trying to process a chemistry equation. He knew what she was saying was important, but he was not capable of addressing it in a meaningful way.

"I'm not trying to shut you out. I'm just trying to put this thing down, and then . . ." Behr said, tapering off like a first-year French student, not sure what else to add.

"Then what? The next one? And one of them goes the wrong way and that's it . . . I'm afraid, Frank. Afraid that one day the lousy Snoogler is all I'm gonna have," she said, referencing that body pillow of hers with the silly name.

"Don't be afraid," he said. But it wasn't a satisfactory answer to her. The conversation became stuck in an eddy after that, and he tried to convince her to go into the bedroom and rest. But she was set on going out, to her office to talk to her boss Ed Lindsay about whether she could come back to work immediately, before the baby was born, and if not, how quickly she could come back afterward. She grabbed her purse and headed for the door.

"Susan," he called feebly, but the closing door was her final response. Behr didn't go after her. He knew she was right about all she'd said, because within a minute he felt his mind pull back to the Kolodnik case, and he let it.

The numbers associated with the tax breaks in the proposed Senate bill were huge—tens of millions, maybe hundreds. On the streets he'd seen people killed over five bucks, so what would that kind of money cause men to do? Once the fever was unleashed, values—monetary, moral, or that of human life—had a way of becoming arbitrary in a hurry.

If he looked at the thing from five miles up, it was clear enough: everyone was acting in his own self-interest. It was as simple as that and something he shouldn't have forgotten. Forces wanted Kolodnik gone. Caro wanted Behr out of the way so things were smooth with the cops. The police wanted to be the only player on the field, as they always did. Not for any grand conspiracy for the most part but for a much cleaner reason: expediency. Behr wanted to find who'd shot at him. Mothers looked out for their babies because that's what mattered to them. All these things only became a problem when agendas conflicted. But then it was indeed a problem.

Behr opened his notebook and pored over what he had and what he still didn't. Then he realized there was someone he hadn't gotten to yet, and it was time to do so. It was time to get a hold of Lowell Gantcher.

59

A Westerner's first impulse when planning a crime is: *How am I going to get away when it's done?* But Dwyer had learned an important mind-set in his days in the field in the Middle East. The first impulse in the extremist—Muslim or otherwise—is: *How can I succeed? The getaway be damned.* This was Dwyer's current attitude. He needed to get it done. Then he could return home to his mountaintop and his Sandy. But a nasty secret had reared up in him as of late. The truth was, he finally had the taste for action back in his mouth after a bit of an absence. He could keep telling himself this was about walk-away money or protecting his reputation, but he knew what it was really about: the juice. And the irony that he was using the extremist approach *in order* to get away with the original crime was not lost upon him. He felt himself starting to stumble and shake a little like a dry drunk.

Dwyer was in the living room of Pat Teague's house, off a small-town crossroads in the middle of the American flatlands. He surveyed the damaged hutch, the cracked mirror, and spilled dirt around the potted plant, and put it together with what he knew. Something had upset Pat Teague big-time. He had used his landline telephone to call a man with a warning, and Dwyer and Rickie had just gotten there and were sitting down the street listening.

"Hey, it's Teague," he'd said.

"Shit, Patty," the voice said, "is it safe to call me?"

"It's not safe anyway," Teague said.

"Oh no . . ." the voice lamented.

"You know who he's talking to?" Rickie asked.

"Nah," Dwyer said, "wish we had caller capture." On the more sophisticated version of the line tap, they'd be able to know the number he was calling, not just listen.

"The wheels are coming off this fucking thing," Teague said. "Are you still around?"

"Yeah, the son of a bitch left me," the voice said.

"Then we should meet and talk about what the hell we can do."

"Where and when?" the voice asked.

"The Steer-In, first thing tomorrow, say eight," Teague told him. "It'll be nice and quiet." Dwyer jotted down the information.

"Good," the voice said.

"Keep your head down, then," Teague advised.

"Ah, Christ," the voice whispered, "I will."

"You want to tail him to this Steer-In, see who he's meeting?" Rickie asked.

"We can't wait that long, you savvy?" Dwyer said. "We'll find out who he's gonna meet, but we're not just gonna sit here and diddle ourselves while this bastard calls everyone in his address book."

As if to confirm the statement, they heard Teague pick up and dial again.

"Hello, hon," he said.

"Hi, Pat," a woman, presumably his wife, said. "How's it going?"

"I had an issue. Got into it with someone. A real prick . . ." Teague said.

"Oh no, you all right? Was it work related?" she asked.

"Yeah, of course it was work related. I'm pretty lumped up, it'd probably be better if the kids didn't see me," he said.

"They're going up to the farm with Mom and Dad to help out after school. They were gonna stay up there for dinner," she told him.

"Good," he said, "I'm heading out to Stookey's for a cocktail—"

"This early?"

"Screw it, yeah," he said. "Then maybe I'll go and stay in the city. You want me to bring you back an order of fried catfish before I go?"

"Sure," she said. "I'm worried about you."

"Don't waste the energy," Teague said, and hung up.

Dwyer and Rickie scrambled to gear up and go in, to intercept Teague before he left, but they were too late. Almost instantly they saw him walking, with a slight limp, toward his car.

"Heading off for Stookey's, I imagine," Rickie said as Teague drove away.

"Fucking doctor of rocket science, ain't ya?" Dwyer said. "Come on, let's be waiting when he gets back home."

A good hour and a half had passed since Dwyer and Rickie had entered Teague's house. Things had finally gotten quiet back in the bedroom, where Rickie was. Dwyer was doing a little stretching in the living room when he heard the garage door start to open and it was on. He moved quickly into the kitchen, where the door from the garage let in. After a moment he heard the car door slam and saw the knob turn. He let Teague step in past him before he burst from the wall and hit the man across the back of the head with the blunt side of his newly purchased hand ax. Teague went down and Dwyer dragged him by the hair and collar into the family room where he shoved the looped detective into a chair. After a few minutes spent with his head lolling about, Teague came around and stared across at Dwyer, who had the Česká in his hand.

"You're him . . ." Teague said, slowly putting things together. "There is no Carrolton."

"No, Carrolton exists, but I'm me," Dwyer said.

"Ah, shit, this isn't my day," Teague said. Then he looked around, assessing his own home, and asked, "Where's my wife?"

"She's not home," Dwyer said.

It *had* been a bit of a surprise when she'd arrived while they were waiting, as based on the call they'd intercepted they didn't expect her until later. But they'd improvised.

"Why's her car in the garage?"

"Don't know," Dwyer said. "She parked and then went off on foot. Lucky all around."

Teague nodded and glanced over Dwyer's shoulder toward the bedroom.

"Who decorated your face?" Dwyer asked.

"Some asshole from work," Teague said.

"Wouldn't be Frank Behr, would it?" Dwyer said, planting a look of shock in Teague's eyes.

"Who?" Teague said, doing his best to fall back on his training that had been too long neglected.

"Look, man," Dwyer said, "you should drop the counter interrogation, and then I won't need to use counter resistance, and we can just move things along. Otherwise I'll go pull the battery out of your car and we'll get to it."

Teague nodded warily.

"Who have you told, and what have you told them?" Dwyer asked.

"Nothing to no one," Teague said. "I thought you were a pro. Hire you, the job gets done, and everybody's insulated. That's what they all said."

"We try," Dwyer said, tamping down his fury at the criticism, "but life's full of imperfections, ain't it?"

"I haven't told anyone anything," Teague repeated, looking over Dwyer's shoulder toward his bedroom once more.

"Try again," Dwyer said.

"No one who didn't know already," Teague said. "Behr found out some of it, all right? Some of the basics. How it got started. But nothing about you."

"Nothing about me?" Dwyer said. "That's good fucking news. Why am I supposed to believe it?"

Teague looked over Dwyer's shoulder again. *Did he see some-*

thing there? Dwyer wondered. *Was it unusual for the bedroom door to be shut?*

"Who are you meeting tomorrow morning?" Dwyer asked.

"How the hell do you—"

"Does it matter?" Dwyer cut him off. "Who?"

Teague didn't answer. Instead he looked back at the bedroom door yet again. Then his face changed, and whatever semblance of professionalism he'd been holding onto started to give way.

"I really need to know my wife is okay," he said.

"Come on now. Focus. Who are you meeting tomorrow?"

Teague shook his head. Dwyer saw the transition as the wondering got to the man and his face crumbled and he sobbed. "Oh, Margie . . ."

"Don't you do it, man," Dwyer warned. "Steady."

But it was too late. Teague was cracked. He went for his hip. But he was hopelessly slow. Dwyer gave him a double tap to the sternum. The report of the shots was muffled, short and sharp in the small room, like dry wood cracking in a fire. Teague fell forward out of the chair onto his face. His shirt rode up and revealed he was wearing a gun. Dwyer stood and fired once more into the back of his head. The door to the bedroom was open now, as Rickie came out to check what was happening, and the sight Teague had been so afraid to see was now finally visible. A leg hung heavily from the edge of the bed, a loose sock dangling limply off the end of the foot.

"How's mum?" Dwyer asked, bending to pick up his brass shell casings.

"She had her fun, but now she's done, the old girl," Rickie said. The kid was really quite amazing.

"We're getting busy," Dwyer said, standing. "We've gotta get you your own banger."

Then they started to wipe down surfaces.

60

The attempt to get face-to-face with Gantcher at his downtown office started off just as easily as the foray at the casino but went wrong just as quickly. Many office buildings in Indianapolis don't have lobby security, and Behr was happy to find that Gantcher's was one of them. He went straight to the elevators and rode up to the eighth floor where the company was housed. A left turn out of the elevator put him in front of a set of large glass doors etched with the initials "LGE," and behind them was the anteroom of Lowell Gantcher Entertainment. A pair of receptionists sat inside, and two things became immediately clear to Behr: that Gantcher was in there too, and that he wasn't getting in. The reason being that a professional security force was camped out right in front. While Behr didn't see the men he'd tangled with at the casino, he spotted four operatives milling around, using the phone, talking to the receptionists, and sitting on the guest chairs. He slowed as much as seemed natural as he passed by and considered the likelihood that there were at least another one or two inside the work area, if not many more. He thought about running a pretext in order to talk his way in—real estate appraiser, mortgage broker, Web site builder—but it seemed like a long shot he'd get past the bunch of pros hanging around, especially in the jeans and T-shirt he was now wearing, so he continued on past, eyes front, without breaking stride until he reached the fire stairs and descended. A repeat scuffle in an effort to get to Gantcher wasn't going to do him any good.

Once outside the office building he made for his car and sat there for a long time, staring out the window at the street, thinking. He needed to interrogate Lowell Gantcher, but he couldn't get to him. He also wanted to get a hold of Kolodnik's adviser Shug Saunders, but Behr could practically picture him on Capitol Hill, overtan, slickly dressed, and cozying up to the boss he was involved in trying to remove. He dialed Kolodnik's office anyway, hoping he could get some information out of the secretary or book an appointment. It'd be worth a drive to Washington.

"Shug Saunders please," Behr said.

"He's not in, but I'll connect you to his office," a receptionist's voice cooed. After a few rings an automated voice mail picked up and offered him the chance to leave a message, which, pointless as it was, he took.

"Hello, Shug," he said. "This is Frank Behr. We met a little while ago over at your offices and I was hoping to talk to you about something important, so please give me a call." Behr left his number and hung up.

He was stuck and frustrated and without direction or answers. Hikers lost in the mountains are advised to stop and stay still and wait to be rescued, but Behr knew no one was coming to find him. Only his experience told him not to give up, that if he could just look at the situation with focus for long enough, an angle would present itself and he would finally see it. He flipped pages in his notebook, scanning his notes, when something caught in his mind and stopped him. It was a question he'd asked and gotten a response to, but it was not an answer he should've accepted.

Who did the hiring? he'd asked Pat Teague.

I don't have a clue. Not a damn clue, is what Teague had told him. Behr pictured the man's face, sweaty and beaten. His eyes, glazed in anger and defeat, had flashed downward. And Behr's own rage, his indignation at being set up, had caused him to career ahead without probing further. That was the moment, and he'd missed it. Whoever it was that had supplied the money—Shugie Saunders or Lowell Gantcher or the two of them together—and whichever one of them had initiated the plot, who involved was most likely to know how to hire a professional contractor? It was Teague all the way.

Goddammit, Behr hissed, already dialing. But he got no answer from Pat Teague. Behr let it ring and ring, and then he put his car in gear. He was going to have to drive out to Thorntown again.

61

The man has money, but he lives like absolute swine, Dwyer thought. He was standing in Shugie Saunders's walk-in closet in front of a row of expensive but garish suits. There was another row of dress shirts, many with sweat rings around the collar and armpits that laundering had only faded but didn't remove. The enclosed space smelled like feet, thanks to the pile of cheap shoes on the floor, many with their soles and heels worn to the uppers. Dwyer had been over the place with painstaking detail, from the dirty dishes in the sink to towels piled on the bathroom floor. First he'd called, then waited in front of the building for a couple of fruitless hours until he was convinced that the man wasn't home and was probably off in Washington, before making entry. The building had an external fire stairway and Dwyer was able to jump from it to a neighboring balcony, cross two more, and reach Saunders's. A six-inch lockout tool easily popped the glass slider and he was in.

What he hadn't found was a safe, but neither had he come upon any documents implicating him and Shugie. Dwyer *had* found a checkbook with a balance of $62,000, and this was in his pocket. Three months earlier there had been more than $100,000 in the account, so the man was on a bit of a spending spree.

Dwyer took in the apartment, which he'd thoroughly tossed, a final time. He wasn't sure why, but he now had the feeling Saunders hadn't left town permanently for D.C., but that he must be staying elsewhere. No discernible amount of clothing and toiletries were missing—there were several large pieces of luggage in the top of a hall closet—so it was likely a short trip if Dwyer was right in the first place. As tempting as it was to wait out Saunders's possible return for another hour or day, Dwyer and Rickie had agreed to rally back at the shite hole after their respective actions. One never knew if one's partner in the field might need support, so he had to keep discipline and make the meet. Dwyer did a quick wipe down of the doorknobs and let himself out the front door.

62

A piece of storm cloud snaked its way into Behr's belly when he reached the head of Teague's street. There were police cars and an ambulance and neighbors lining the block, and like a funnel of bad news it all led to Teague's door. Behr parked as close as he could and advanced through the onlookers toward the house and was just in time to see a stretcher bearing a loaded body bag being carried out.

"What happened?" Behr asked those in his general vicinity.

A woman with a tearstained face didn't turn toward him, but just kept her eyes on the stretcher as she spoke. "Someone killed the Teagues."

"All of them?" Behr asked, sick with the knowledge that Pat had four children.

"Both of them," a man in a checked shirt said, rubbing the back of his brush cut head. "Pat and his wife. The kids weren't home . . ."

"Thank god," the woman said with a half sob, "those poor babies . . ."

There was assorted talk about who could've done the crime in this quiet community, and the quick consensus was gangbangers down from the city looking for easy drug money via robbery.

"Son of a bitches," the man in the checked shirt said through gritted teeth. "I've got a Remington twelve gauge's gonna be waiting by my bed if them junkies want to try this town again."

Behr wondered if any of the neighbors had seen *him* coming or going earlier, or if Teague had told any friends of their run-in and *he* was the one headed for a police interview room. He drifted away from the group and moved closer to the house and found a spot near some officers by the door where he listened to fragments of their radio chatter.

". . . yeah, the resident was male, Caucasian, early fifties. GSWs to chest and head, over."

". . . deceased was law enforcement, or ex-law enforcement, retired FBI . . ."

". . . victim two, spouse, also early fifties . . ."

"GSWs, over?"

"Negative. Stabbing . . . or, well, slashing, chopping really, with a bladed weapon, over . . ."

". . . Homicide and robbery units on scene, copy . . ."

Behr dropped back from the house and passed through the crowd toward his car.

"What they ought to do is check his old cases, see if some serial killer or felon he put away was recently released," a bystander voiced to some murmured agreement.

Behr knew he wasn't getting inside. He had no pull with the cops out here, and no standing as one of Teague's coworkers anymore. It didn't matter. There'd be nothing in there for him by way of evidence. The doer was a professional, and while the neighbors may have wanted to speculate over vengeful master criminals with vendettas, the killing of Pat Teague represented another loose end snipped off by the cold player he was chasing. He imagined the wife was an accident, collateral. Perhaps she'd walked in at the wrong time or the guy couldn't wait until she'd left. Or he'd used her to get Teague to talk. Regardless, this guy was stone coldblooded in everything he did.

It wouldn't be long before Potempa and the rest of Caro received word and traveled out in a caravan to gather up around the surviving family. Behr, as he returned home, imagined he was driving east past them as they went west to Teague's.

63

Dwyer was sitting in the shite hole drinking a Newcastle and looking out the window when Rickie arrived, and he couldn't help laughing at the sight of oversized Ruthless in his silly little Japanese motor. He could practically stick his arms out the windows and his feet out the floor and carry it around his waist as if going to a costume party dressed as a car. When he got out, he looked a little weary but otherwise unfettered.

He carried a plastic rubbish bag in his left hand and walked into the room.

"I'll have one of those, please," Rickie said of Dwyer's Newcastle. Dwyer pointed to the remainder of the sixer in a plastic ice bucket.

"Did you get him?" he asked.

"Nah," Rickie said, popping open the ale. "I waited as long as I thought it was wise."

"So, nothing then?" Dwyer asked.

"Well . . ." Rickie said, and went into the bathroom. Dwyer heard him empty the contents of the bin bag into the sink and turn on the faucet. He got to the door in time to see the water run pink over the tools in the basin.

"What happened?" Dwyer demanded.

Rickie met his eyes in the mirror. "I had to do the big guy's wife."

64

The first thing Behr saw when he walked into his house was blood—what looked like gallons of it—on the diamond-tiled floor near the door, slowly spreading in every direction, and lapping over plastic shopping bags from Target. His world flipped upside down in that instant and he fought a roaring surge of panic. A dead woman lay on the floor in his entryway. She was pregnant and blond, her throat slit and bled out, her hands folded over her abdomen. His mind fought to process what he was seeing . . . she was six inches shorter and five years younger than Susan, and there were some dark roots showing along her scalp, which was mostly soaked red. A cold wave of relief and crushing dismay collided within him. The dead woman was Gina Decker.

He crouched to touch her neck for a pulse, but saw it was more than just cut—it was opened up in horrific fashion, chopped away in a deep, wide arc from ear to ear beneath her chin. She hadn't lost all her heat yet, but it was going quickly. He put a hand on her belly, which was still and without life.

Behr muttered a stream of epithets and what passed for prayers as he dialed Susan. His call passed straight to voice mail and he went white with fresh fear before he remembered that she was at a doctor's appointment. He speed-dialed the gynecologist and got a receptionist who told him, "She's in with him now. Any message?"

"Tell her not to leave alone."

He hung up on her and dialed 911, calling the police and an ambulance to his house and police to the doctor's office for Susan.

His next call was to Eddie Decker, and he felt his voice go flat.

"It's Frank Behr. My place. Get here now," was all he said.

He looked around for evidence or clues of any kind, but nothing looked out of place. The thing appeared to have been coolly and expertly handled. His head was swimming, though, so short of whoever did it crouching in the corner, he had to allow he was probably going to miss anything subtle.

Two patrol cars arrived first, the whoop of sirens breaking him out of his head-down, trancelike stare at the body. Four officers—three men and a woman—appeared at his entryway, and he moved aside to let them in. They were silenced by what they saw, save the youngest male in the group who looked like he was fifteen but must have been past twenty-one, who doubled over and gulped and dry-heaved but managed not to vomit.

"What happened?" asked Sergeant Ryan, the female officer, who seemed to be senior in the group.

"My name is Frank Behr," he said, showing his old three-quarter tin and his driver's and P.I. licenses. "This is my residence. I returned home to this. Her name is Gina Decker. She's my wife's friend and married to an IPD officer."

They reacted to this news, but before anything else could be said, another car raced up and ground to a halt outside. Behr saw it was Decker, in uniform, getting out of his cruiser, and hurried down to meet him.

"Behr . . ." Decker said.

"This thing I'm in the middle of . . ." Behr began, "someone came for me. Susan was going to be collateral. But Susan, she wasn't here . . ." Behr felt Decker's black, knowing eyes search his own.

"Gina," Decker said. He must have known his wife's schedule. He practically ran through Behr up the steps and knocked the young officer, who was exiting the front door, flat on his ass.

A blood-in-the-esophagus wail echoed from inside when

Decker saw her, and the officers inside were not equipped for what happened next. By the time Behr got there Decker was tearing the place apart. A chair exploded against a wall. A left-right combination blew holes clean through the drywall next to it. A kick turned more drywall to powder, but also found a stud that cracked in half under the boot heel. None of them could get close to him. Decker turned, his eyes wild with pain and rage, and he moved for the door. The older male officer tried to put a comforting, restraining hand on Decker's shoulder, but he ended up slumped against the doorframe for his trouble. Behr followed Decker down and out into the street. He was headed for his car.

"Uh-uh, Eddie," Behr shouted. He knew if Decker got behind the wheel, somebody was going to die.

Behr reached him just as he was opening the driver's side door. He didn't pull Decker, but instead pushed him forward, using his own momentum, into the side of the cruiser, and tried to wrap him up from behind. Decker caught Behr's elbow and spun him, slamming him into the rear door. Behr fought to hang on to him, and finally got his arm over and around Decker's in a whizzer, then clapped his other hand around the back of Decker's head, who in turn got an under hook on Behr, and then they clinched.

Decker drove Behr back into the police car again, standing him up. Decker was strong, that much was clear. The man was a beast. He wasn't just stronger than Behr, he was exponentially so, like a lion or a gorilla would be. Behr tried to use his height for leverage, leaning down upon and sinking his weight onto Decker's shoulders, but Decker fired his legs and whipped Behr around like a rag doll. Behr stumbled but kept his feet. Barely. He recranked the whizzer and then jerked hard and fast to the other side, unbalancing Decker. Decker went with it, though, yanking them both to the ground, as if he were pulling guard, but instead of wrapping his legs around Behr's body, he jammed them inside Behr's legs—butterfly guard—then rocked back, extending his legs. Behr felt himself travel up, flying through the air in an elevator sweep, and landed hard on his back. It was no massage, but nothing broke or tore either, and he managed to grab Decker's wrist as it was being yanked away, and keep it. He used it to pull himself forward, and Decker toward him, until he caught the sleeve of Decker's other arm. Behr gator-rolled, keeping them on the ground, spinning them in a cloud of dust. After three revolutions, the rough dirt and gravel scraping their elbows, hips, and knees, Behr stopped them and went for a front headlock that he hoped to convert to an anaconda choke. If it's not applied perfectly and sunk deep, the anaconda becomes something of a strength move which doesn't work on a powerful, educated opponent; and Decker was on his way to ripping loose from it when the other cops on the scene got with the program.

Behr felt Decker torn free of his grasp as the four officers tackled the wild man to the ground and restrained him. Decker was in the process of wearing out—Behr certainly was—and his fury gave way to grief, and the howling sound that issued from beneath the pile of officers was more animal than human.

The scene got thick with official vehicles within moments: more police cars—marked and unmarked—an ambulance, and a coroner's van. A hoard of officers descended to keep neighbors and a few arriving news crews back. Another group gathered around Decker. Sergeant Ryan and her partner had sat him in their cruiser and were attempting to comfort him, before they finally got him into an ambulance and Behr was oddly left alone for the moment when the dark Crown Vic that Breslau drove rolled up.

The lieutenant jumped out and crossed inside the perimeter to Behr, but this time his attitude was different from the other times they'd spoken.

"We're in this thing now," was the first thing Breslau said. "I just want you to know that. You can't murder an officer's wife. There's no fucking way, and we're going to make that clear . . . Now, who came after you?"

"I wish I knew. Believe me," Behr answered.

"Bullshit," Breslau grunted.

"You think I'd bullshit you on *that*?"

"Then what do you have?" Breslau asked.

Behr gave him a thumbnail of what he'd learned, including what he'd just seen over in Thorntown. Breslau was silent, working his gum with his front teeth as he wrote it down in his notebook.

"I left here a few hours ago, and what happened to Teague was pretty fresh," Behr said. "I must've just missed the guy."

"Unless there's more than one," Breslau pointed out. It was a good point, one that a layer of objectivity provided. Behr should've thought that way on his own.

"What do you have on the guy who got burned?" Behr asked.

"A whole lot of nothing. He rented that apartment with cash. Security deposit was a money order. There are tracks to another apartment and another alias," Breslau said. "Do you have anything else? Any ideas?"

"You've got to grab Shugie Saunders, Kolodnik's political adviser. He's probably in D.C."

"I know who he is. Why would he want to cancel his own meal ticket?" Breslau said.

"Don't do it, then, just let the city turn into a goddamned butcher shop," Behr said. He'd never encountered human death in such a concentrated way, and it was preying on his remaining sense of balance.

"All right, don't get fucking testy," Breslau said. "I'm just saying how?"

"He found a better ride," Behr said.

Breslau looked at him and nodded for him to continue.

"One of Kolodnik's old partners. Lowell Gantcher."

"You got reports, hard linkage, substantiation?" Breslau asked greedily.

"I'm working on it," Behr said. "I got a woman who was the nexus between Saunders and Teague. Not Gantcher, specifically, but there must be some connection there, too."

"What 'woman'?"

"One who knows," Behr said, seeing a cruiser pull up with Susan in it, "but not a very presentable witness."

"Junkie?"

"Close. Escort."

Breslau winced. "Not being a jerk off here," he said, "but I can't go bunge up some solid citizen with *that*."

"What the hell *are* you doing, then?" Behr asked.

"Exploring all the known business associates, digging into other shit. We've got to be exhaustive now," Breslau said. "You know how it is." Behr did. If it wasn't a lack of resources these days, it was fear of being sued. It had law enforcement pretty well shackled.

Susan was out of the cruiser now, taking in the scene with confusion.

"I'm telling you, give Saunders a look," Behr said. "*He's* not so solid that you can't get away with it."

Behr broke off and went to Susan.

"Frank . . . ?" she said.

It was a disaster. He told her and stopped her from going inside. But she screamed and cried as he talked to her and tried to hold her. He gave her water, which she batted away, and tried to sit her in his car, which she refused. She hyperventilated and nearly collapsed, though he managed to catch her; and the paramedics on-site, who could do nothing for Gina, swooped in and gave her oxygen and checked the baby's heart rate, which was elevated, but not dangerously so.

She finally calmed, but then said, "Gina made a run to Target for baby stuff for us, and was dropping off mine—" which set off another paroxysm of grief. Behr tried to ride the waves and noted when various arms of the police finished their work and departed. The homicide unit was done with the scene, having photographed it and tried for prints. He saw the coroners carry out the bagged body, the plastic higher in the middle from the baby bump, and he physically held Susan's face, keeping her eyes on his so she wouldn't see it. Not long after that they were done inside, and an officer gave him a wave.

"Babe, I need three minutes before I bring you in," he said, because he knew that while the authorities do cart the bodies away, they don't clean up.

Somewhere close to catatonia, she nodded, and he hurried away.

Passing by a departing deputy coroner, Behr paused to ask, "What did this?"

"Initial guess, based on the tissue damage, some kind of hand ax," the deputy said, continuing on. Behr gathered himself and moved inside.

He had worked three months in a slaughterhouse one summer many years back, right before college, and beside the sights of shit-stained animal flanks and offal running in cement trenches, the sounds of electric saws and bolt guns, and the lifers who thought nothing was funnier than flicking blobs of fat and meat off the end of their boning knives into the necks of the new-bies like stinging projectiles, the fecund smell of blood and fear was one he'd never forget. It was in his nose now, as he crawled about and went through three rolls of paper towels, soaking his knees while trying to blot up the coagulating fluid and make the entranceway passable. He splashed pine-scented cleaning solu-tion onto the tiles, the grout in between them turning pink, in hopes of knocking down the odor. Sweat ran into his eyes and burned them until they teared.

When he had done what he could, he went and tried his best to clean his hands and then saw Susan in. Being inside where it had happened, seeing the broken walls and furniture, which had actually been damaged by Decker, and stepping over the still damp and not properly clean floor, set her off again. By now, though, her grief had lost some of its force to exhaustion and Behr got her into the bedroom, and sat her down on the bed where he stroked her hair for half an hour, hoping she would pass out.

The situation outside had calmed. The neighbors and other onlookers, including the news crews, had called it a day. There were only a few police cars left. One belonged to the last pair of officers at the location; the other was Decker's. He had been carted away in an ambulance filled with his brother cops at some point. Behr had lost track of Breslau too and he, as well as his Crown Vic, was now gone. But there was another Crown Vic outside. This one was silver. It was his old boss's car. Major Pomeroy. Behr walked outside and saw him behind the wheel on his cell phone. When Pomeroy saw Behr, he hung up and got out.

"Major," Behr said, greeting the tall, silver-haired man. He hadn't tended to the thin side, but now he was cadaverously so, as if the worries of higher command had counteracted all the big lunches and desk work of his captaincy and eaten away all nonessential flesh. His eyes were like dark agate marbles sunk in pale dough.

"I recognized the address when the call came through," Pomeroy said. "How's Officer Decker in this?"

It was no social drop-in. "The women were friends," Behr said.

"I see . . ." Pomeroy said. "I've been made aware that he put himself in this thing, that he might've shared department information with you."

"He didn't put himself in it," Behr said. "Some asshole showed up looking to kill me, or me and my girlfriend, and his wife happened to be here."

"And the information?" Pomeroy pressed.

Behr said nothing.

"Right . . ." Pomeroy said. "Well, I've gotta have someone on this." Behr could only admire the unbelievable, self-cleaning organ that was the police department. "Seems like Decker's paid enough."

Behr could only nod.

"Due to the . . . political nature . . . of it, it's raining big juice on this one, and you can't stand under our umbrella. Lay off it, Frank."

"Unbelievable." Behr nodded once more. He knew what it meant: he was done with the department. Whatever anemic courtesy he might have ever gotten was now history. He'd been on this side before, for a long time. He'd only recently been in good standing. It was a shame to have to go back so soon, but he'd survived it in the past and he would again.

"You have no idea how the upper ranks of the department work—it's like the Vatican," Pomeroy said by way of absolving himself.

"Decker will be untouched?"

"He'll be untouched."

"Just so you know, I didn't go looking for any of it—someone shot at me," Behr said, walking back toward his house.

"Hey, this is the business we've chosen," Pomeroy said, his arms outstretched and palms turned up.

When Behr came back in, he took care to be quiet in order not to disturb Susan, but soon found that she hadn't been resting. She'd been packing.

"What's going on?" he asked when he saw her in the kitchen filling a water bottle, a shoulder duffel and her pillow in a garbage bag at her feet.

"I've gotta go, Frank. I'm sorry."

"What?"

"I just can't be here now."

"That's understandable, Suze," he said. "How about if we go to a hotel? Where you can relax . . ."

"I don't think so," she said in a tone that sent a chill through him.

"You're leaving? For good?" Behr said, a near-desperate feeling taking hold of his insides. "You can't. It's not safe, if someone's looking for you I need to be able to—"

"They're looking for *you*, Frank," she said with regret. "I'll—we'll—be safer . . . away from you."

"Where are you going?"

"Chicago. To my parents, I think," she said.

"What about the doctor, and the delivery?" he asked.

"I don't know," she said. "There are doctors there. That's two weeks from now anyway—"

"If he waits—"

"If he waits. I have to worry about today. About tomorrow."

Behr just shook his head at what had fallen, one domino at a time, and how they had ended up here.

"I need you to drive me back to my car. It's at the doctor's office."

65

It was an evening of what Dwyer called "hopeless sits." They'd been out to Kolodnik's residence, gotten a vantage, and found the massive home darkened. They sat silently in the woods for an hour, hoping someone—Kolodnik himself even—might arrive. Dwyer had been following news of the man and it seemed he was off for the country's capital for his coronation, or whatever the hell it was called. But one never knew when a subject's plans changed or when the news cunts might be wrong. Night stalking like this always reminded him of diving, the limited yet purposeful actions, the effort to preserve stillness and quiet. After another few minutes in their positions, it was time to play the percentages, and Dwyer tapped Rickie on the leg and signaled: back to the car.

Then they'd made their way downtown to Saunders's building again. They'd called and gone up and knocked, but there was no answer. They returned to the car to wait for a bit, though Dwyer had all but changed his mind and accepted that the man must have left town with his boss. While they sat, Dwyer used the laptop to book them back out of town the following afternoon, Rickie from Indianapolis, and he from Chicago. Once they had staked out Teague's intended morning meeting and seen what it was all about and had visited Gantcher one last time to collect the money, their business would be done. Then, since the element of surprise had been ceded, they could go straight on and hard at this Behr, clean that up, and head directly for the airport. When he'd finished the bookings and closed the laptop, Dwyer turned to Rickie, who had been unusually quiet.

"Brief me on your action of this afternoon," Dwyer said.

"I don't really feel like it," Rickie said.

"I don't really give a fuck how you feel," Dwyer said. "Do it." A harsh order could be comforting to a certain kind of lad.

Rickie nodded. "I'd just gotten there, and I mean literally just inside the door, when I heard the car and looked out. I saw her parked at the curb and coming to the door with her hands full of plastic shopping bags and her keys around her knuckle. So I timed it with her walking up the steps, opened the door, and yanked her in. Pretty certain no one outside could have seen it."

"Good. Then?" Dwyer asked.

"Then she screamed and I closed off her mouth, and put her to the floor and started an interrogation. Bad bit o' business she was knocked up, but I figured it would make her talk quick," Rickie said.

" 'Where's your husband?' I asked her. 'He's at work,' she said. So I says, 'What's he working on? When's he home?' And, believe me, she was in no position to lie." Rickie paused and made a hatchet-against-neck gesture.

"Fucking Ruthless," Dwyer said.

"That's me," Rickie said. "She keeps on with the 'I don't know,' and adds 'His shift's over at six.' I thinks, 'Six is too bloody long to wait 'round.' We go back and forth another few times— 'Where's your husband? Where's Frank? What does he know?' 'I have no idea,' she says. 'No idea.' The cheeky little gash wouldn't give him up. Then one last time, 'Where's your husband?' And she says, 'He's a cop, you can't do this.' But by then she'd seen me, so I had to do it, o' course."

"Cop?" Dwyer said.

"Yeah. Cop, private cop—what's the difference?"

"What'd she look like?" Dwyer said, suddenly troubled.

"Good looking. Blond and preggers, like you told me. Young, ya know," Rickie said.

"How young?"

"Late twenties. 'Bout five foot and a few—"

"You mean near six foot," Dwyer said.

"No, she was a little thing. Come on, man, you're starting to make me feel bad."

Dwyer turned to him. "You sure of who you grabbed over there?"

"I was a go on the guy and a pregnant blond slag, Waddy, I wasn't checking IDs. How many of 'em they have running around here?" Rickie said.

Dwyer shrugged. "May have been a wrong woman. Friend or neighbor."

"Fuck me backward," Rickie said with force, and then the big kid's shoulders sagged.

"Shame about the wee one . . ." Dwyer said.

"Yah," Rickie agreed.

"Well, don't get down about it," Dwyer said. "It'll be over tomorrow. That fancy bastard will either pay, or he'll pay, and we'll be done."

They sat there in a long moment of contemplation and then Dwyer put the car in gear.

66

Behr dropped Susan off at her car in her doctor's parking lot and stood there and watched everything he loved drive off into the night. He'd been unable to convince her to do otherwise. He considered putting a fist through his passenger side window, but suddenly felt overwhelmingly tired. He staggered around the car and got in and drove back across the city. The downtown area felt deserted, as if everyone had decided en masse to go inside or otherwise hide.

He passed by the statehouse, big and brilliant white and lit up, the place where laws where supposed to be tended and fairness and justice meted out. Instead, it seemed to be the central nest of rot. It needed some brighter lights, Behr thought, or, better yet, turn them out altogether. He braked at North Capitol for the only other vehicle in sight—a white carriage pulled by a dappled draft horse, head nodding at each step with the effort. Behr listened to the clopping of hooves on pavement along with the rattle of wooden wheels. A man in a fleece vest and a top hat steered by and touched his brim in greeting. Behr watched for a long time and then drove on.

Before long he reached Crows Nest, one of the ritziest enclaves of high-dollar houses in the area, which Lowell Gantcher called home. He was running on fumes, but needed to get to the man. Behr drove down Sunset Lane, looking at the impressive mansions, checking the gold numbers affixed to mailboxes near wrought iron gates and wooded driveways. He spotted Gantcher's home, regal and imposing, if not a little newly built looking next to some of its ivy-covered companions. The designer had been conscientious, though, because a ruff of thick old growth trees that circled the rear of the house had been left standing. Behr slowed at one end of a large U-shaped driveway. The news was bad once again. There were three vehicles parked in front of the house and all the lights were on. A pair of strapping men stood outside the front door, and through a large window Behr could see about three or four more men moving about in shirtsleeves and what looked like handgun shoulder rigs. It was about this time the guys at the door started noticing him and were moving down the driveway toward him, so Behr took the opportunity to motor on.

When he got home, his place smelled of pine cleaning fluid, a chilling reminder of what had happened earlier, and it was too quiet, as if the walls were mourning the deaths and departures of the expectant mothers. Behr pulled the cork on a bottle of Harlan Estate and didn't wait before filling a Ball jar and drinking it down quickly. He sat there, still and dumb, and watched the wine go down past the label and finally to the bottom and it wasn't enough. He pushed himself up and got a gallon slugger of Wild Turkey, the same one he and Decker had put the dent in so recently.

Gina Decker. He'd barely known her, but she was a lively little sprite. Neither she nor her child nor Decker himself, regardless of the sins he'd committed, deserved what had befallen them. Every creak in the settling house made him wonder if he—the professional contractor, or *contractors* plural—was coming for him. He rested his gun on the table next to him.

He'd lost Susan and it hurt, but he wasn't sure if it was something he should be sorry over, because he and his way of life were toxic. That much was as clear to him now as ever. He was poison to everything and everyone around him. It was starting to get easy to be glad that she and the baby were gone. They were safer, better off away from him. He poured another bourbon, grabbed his phone, and moved to the couch. He set his gun on the arm of the couch and checked his lone incoming text. It was from Susan: *I made it.*

He punched out an inadequate text to her: *Good.*

When that was done he sent one more: *Decker—call me if you want, Behr.* At some point he fell asleep in his clothes.

67

Behr's phone beeped and he sat up. It was early morning and he was still on the couch, and though it had been set to vibrate so he hadn't heard it ring, the tone signaled that he had a voice mail.

"Behr, it's Breslau . . . Look, we can't find Saunders. We don't have any contact info for him in D.C. We tried the home, we tried the place of business. You have any ideas where he might be, you let me know."

Behr didn't, not at the moment. He went and stood under the shower, freezing needles of water driving away the alcohol portion of his hangover. It was going to take a lot more than that to get rid of the emotional part. As he turned off the water a sentence came into his head. *"Due to the political nature of it . . ."* It was what Pomeroy had said. It was what was driving all the pressure.

When he dried off and dressed, he knew what he had to do. He dug around on his dresser and found the heavy stock business card that Kolodnik had given him. He looked at the name and the cell number for a long moment before dialing. He could only hope that Kolodnik hadn't changed numbers or been issued a U.S. Senate phone or any number of circumstances that would cost him a trip to Washington. But after four rings a voice answered.

"Hello?" It was Kolodnik. It was 7:00 a.m., but the man hadn't been sleeping.

"It's Frank Behr," he began, suddenly dry mouthed. "I need to talk to you about what went down in that garage and I need you to be forthcoming, because bodies are stacking up like cordwood around here."

"Oh lord . . ." A long pause elapsed, then Kolodnik let out a slow breath. "All right, Behr," he said, "we'll go ahead this once. But you're not to repeat it to anyone, or I'll deny it forcefully, and regardless this will be the last time we speak."

"Fine," Behr said, seeing as he had no choice.

"Are you on a landline?" Kolodnik asked.

"Yes," Behr said.

"Well, I'm not. Give me your number."

Behr did so, and Kolodnik abruptly hung up. A momentary sickness hit Behr in the gut. He knew Kolodnik wasn't calling back, and that'd be the end of it. But the phone rang almost instantly. The man was as good as his word.

"What is it you want?" Kolodnik asked.

"You know who was behind the attempt?" Behr asked.

"I have an idea. I don't have every nut and bolt."

"A business partner and an employee," Behr said.

"Yes. Ex-business partner, if we're being specific."

"Then you got into it, didn't you? The way the case was handled by the police."

"I did."

"The security tapes. You squelched 'em."

"I asked a favor. Look, the truth is, they were grainy. The shooter was wearing a hood. The cops got a license plate that everyone knew would come back a dummy."

"The plate wasn't a complete dead end," Behr said.

"I heard something about you and a fire. I really hope you take care of yourself and this doesn't cost you any more trouble, Behr," Kolodnik said. The man had no idea what it had cost him. "If there comes a time when certain individuals are facing prosecution, I won't get in the way. I'll even support the case any way I can . . ." The next part seemed like it took plenty for Kolodnik to say, but he went on with a clear voice. "The cleanest part of the video was me flopped on my belly with my hands over my head.

You, on the other hand, looked like G.I. Joe, but I just couldn't launch my political career with that footage out there on the Web. My adversaries would've used it for decades to come."

So instead you went with good old vanity and suppression. Behr thought it, but he didn't say it. He still felt a current of respect for the soon-to-be sworn senator on the other end of the line.

"And Saunders gets a free pass? 'Keep your enemies close?' " Behr wondered.

"Not exactly," Kolodnik said. "Shugie is smart, but he's weak and greedy, and he let himself get distracted, but I didn't give him a free pass. I left him behind to look after my local interests . . ."

"He's *here*?" Behr gripped the phone tighter.

"Yes."

It was a chilly, bloodless thing for Kolodnik to do, because he was more than smart enough to realize what was going to happen to Shugie Saunders now. Behr knew it was the last conversation between them, as Bernie Cool had stated, and that he would undoubtedly have a thousand questions fly into his head later, but he had the sudden need to get off the call. If Shugie Saunders was still in Indy, the contractor would surely be going after him and that might represent Behr's last shot at him.

"I do appreciate that night, Behr," Kolodnik said, "and so does my family. And I know you're aware that if any of this gets out, it'll badly hurt the state. You don't want to hurt the state, Frank, do you?"

"No, sir, I don't want to hurt the state."

"Now, I have to go on and do this Senate thing, see where it leads. I know you're going to do what you have to, and I wish you luck."

"Roger that," Behr said, hung up, and went for his car.

He didn't get that far, because as he walked outside beneath heavy and darkening clouds, he found Eddie Decker pacing around his silver Camaro, which was parked in Behr's driveway.

"Hey," Decker said, looking at him with abject pain in his black eyes, which were barely visible for the dark circles beneath them.

"Hey," Behr said. "How long you been here?"

"Two hours?" Decker shrugged.

"You okay?" Behr asked.

"Nope," Decker said, then extended an envelope. "Here."

Behr looked inside and saw seven hundred in cash.

"I shouldn't have tore up your house."

The damage and the money didn't matter to Behr, but he understood Decker had to make the gesture.

"Thank you," Behr said, "I accept." Then he extended the money back to Decker. "And I want you to accept this, for funeral expenses. *I* insist." Decker met his eyes. There wasn't much resistance there. He nodded and took the money back, and it was clear it was not something that they would discuss again.

"You got anything on who did it?" Decker asked.

Behr hesitated and felt the grimace on his own face. Whatever he might find by catching up with Shugie Saunders would not be helped by having an emotionally on-edge Decker along with him.

"I want in," Decker said, reading his thoughts.

"You think it's a good idea?" Behr asked.

"No."

"Take some time?" Behr offered.

"Hell no."

"You drive," Behr said, moving for the Camaro.

68

Shug Saunders sat in a back booth of the Steer-In and poured a swirling ribbon of cream into his ink-black coffee. His triglyceride level dictated he ought to be using skim milk or better yet no dairy at all, but now what difference did it make? He felt like he was in quicksand, falling down a hole, with the hole closing right on top of him.

"We're going to need you to stay back, be the home base guy for the time being, Shug."

"But, Bernie, I—"

"Yes, you had much to do with this, and the gratitude is there, but everyone needs to do his part now . . ."

That was how the brief meeting with Kolodnik had gone a few days back, when Shug had been told he wasn't going to D.C. It felt like a life sentence. He'd analyzed every word of their conversation, as he had every conversation between him and Kolodnik since the night of the incident.

Does he know? It was the question that burned in Shug's brain 24-7 now. At first it had been there only during his every waking moment, but there was little sleep lately. Some wise man once said: "The guilty wish to be caught."

Yeah? Well bullshit to that, was Shug's feeling on the matter.

The waitress headed his way. "You ready to order, or you still want to wait, sugar?" she asked.

Where the hell was Pat Teague? Shug wondered.

"Guess I'll keep waiting," he said. Then a slight smile suddenly appeared on his lips. It was odd considering his situation, the danger of it, but despite all that, the last two days had been the most wonderful, amazing days of his life. "You know what?" Shug said, "bring me a 10th Street Skillet."

To hell with the lipids, Shug decided. Spending this much straight, uninterrupted time with Lori was his idea of heaven. He couldn't believe he'd gotten her to go for it. Sure, it was costing him a fortune, but recent events had given him a new perspective: *life is now.* Maybe Lori had shown him that, or he'd just figured it out in her vivacious presence, but she was better, and *more* than he even expected. Whether it was ordering in dinner or him driving her to the gym or just watching TV on the couch, her in her nightclothes with her feet across his lap, he'd never felt such intimacy. Not even with his first wife. And in the bedroom . . . oh my, it thrilled him just to think about it. He didn't even mind going to sleep on the pullout sofa afterward. It could've been a lifetime of this, if that night in the garage had worked out, and with Bernie Cool out of the way Gantcher and the rest had gotten the tax rebate and he could've cashed in his share of Indy Flats for full value. *Sometimes you just get what you get.* He shrugged.

Shug rubbed his hands together in anticipation of his breakfast skillet, and getting back to her. He reached for a newspaper resting on the edge of the counter that a departing customer had left behind. It was folded back to the business section, so he flipped it over to start from the front page and felt his throat go thick.

Ex-Fed Slain in Thorntown, bannered the article, with an old FBI class photo of Teague twenty-five years and fifty pounds ago. Shug read on in organ-gripping dismay:

> In what appears to be a home invasion robbery gone awry, Patrick Teague, a former FBI agent and current security specialist, and his wife, Margaret, were found dead in their Thorntown home . . .

It went on from there, reporting too many mundane details and leaving out the most important ones, like who did it and where was he? Shug felt his eyeballs might roll out of his head onto the table beneath him. He began waving at the waitress— trying to short-circuit his breakfast order, to ask for the check, to announce he was leaving. His flapping lips and gasping breath were no help. Finally, he rose, gathered his feet under him, and pulled some cash from his wallet. He staggered out the door, both hands on the glass, and out into the parking lot, raising his face toward a cover of chunky gray cloud belly hanging low in the sky. The air felt close, and he throttled the air conditioner the minute he climbed into his Acura and drove away toward Lori's.

69

"Lookit that," Ruthless said when the lone man crossed from his car to the diner, "that's fucking Saunders, ain't it? The bloke who's supposed to be in D.C."

It was. Waddy Dwyer and Rickie Powell were sitting at the far end of the Steer-In parking lot, as they had been for over an hour, waiting for Teague's meeting partner to show up. They figured they'd be able to spot the likely candidate, but now they were beyond sure. They knew Saunders's face from photos on the Internet, and considering they thought he'd slipped away, it was unbelievably good fortune.

"Stand in the right place and the ball falls right on yer fucking foot sometimes . . ." Dwyer said.

After a brief wait the restaurant door swung open and Shug moved toward his car. Dwyer turned over his engine and put it in gear. As Shug's car jutted erratically into sparse traffic on 10th Street headed west, Dwyer and Rickie Powell dropped in, smooth and unnoticed as a creeping shadow behind him.

"I imagine he's heading back to his flat," Dwyer began. "When we get there, there's a way in through the—" But Saunders turned in a different direction. "Belay that," he said.

They veered toward a more commercial area than Saunders's, before he parked near a brick factory building that looked like it had been converted to residential space.

"Come on, then," Dwyer said to Rickie. "Gear up. You've got to follow him in and find out what floor he goes to."

"Copy," Rickie said, opening the door.

70

"Where are we headed?" Decker had asked as soon as they'd gotten in his car.

"Up to Franklin, take it to East Wash toward town," Behr said, hoping to keep the information in small, digestible pellets that would prevent Decker from getting too wound up or ahead of himself.

"I mean who?" he practically snarled.

"Shugie Saunders, Kolodnik's political adviser," Behr acquiesced, and gave him the address.

"How's he in this?" Decker asked, driving to the location at a speed usually reserved for a pursuit with siren.

"Like the center of a Tootsie Pop," Behr said.

"Motherfucker," Decker breathed, picking up the pace.

When they arrived at Saunders's building, Decker shut the car engine off and pulled his Glock .40-caliber duty weapon.

"Whoa, whoa, whoa," Behr said. "*You're* waiting in the car. I'm talking to him first—"

"Come on—"

"I need information on all the players before you go and put a round in him and end up in jail yourself."

"Not in the head for this bullshit—"

"You're waiting in the car," Behr said, a hard edge to his voice, disturbed that Decker didn't bother denying what he'd just suggested.

In response, Decker released the Glock's magazine onto his

lap, popped the chambered round, and worked the slide once, five, ten times and kept going and going, snapping it back and forth with rhythmic, unnerving repetition.

"Don't go anywhere, don't do anything," Behr said.

"Yeah, I won't—" Decker said, but Behr cut him off by closing the car door.

Behr crossed the sidewalk and entered the building. He took the elevator six floors up, went to Shugie's door, and began knocking. Before long he was pounding in frustration because there was no answer.

He was trying the knob, which was locked, and considered making entry when an across-the-hall neighbor's door opened. A middle-aged woman in a business suit stepped out holding a cup of coffee in one hand and a tube of mascara in the other. Jumping and yapping around her feet was a tiny white dog, a Maltese, he believed.

"What the heck?" she demanded. "I thought someone was trying to break *my* door down."

"Sorry," Behr said, "but I really need to locate Mr. Saunders." At a moment like this, Behr wished he were wearing his blue Caro business suit for respectability's sake.

"Yeah, well, if you find him, tell him I'm holding these for him." She opened her door a bit and pointed to three rolled up newspapers.

"So you don't know where he is?" Behr asked.

"No. I'm just glad he decided to take his . . . nightlife activities elsewhere. Cops were here earlier, scaring the poop out of Chessie," she said, pointing at the dog. "But, like I said, you find Shug, tell him in another day or two his papers are gonna be Chessie's wee-wee pads."

"Sure thing," Behr said, stalking away down the hall.

The rain had started falling in fat, greasy splotches as Behr slid back into Decker's car, where he found him still working the slide on the Glock like a maniacal puppet.

"Anything?" Decker said.

"Not home, hasn't been for a few days."

"Shit," Decker barked, punching the dash. "What else do you got?"

"Let's try Kolodnik's company," Behr said. "Maybe the ass-hole went to work."

Decker put the loose round back into the magazine, which he fitted back into the gun, then worked the slide a last time, charging the weapon, which he stowed in his Kydex hip holster. Behr clicked his phone for the street address as Decker put the car in gear.

His nightlife activities . . . Shug's neighbor's words rang in his head.

"Make a left," Behr said. "New destination. McCrea Street."

Behr suddenly knew where Shugie Saunders would be.

71

Decker wheeled his car to a hard stop in front of the loft building that was home to Saunders's escort-lover Lori, and they saw the lobby door had been jimmied open. The metal frame was bent and now it wasn't closing properly.

"Come on," Behr said, his pulse rate shooting skyward. He didn't have to ask twice, Decker was out and heading toward the building through the spattering rain, his gun drawn.

"You take the elevator to four, I'll take the stairs. Apartment F."

"Who am I looking for?" Decker asked.

"Buddy, I have no idea," Behr said, and charged up the fire stairwell.

Behr beat the elevator and was breathing hard when Decker stepped out. He gave a low whistle and a head signal that Decker should follow him. He had his Bulldog .44 out because he could see by the light in the hallway that Lori's door had been rolled slightly ajar. They proceeded toward it in a staggered formation, each with a distinct field of fire should anyone emerge. Behr lunged past the doorframe and put his back to the wall, and Decker did the same on his side.

With a finger tapped against his chest and then pointed toward the door, Behr let Decker know he was going in first. Decker nodded and Behr spun and led with his shoulder, rolling the door all the way open. He entered in a crouch, gun sweeping an arc in front of him, and saw right away they were too late. Bile came to the back of his throat at the sight of Shug, on the ground, facedown in a pool of blood, the back of his skull collapsed and a pair of entry wounds in his upper back. A chewed-up foam pillow apparently used for sound suppression was singed black with muzzle burn and thrown to the side. Decker followed Behr into the apartment and took one glance at the body.

"We have to clear this place," he said low.

Behr nodded, and they went for the kitchen, moving around a wall that divided it from the main living area. The space was empty, although a butcher block full of sharp knives had been knocked over and a few implements were missing. They checked a walk-in hall closet before moving toward the back bedroom, each using his weapon to cover the zones the other couldn't.

They entered the bedroom and discovered an awful sight. The kitchen knives and more had been put to use. The young woman, Lori, was dead, her blood spread all over and soaking into the white duvet on her bed. Decker continued into the bathroom, which was empty.

"Clear," he said.

"Clear," Behr echoed. "Good Christ." He was disgusted by the scene and sick with himself for being a step slow all the way around.

"Motherfucker," Decker said, staring at the girl's blood-soaked form. Behr recognized a look of deep distress on the young cop's face. Despite all he'd witnessed in his life, this was too much on the heels of what had happened to his wife.

"Come on, Decker," Behr said, putting a hand on his back. "Let's get you out of here."

That's when they heard a moan from the front room. They sprinted out to find Shug's head lifting off the floor somehow, his face drizzled in streamers of blood. His mouth moved in a disorganized fashion, faint, unintelligible sounds issuing from it. Behr crouched next to him, not willing to turn him over, afraid he would inadvertently finish the man off.

"Who was here, Shug?" Behr said.

There was a long moment of silence, a whispered breath, and a gurgle from him.

"Saunders, who did this?" Behr demanded, hoping to jar the man into lucidity. "How many were there?"

"Dwyer," Shug breathed. Behr lay down, practically in the pooled blood, putting an ear next to Saunders's mouth.

"Dwyer? Give me a full name?"

"Another Brit . . . big . . ." Shug croaked.

"Two of them? Are they both Brits? Give me a full name," Behr said. "What's with the pen—did they make you sign something?" he asked, noticing a blue ballpoint a foot away from Shug's right hand.

"Lori . . ." Shug gasped. There was as much pain in the word as Behr had ever heard spoken. He knew what the dying man was asking.

"She's okay," Behr said, and looked to Decker, who nodded slightly. "She got away."

Shug's face relaxed and a bit of serenity came to his eyes before they closed.

"Shug . . . Shugie . . . Saunders!" Behr shouted. But the man was gone.

Behr climbed to his feet. He was stunned, becoming overwhelmed by the violence, and he fought to keep his mind clear. Behr wasn't a chess player, but he had overheard some talk when a chess club was at Cici's Pizza at the same time he was. They were discussing endgame, when very few pieces remained on the board with limited moves left to be made. That's where they were now.

"You know we just missed 'em," Decker said.

"I do," Behr nodded, moving for the door.

72

They'd given him the night, but when morning came, they'd pulled out. Every last one of the six of them, armed and capable, hale and comforting, were gone, and now Lowell Gantcher was alone. He still saw the newspapers and magazines scattered around and the cups and plates used by his executive protection team. He didn't blame them. They were professionals. When he'd hired them, he'd managed to talk his way around the wiring of the customary $10,000 retainer they required; after all, he seemed like such a big wheel. The minor scuffle in the casino gave him legitimate reason to act distracted and delay the payment even further. And when the two guys got busted up at his house, the company was apologetic and pissed off and agreed to stay on and beef up the team. But when another few days had elapsed, a manager type from the security company had called and given him the drop-dead to transfer funds, so Gantcher had written a check for the full amount. And last night the same manager had called again.

"That check was a Super Ball, sir," he'd said. "I'm pulling my guys."

"You can't do that," Gantcher pleaded.

"It's done. First thing in morning. Pay your obligations, sir," the manager had said, hanging up.

The last words rang in Lowell Gantcher's ears. He had no

more funds, but he was surely going to pay. He thought back to a time not two years ago when he used to spend and allocate money in hundred-thousand-dollar blocks. If his wife bought a couch for fifteen thousand dollars it wouldn't even get on his radar. He had dreamed of, and saw close at hand, a time when he wouldn't pay personal attention to anything less than big rocks—seven-figure transactions. But things had reversed course. The accounts had shrunk, and the liquidity vanished. There was nothing left now. Thousands would be a dream to have in hand at the moment. His wife was living on their last few hundred dollars cash up in lake country, though she didn't know it. As for him, he was down to a few twenties in his wallet and a couple of traveler's checks in the basement safe.

In the wake of the security team's departure was a dread as pervasive as water rising inside a sinking submarine. Everything that constituted life had dwindled and was being squeezed out with that dread taking its place. Gantcher opened a rectangular metal case on the coffee table in front of him, revealing the sporting weapon broken down into two parts. He was suddenly glad he hadn't been able to find a buyer for his Orvis over/under. He picked up the barrel piece and snapped it into the stock. He fished around in a shell bag and loaded both barrels, sorry that the gun was only a 28 gauge and the ammunition number six birdshot, good enough for fragmenting clay pigeons but woefully light to deal with the monster coming for him. Still, he thought, gripping it, raising it to his shoulder, it might do the trick.

He thought about what to do next. It was time to get in the car and run. The tank was full. The only question was: where? Nancy was up north with the kids. He'd give anything—not that there was anything left—to see them, but he couldn't risk leading Dwyer in their direction. So he could go south, but the country would run out too quickly, and he hated the thought of being cut down in some Louisiana swamp. The west seemed to hold more possibility. If he could make California, he might be able to get lost in the endless overpopulated sprawl. Maybe he could catch on with a construction crew and get paid in cash. He'd be packed and out of the house in five minutes. It was time to go.

He felt a draft, a slight breeze that spread through the family room when the kitchen door was open. He didn't hear anything over the rain, though . . .

73

Behr took the keys from Decker and drove hard north, the direction of both Gantcher's office and home. They'd called 911 on their way out of the loft, but hadn't even considered waiting for the response to come. There was no point.

"Scroll my contact list and dial Lowell Gantcher Work," Behr instructed Decker, handing over his cell phone.

Decker did so, waiting with the phone to his ear.

"Lowell Gantcher," he said. Then he covered the mouthpiece with a hand and told Behr, "She's saying he's not available."

"It's urgent, if he's there, you have to put him on . . ." Decker continued. "You can't? All right . . . Message? You tell him he better watch his ass." Decker hung up. "She said she couldn't *reach* him. Not that he couldn't come to the phone. Tells me he's not there," Decker said.

Most people would probably just take Meridian to get up to Crows Nest. It was a straight shot and the main thoroughfare, but because of that it could be slightly slow going. The car had muscle to burn and Behr flew along N. Michigan, which though it angled slightly away from the center of town was free of traffic. He cut right on West 56th, and only hoped he was making up some time.

"You might want to take her easy," Decker said over rain that sounded like marbles bouncing off the roof, "she's American so she runs good straight, but she's not much on the corners."

Behr's response was to gun it. He kept his hands on the wheel, his eyes on the road, and did his best to rope down his thoughts, which were jumping around inside his head. Trying the home address first was a gamble, but if they chose not to believe the secretary and went to the office first and he was at home, they'd be too late once again and it'd be over. Of course the reverse was true, too. Decker, for his part, was twisted around backward, reaching into the backseat and coming around forward with a multipocketed tactical vest, which he put on. Behr fought to empty his mind and drive. This was his last chance to get the bastards who'd nearly killed him and his family and who had destroyed Decker's.

Behr took his phone back and dialed Breslau, who answered on the first ring.

"It's Behr. Don't know if you caught the nine-one-one, but Shug Saunders is down."

Behr wheeled onto Sunset Lane, blazing past the homes of the rich and locally famous. Gantcher's place was up ahead on the left.

"Fuck, I know it," Breslau spat. "Where are you headed now?"

"To Lowell—"

Behr stopped talking because his cell phone connection had gone suddenly and completely dead.

"Shit," Behr said. Glancing at the phone he saw the words "no service," in the signal readout space. "You have reception?"

Decker checked his phone. "Empty triangle," he said.

"The weather?"

"I don't think so . . ."

"Signal jammer?"

"It'd mean they're here," Decker answered.

"Well, we can fall back, call it in, and wait," Behr offered, pulling over.

"Uh-uh," Decker said, reaching for the door handle. "Even if you want to, I get out here."

Behr held the wheel, considering it for a moment, then turned to Decker. "There are two of them."

"That we know of," Decker amended.

"That we know of," Behr agreed. "I'll go in the front, you go in the back."

"Front's a bad approach," Decker said, appraising the house with an expert eye.

"Choices?" Behr asked.

"None."

"Hit the doors at the same time and meet inside."

Decker nodded. "Wish I had my body rifle to cover you," he said, opening his door gently and slipping out of the car. Behr did the same. "Gimme four minutes to work my way around." The rain muffled their words.

"Four minutes. I have twenty-five after," Behr said, crouched below the roofline of Decker's car.

"Good," Decker said.

He watched as Decker adopted a stealthy, stooped gait completely unlike his usual one. It resembled that of an Apache on a stalk, Behr imagined. Decker moved lightly and disappeared into the neighbors' tree line, bending, ducking, and turning sideways, not disturbing a single branch. Within seconds Behr had lost sight of him altogether.

Behr was conscious of the heaviness of his own step as he dropped below the tops of the rhododendrons that ran along the street side of Gantcher's front lawn and connected the open end of the U-shaped driveway. When he had crabbed across and reached the far side, Behr stayed low and leaped across the opening. He moved along parallel to the driveway, hugging some close-planted Japanese cherry trees. Their trunks were too slender to give him real cover, but he hoped they'd break up his silhouette a bit.

He made his way toward the house and paused beneath the last tree, standing very still, thick droplets of water slapping the leaves around him. He saw now that he'd have to cross the courtyard, out in the open, in order to make it to the side of the house and then ultimately a window or the door, or better yet a set of

French doors off what seemed to be the dining room or kitchen. He glanced at his watch. Two minutes. He couldn't let Decker hit the back door alone; God only knew what he'd be walking into. Behr drew the Bulldog .44 from the holster at the small of his back.

He dropped as low as he could—which wasn't very, considering his height—and made his move. The gravel crunched softly beneath him. The windows appeared black through the rain, and it was impossible to see clearly inside the darkened house, but Behr thought he detected a streak of movement inside. It caused him to crouch further and raise his gun, but then his feet were ripped out from under him and he was slammed to the ground on his back. He had no air in him and saw white in front of his eyes. The triple hammering sound of three rounds, muted and distant, arrived almost like an afterthought.

Hit.

When his regular sight returned he saw translucent rain beads falling from black clouds and then he breathed and all the pain in the world concentrated in his chest and shoulder. He was railroad spiked to the ground and the oxygen blew in and out in a stabbing manner, but it was like pumping a ruptured inner tube—things were flapping around and not really inflating.

Get up, Frank, he urged himself. Nothing happened. He felt his arms swimming against the gravel beneath him, but couldn't tell if he was moving them or if they were merely in spasm.

The bullet that he'd avoided in the parking garage had finally found him. Other words and thoughts washed through his head, along with images. Decker. Susan's face. The sonogram image of his tiny son. Breslau's wide nostrils and clenching jaw. Gina, awash in blood. Kolodnik. The police, politicians, the Caro Group—he was as done with organizations as they were with him.

Family, he thought, *and friends—if he could ever collect a few, and keep them—were all there was, and he'd hold on tight to that if he could just get up . . .*

But he was down and he was going to stay down, and he wasn't ever going to see his child, because whether he bled out or was finished by someone standing over him at point-blank range, he was going to die here.

Get up, man.

74

It came as a roar.

Three shots smeared together, almost as one, belched out of the ugly black gun in Dwyer's hands. The kitchen filled with the malevolent stink of gunpowder. It must've been a hit because Dwyer stepped away from the shattered window, lowered the weapon, and handed it off to his huge friend.

"Some piece," the man said.

"Alternated buckshot and deer slugs," Dwyer said.

"Nasty."

Gantcher struggled to free his hands, but they—like his knees, ankles, and mouth for that matter—were held fast and painfully with silver duct tape.

"Now where's the bloody safe—in the study or the basement?" Dwyer asked.

Gantcher didn't answer. He had no idea how they'd gotten inside. He'd felt a breeze and had stood to investigate and lifted the over/under and was suddenly tackled off his feet and found Dwyer's knee, like an anvil, on his chest. He saw Dwyer rear back for a punch, glimpsed a piece of black metal in his hand—and had woken up in the chair. He hadn't even fired a shot.

Dwyer had been asking about the safe just before the tall one with the buzz cut had whistled him over to the kitchen window. They'd seen something—someone—and Dwyer had lined him up and fired. Gantcher couldn't care less about them finding his lousy safe, that wasn't the reason for his holding out, nor was it heroics. It was more his profound feeling that when the safe was open, and Dwyer found it held only three hundred dollars' worth of paper issued by the American Express Company, it was going to all finally be over and they were going to kill him. And beyond that, Gantcher had suddenly gained the elemental knowledge common to all living beings close to their end: every last second mattered a great deal.

He heard the clatter of steel kitchen implements, but couldn't turn his head to see what was happening. The information soon came to him, as Dwyer stepped back in front of him, this time holding one of Nancy's long, stainless steel, two-tined barbecue forks. Dwyer put the points of it maddeningly close to Gantcher's eye and said, "Now is it in the fucking basement or the study? Or should I take an eyeball to each place to help me look?"

"Basement," Gantcher said, though the tape muffled it.

"Basement. Grand," Dwyer said. Gantcher understood another elemental truth, this one specific to him: even close to the end, agony and disfigurement were still frightening propositions. Then Dwyer grabbed a paring knife to cut Gantcher loose at knee and ankle and dragged him out of the chair toward the door that led to the stairway down.

"Go make sure that fuck in the driveway is finished," he instructed his friend, leaving the big shotgun with him, as he pulled Gantcher along.

I'm going to die in the basement, flashed through Gantcher's brain as he stumbled down the steps.

75

Behr freight-trained through the French doors into the kitchen, splintering them in a shower of wood and glass, and landed on his face. Images flickered in front of his eyes as if played by an old film projector with a bad bulb. What was once a high-tech kitchen was destroyed. The table was upended, same with the chairs. Water sprayed out of a small sink, its faucet snapped off. A heavy black shotgun and shells were scattered across the floor. Bullet holes in the Sub-Zero refrigerator and a shotgun blast pattern in cabinets on the opposite side explained the popcorn sound Behr had heard as he entered. Somehow he found his way to his feet again, just as he had in the driveway. If this was the end of it, at least he kept getting up.

Decker was there, having arrived after the first gunshots, and was fighting on the ground with a tall man whose hair was buzzed military close. Both were bloodied, climbing to their feet and squaring. The tall man had a pair of round holes, a tight double tap, torn into his T-shirt, which revealed personal body armor underneath. Decker's Glock was nowhere to be seen. The tall man's hand went to his belt buckle in the instant before they lunged at each other with near simultaneous Superman punches. Decker's landed hard, stunning the man. But the tall man's landed too, and caused a geyser of blood to spray from Decker's throat. A glint along the metal loop around the man's knuckles revealed a HideAway knife, a razor-sharp two-inch point that had been camouflaged as a belt buckle. Decker sagged for just a moment and the man yoked him behind the head, raising his fist for a carotid punch with the blade. Behr blinked away the blood, sweat, and rain running down his face and emptied all five .44 special rounds from his Bulldog into the man, who went down bucking, like a sledgehammered farm animal.

76

All bloody fucking hell had broken loose upstairs from the sound of it, and Dwyer ran for the stairs. *Had that big fucker managed to stand and trade shots with Rickie?*

Dwyer had popped the safe with the combination Lowell Gantcher had generously volunteered and then saw, with much disgust, what it contained. He'd ripped up the lousy traveler's checks right in front of Gantcher's eyes, while they were still open, though the paring knife was already lodged in his liver. It was a German make, a Wüsthof, a damn good high-carbon steel, laser-edged blade that did its work efficiently. Gantcher had gone crying softly, something mumbled about a wife and kids through half-chewed duct tape, not much fight left in him, but nothing too unmanly.

Now Dwyer charged the door leading to the kitchen, the Česká drawn, and rammed his way through. Behr was on a knee, hit and bleeding badly but not dead, and currently stuffing shells into a revolver. Other bodies were visible on the floor in the corners of his eyes as Dwyer lined up his shot: Rickie twisted in a heap and another fellow on his back, weakly pulling a small-framed concealed carry auto from an ankle holster. Dwyer redirected his sights to the armed man, who in turn fell back and fired, peppering the doorframe around Dwyer's head.

Dwyer had a poor angle but zeroed in on the man's skull and squeezed just as Behr hurtled into him from across the room.

His shot flew high and wide and Dwyer gave up the gun, letting it clatter away in order to grab Behr under the shoulders and whipsaw him into the kitchen island. Behr crashed into it with a thud, but rolled and faced Dwyer and they locked eyes. Before any physical movement, whether it's conscious or subconscious, the intent forms in the brain, and if one is sensitive or experienced enough, one can see it in the opponent's eyes. Most of the time it's infinitely subtle, but what Dwyer saw in Behr's right now, despite his being half bled, was the intent to kill him. Dwyer imagined the same message was flashing like neon in his own.

He charged Behr, dropping for a double leg, which the larger man somehow stuffed by sprawling. Dwyer felt a hard elbow thump into the back of his skull and he dove down toward unconsciousness, but managed to fight through it and stand and wedge a forearm beneath Behr's throat as he put him into a guillotine choke. Behr pumped his legs and found a reserve that Dwyer hadn't banked on. He stood up through the choke, snaking his arms around Dwyer's lower legs and churned forward. They left the kitchen, careening through a doorway into a butler's pantry, where they both hit the ground in a crash and clatter of cabinetry, dishes, and serving implements.

They faced each other, panting, for a split second, the gamy physical stink of death coming off them in waves. On their elbows and bellies atop broken glass, shattered and pebbled, it was all between them now, the few-foot expanse that was survival or death. This was Dwyer's terrain. His eyes cut around the space for something sharp or edged or heavy. He saw Behr's do the same. *Nothing suitable.*

With grunts and the pop of glass ground to dust underfoot they ran at each other and locked up and Dwyer got his hands around Behr's neck in a double collar tie. He yanked, then flung his hips back for a snap down, a technique that always left his opponents on their faces, spitting teeth. But this one didn't go. He merely doubled over some. *The wound,* Dwyer thought, as he drove down and felt Behr's clavicle there, shot apart and jagged, under his forearm. He'd broken countless healthy men with the move, and he pushed with all the leverage his stout body possessed. But this one wouldn't break. Then, with a guttural bellow, Behr caught him around the waist, lifted him off the ground and high into the air before dumping him with a vicious body slam that caved in his rib cage. He felt the air squeeze out of him and black pain flood in. The effort of it caused Behr to drop to his knees. Dwyer looked up and saw that the other wounded man had twisted his way into view of the doorframe, a smeared blood trail behind him, and had managed to roll and was attempting to work himself into a modified Creedmoor shooting position, his gun across the outside of his calf. Dwyer summoned the last strength he'd trained into himself over decades to gain his feet and run straight through the glass door of the pantry. He kept waiting for shots to sound and bite into him as he hit the ground outside and clambered for the cover of the side of the house, but they didn't come . . .

77

Behr tried to give chase, but found his legs wouldn't respond anymore and he stumbled down to his knees again. Back in the kitchen he scrabbled around on the floor for the Bulldog and the shells he'd dropped when he made his tackle, but he was weak, uncoordinated, and light-headed and he hadn't fitted a single one into its chamber before Dwyer was out of sight. Decker lay there, his gun still up, but there was no one left to line up on. Behr crawled for the kitchen phone, yanking it down and putting it to his ear, only to find it dead.

He made his way, on hands and knees, toward Decker, grabbing a wadded-up dishtowel from the floor on his way. Behr reached him and pressed the linen hard onto the wound, which was a wickedly clean seven-inch laceration that went clear down to the bone and ran the length of his jaw, and was still gouting blood. Another inch lower and it would have been his jugular and an early good night.

That's when a low-grade explosion erupted outside and a compressed whump rocked the kitchen. A kind of smile creased Decker's face. His teeth shone bright white against the dark blood around his mouth for a moment.

"Mud cutter," he said, "made it myself," his back sinking against the floor in something resembling satisfaction. Behr understood he'd set off some kind of booby trap near the back door on his way in.

The two of them lay there breathing raggedly for a moment. Behr dialed 911 on his cell phone and pressed Send over and over. The last thing he saw was a signal bar flicker into place and then his head dropped and blackness came.

78

Waddy Dwyer was completely arsed up. Hurt and alone, ribs crushed, the soft tissue of his legs shredded and his face blown up, burned, and peppered. The kind of damage he'd managed to avoid his whole career, and the kind a man never fully comes back from. He'd be completely unable to cash the $62,000 check he'd made Shug Saunders write him. He'd need to stay away from banks and most public places with cameras, especially during the day, being so recognizably disfigured now. The whole trip was for naught. Gantcher had run dry of funds and there was no one left to squeeze for his payday. It had become a complete fucking debacle. And now he was doing something he hadn't in his whole bloody life: he was running.

One of them, probably the younger of the two, had mined the ground near the rear steps. He'd used something frag-mentary and incendiary that was homemade yet effective and would've killed him outright had he not felt the hard metal underfoot and dove away just in time. Dwyer should have been looking for it, or something like it, after seeing they'd killed his SAS boy. Only true players could have done that to Rickie. What was it that Ruthless had said? *When pros lock up, everyone gets hurt.*

Dwyer's own arrogance, the way he'd taken Behr lightly and only thought of killing him and not the reverse, was the true sign of his age. Suddenly his belief in his skills outstripped his ability. Miraculously, he'd made it to the car, used a sweatshirt to blot his tattered face, and drove out of there before any police had arrived.

Now, at a rest stop off I-65, he rinsed his torn-up thighs with bottled water and used the rest to wash down half a dozen codeine and acetaminophen and two Adderall. He was far off the road, away from the abandoned car park, tucked into thick trees where he fed Rickie's belongings into a fire he'd built in a metal rubbish barrel. The clothes were burning well, already beyond recognition or provenance, the same with the Elvis glasses, which melted immediately when he tossed them into the flames. He added the GSM mobile jammer, along with the rest of his equipment, to the mix. It was time to travel light. Finally, he dropped Rickie's passport in and watched the crimson cover curl, peel back, and liquefy, revealing the photo page. Black ringed holes spread across Rickie's young, unsmiling face, before he disappeared altogether.

Dwyer limped back to the car and used the map feature on his smart phone to plot his route: straight north to Lake Michigan, then northeast on I-94 to I-196, until Route 31 would take him straight into the wilderness country of Michigan's Upper Peninsula, to Traverse City if he could make it that far on land, where he'd boost a boat and steer it around Mackinac Island into Lake Huron and Canada. From there, depending on how and if his face healed, he could bus over to Nova Scotia and catch on with a merchant ship headed for the UK, or maybe even a flight to London if the heat dissipated enough. Dwyer sketched the route in detail on paper, then texted home a coded message: *kits in dens*. That would give Sandy an idea of what was going on and what to do. Then he took the SIM card out of the already clean phone and cracked it into pieces and let them blow away on the post-rain breeze.

He started the car. He would have to dump it soon and switch into a stolen one for the second half of the drive. He had so far to go, but all he could think about was getting back to Wales. All he could picture was Sandy, her fine hands treating his face with boric acid solution and spreading calendula and comfrey salve over the burns on his legs. He pulled out of the rest area, back onto the interstate, and started traveling.

79

There was noise, and white lights flashing in his eyes, and it was bone cold. He felt steel against his skin and heard tearing, then felt even colder as his shirt was cut away. There were voices, talking to each other, not to him, and scraping and digging in his body. His every nerve felt raw, as if they were plugged into a surging electrical current. Then there was a sharp jab. A needle. It was held in place with tape. A burning erupted at the spot of the puncture, it was agony, but soon a warm, floating sensation carried him away, as if in a bubble of saline. Sound became muffled as he entered a gauzy tunnel. *Was he dying or already dead?* He might've been. But he didn't think so. Then, black.

His eyes opened. It was much later and everything hurt. He was flat on his back. He felt pinned in place, but not by any restraints, just his own inability to move. He stared up at the plastic diamond grid of the light fixture above him for what felt like hours, gathering himself, and then was finally able to turn his head. He saw her there, her blond hair spilled along the edge of the bed where her head was down.

"Suze." The word was a croak, a gasp.

She rose up, a look of abject relief on her face.

"You came back."

"I came back," she said.

He felt himself smile. It felt like everything inside him was going to tear apart.

"You crazy jerk," she said. "You had surgery. A collapsed lung. They gave you blood. You were a couple quarts low."

"How long have I . . . ?"

"Thirty hours or so, maybe a little longer," she said. She was completely scrubbed free of makeup. He'd never seen anything as beautiful as her face.

"Dwyer?" Behr asked, his eyes cutting toward the door.

"The guy you were chasing?" she said. "There was—what did they call it?—a blast crater and lots of blood, but he was gone. Police are looking for him all over the place. They said they're sure they'll get him. Soon."

His eyes closed in pain. *No they won't* . . . Behr knew the man was gone again on the same dark wind he blew in on.

"And Decker?"

"He's . . . okay. They sewed him up—a hundred and thirty-seven stitches—and he left. He just walked out," she said. "They released Gina's body to him and he had her . . . them . . . cremated this morning."

Behr pictured Decker, alone in his Camaro, a blister on the highway, driving toward some unknown destination, bent on ungettable revenge.

"Was there a service?" he asked quietly. The words were coming more smoothly now, but it was easier to whisper than talk. "Were you there?"

"Not sure if anyone was . . ." Susan said, "I was a little busy."

That's when Behr realized she was dressed in a robe, over a hospital gown. "You had him?" Behr asked.

"He wouldn't wait. I went into labor while you were under. Dr. Bezucha has privileges here, and he came."

"And I missed it."

"You did. Won't say you didn't miss a lot, but I'm sure it wasn't pretty."

"You okay?"

"Yeah. I am."

"And how is he?"

"He's unbelievable," she said. Behr couldn't lift his head to see. She wheeled a clear plastic bassinet around the foot of the bed and close to him. In it, like a cotton-wrapped doll, was the baby, with a furrowed brow and his pink nose peeking out between a swaddling blanket and tiny watch cap. She lifted him, his eyes closed like a kitten's, and showed him to Behr.

"Your son," she said, with the first smile he'd seen on her in weeks. "Weighed in at eight-eight, so thank god he didn't wait any longer."

"Kid's a light heavyweight," Behr said, hardly recognizing his voice for the mystified joy in it.

"So, Frank Junior? Little Frankie?"

Behr, feeling as weak as he ever had in his life, shook his head with all the force he could muster. "No. He's gotta do better—be better than me."

Her eyes brimmed with tears as she held the boy up to him.

"Then it's Trevor, because we wanted to go with a 'T,' " she said. "And Frank is his middle name. Don't even try and argue."

There was so much to be strong for and to protect. With effort he reached out and touched the tiny fingers in front of him and held them for a moment, before his arm tired and fell away. The baby woke then, and Behr's head sank back onto the thin pillow as he stared into the eyes of his son.

ACKNOWLEDGMENTS

I would like to express my deep gratitude to Theodore Petrara, gunnery sergeant, USMC, Ret. (3rd Force Recon Platoon, 3rd Recon Battalion, 12th Marines, 24th Marine Amphibious Unit, Lebanon), and Steve Moses, deputy constable, Dallas, Texas, for sharing their incredible expertise. They are as generous as they are knowledgeable.

An excerpt
from David Levien's *City of the Sun,*
Frank Behr's **relentlessly suspenseful** debut

1

Jamie Gabriel wakes at 5:44, as the clock radio's volume bursts from the silence. He rolls and hits the sleep bar, clipping off the words to an annoying pop song by some boy-band graduate who wears the same clothes and does the same moves as his backup dancers. The worst. Kids at school say they like him. Some do; the rest are just following along. Jamie listens to Green Day and Linkin Park. It's three-quarters dark outside. He clicks off the alarm and puts his feet on the floor. Waking up is easy.

In the master bedroom sleep Mom and Dad. Carol and Paul. The carpet is wall-to-wall, light blue. New. The liver-colored stuff that came with the house when they bought it is gone. The blue goes better with the oak bedroom set, Mom says.

It was a good move for the Gabriels, to the split ranch–style on Richards Avenue, Wayne Township. Trees line most all of the blocks here. The houses have yards.

Jamie walks past his school photo, which hangs in the hall on the way to the bathroom. He hates the picture. His wheat-colored hair lay wrong that day. He takes a pee. That's it. He'll brush his teeth when he gets back, after breakfast, before school.

He moves through the kitchen—*Pop-Tart? Nah*—and goes out the utility door into the connected garage. Mom and Dad love it, the garage on the house, the workbench, and space for the white minivan and the blue Buick.

He hoists the garage door halfway up; it sticks on its track. A streak of black fur darts in and hits him low in the legs.

"Where you been, Tater?"

The gray-whiskered Lab's tail thumps against the boy's leg for a moment. After a night of prowling, Tater likes the way the boy ruffles his fur. The boy pushes him aside and crawl-walks under the garage door.

A stack of the morning *Star* waits there, acrid ink smell, still warm from the press. Jamie drags the papers inside and sets to work, folding them into thirds, throwing style.

He loads white canvas sacks and crosses them, one over each shoulder, then straddles his bike. The Mongoose is his. Paid for with six months' delivery money after the move to Richards Avenue. Jamie ducks low and pushes the bike out underneath the garage door, when Tater rubs up against his leg again. The old dog begins to whine. He shimmies and bawls in a way that he never does.

"Whatsa matter?"

Jamie puts his feet on the pedals and cranks off on his route. Tater groans and mewls. Dogs know.

"Should've gone to McDonald's, you fat fuck," Garth "Rooster" Mintz said to Tad Ford as he reached across him for a French Toast dipper. Tad's face squeezed in hurt, then relaxed. The smell of gasoline, the fast-food breakfast, and Tad's Old Spice filled the battleship-gray '81 Lincoln.

"You're eating same as me," Tad said back. "You're just lucky it doesn't stick to you."

Rooster said nothing, just started chewing a dipper.

Tad was unsatisfied with the lack of reaction, but that was all he was going to say. Rooster was seventy-five pounds smaller than him, but he was hard. The guy was wiry. Tad could see his sinew. He'd once watched Rooster, piss drunk, tear a guy's nostril open in a bar scrap. The whole left side of the dude's nose was blown out, and just flapped around on his face with each breath after the fight was broken up and Rooster was pulled off.

Tad had plenty of targets of opportunity with Rooster—the small man stank much of the time. He didn't shower most days. He left his chin-up, push-up, and sit-up sweat in place, only bothering to wipe down his tattoos. His red-blond hair hung limp and greasy as well. Then there were the scars. Nasty raised red ones that ran up and down his forearms like someone had gone at him with a boning knife. When Tad finally screwed up the nerve to ask where he'd gotten them, Rooster merely replied, "Around." Tad left it there.

"You're just lucky it doesn't stick to you," Tad repeated, chewing on his own French toast.

"Yeah, I'm lucky," Rooster said, turned, and looked down the street, still dark beneath all the goddamn trees. "Should've gone to McDonald's."

Jamie Gabriel, rider, pedals. He flows by silent houses, houses dark on the inside. He tosses papers into yards and onto porches. He works on his arc and velocity with each throw. An automatic sprinkler quietly sweeps one lawn, still blue in the bruised morning light. Jamie slings for the front door of that house so the paper stays dry. He works his pedals. A line of streetlight goes dark with a hiss as morning comes. Dad thinks it's great that they moved to a neighborhood that supports tradition: newspaper routes. Mom's not so sure—her boy needs his rest. Few people know the streets like Jamie does. Dark and empty, they're his streets. Jamie wasn't so sure either, at first, when he was still getting used to the work and slogging through the route on his old Huffy. But then he earned the new bike. He read an old story of a mailman who became an Olympic biker. *Why not him, too?* He has a picture. The black man's thighs bulge and ripple. He looks like he's set to tear his bike apart more than ride it. Jamie checks his watch. His time is looking good.

Rooster glanced at the clock inside the Lincoln. Goddamn Lincoln now smelled of an old fuel leak and Tad's farts over the sickly sweet of the aftershave. But the car was clean. Riggi bought it in a cash deal and dropped it off with fixed-up tags. Rooster hated these goddamned pickups. He flexed his forearm, felt the corded muscle move underneath his wounded and roughly healed skin and light red arm hair. His forearm was thick for his stature. He was ripped. He was disciplined with working out, but he was a lazy bastard, he suspected, when it came to certain parts of the job. Yeah, he hated the fucking snatches.

Anybody could do 'em. It wasn't like the house work. *That* was rarefied air, sir.

"Start the car," Rooster said low, glancing sideways at the clock again. He scanned out the windshield of the Lincoln. The goddamn thing was like the bridge of the starship *Enterprise*.

"Oh, shit," Tad said, his last bite of hash-brown cake sticking in his gullet. The car turned over, coarse and throaty.

They saw movement at the corner.

Jamie puts his head down and digs his pedals. He's got a shot at his record. He's got a shot at the *world* record. He throws and then dips his right shoulder as he makes the corner of Tibbs. The canvas sack on his left has begun to lighten and unbalance him. He straightens the Mongoose and glances up. Car. Dang. Jamie wheels around the corner right into the rusty grill and locks them up.

Tires bite asphalt and squeal. Smoke and rubber-stink roil. Brakes strain hard and hold. The vehicles come to a stop. Inches separate them.

With a blown-out breath of relief, Jamie shakes his head and starts pushing toward the curb, bending down to pick up a few papers that have lurched free.

Car doors open. Feet hit the pavement. Jamie looks up at the sound. Two men rise out of the car. They move toward him. He squeezes the hand brake hard as they approach.

David Levien, author of *City of the Sun* and *Where the Dead Lay,* has been nominated for the Edgar, Hammett and Shamus awards in the US, and is also a Hollywood screenwriter and director. He was co-writer of *Ocean's Thirteen* and *Runaway Jury* among other films. He lives in Connecticut.